This is a work of fiction. All of the characters, organizations, and events portrayed in this novel are either products of the author's imagination or are used fictitiously.

www.melodramapublishing.com

Library of Congress Control Number: 2011927245
ISBN-13: 978-1-934157-63-3
Mass Market Edition: January 2013
10 9 8 7 6 5 4 3 2

Interior Design: Candace K. Cottrell
Cover Design: Marion Designs
Cover Model: Vanessa

Bad Apple

THE BADDEST CHICK

NISA SANTIAGO

Buy

for Melodrama

Chapter 1

The shabby three-bedroom apartment in the Lincoln projects of Harlem reeked of cigarette smoke and weed. The place was in dire condition, with its weathered furniture and tattered carpeting littered with stains and cigarette burns. The plumbing was shot, dirty dishes cluttered the kitchen, roaches were crawling all over, and the unkempt floors and walls were soiled with dirt and other grime. Still, it was home to the same family for years—two generations to be exact—so everyone in the apartment was accustomed to the filthy conditions.

Hot 97 blared throughout the apartment, and Lil Wayne's "Lollipop" made Apple nod and sing along. She sat near the window of the fourth-floor bedroom she shared with her sister, Nichols and stared down at the corner bodega, her eyes transfixed on a certain young man lingering in front of the store. She watched him closely, admiring everything about him—his swag, his wardrobe, the gleaming black Range Rover he drove, and the way he had respect from his Harlem crew.

Seventeen-year-old Apple had a crush on Cross, a young Harlem hustler, for years. She felt blessed to be able to watch him chill and do his business from her bedroom window. It was the perfect position for her. She dreamed of Cross constantly, hoping someday he would wife her and whisk her away from the madness and poverty she lived in. If Apple hadn't lost her virginity at fourteen, she would have waited for Cross to take it, because she knew one day he would finally notice her and realize how beautiful she was.

Cross had ladies chasing him on the regular, from young to old, and Apple knew he got around. Still, she knew she could be the better woman for him someday. All she needed was time with him. He'd never had a wifey, and Apple was ready to become his ride-or-die chick.

Apple sat near the window for an hour, her beautiful, long, light-brown legs clad in a dark blue and white pinstripe skirt. The white T-shirt she had on accentuated her full breasts, and her long, sensuous hair fell down to her shoulders, making her look like a black Barbie doll. She knew she was beautiful, with her curvy waistline and succulent figure, because the men who chased her on the daily reminded her. Having chestnut eyes, perfectly curved eyebrows, tight light-brown skin, and sweet glossy lips made her and Kola, her identical twin sister, the envy of Harlem.

Apple was older than Kola by forty-six minutes, and she reminded her of that every chance she got. The two sisters were like night and day. Apple, who could be more reserved and patient, kept to herself sometimes. She knew her time to escape poverty and the projects would come. Kola, on the other hand, was a firecracker and a very promiscuous young girl—getting money and having sex whenever she could. Both sisters had their untamed ways and share of men. Apple wasn't any angel herself, but Kola was the more ambitious and raw of the two.

Apple hated when people confused her with her sister. One day, while she was in the Chinese restaurant with her friend Mesha, a young teen felt on her booty and whispered to her, "So when you gonna let me hit that again?"

"Get your fuckin' hands off me!" Apple shouted. "Who the fuck is you?"

The young teen quickly realized it was the wrong twin. "Damn, my bad, shawty. I thought you were your sister."

"Well, I ain't," she spat.

"I'm sayin', ma, you ain't gotta act like that. Fuck is wrong wit' you?"

"What the fuck is wrong wit' *you*? Don't get me twisted, fo' real."

Mesha had to pull Apple out of the Chinese spot before things got more heated. After Mesha calmed her friend down, the two went on with their day without any more incidents. But Apple was tired of the repeated mix-ups between her and Kola. She'd even thought about cutting her hair one day, but when word got back to her that Cross loved women with long, black hair, she quickly erased the thought from her mind.

Apple continued to stare at Cross from high above, admiring his strapping physique in the wife-beater he had on, and the way his dark brown skin shimmered on the hot spring day. Cross had on a pair of stylish beige cargo shorts, with a pair of spotless white Uptowns. His tattooed arms were rippled with definition, and his long corn rows hung down to his shoulders. He sported a thick Cuban link chain with a diamond-encrusted cross around his neck, along with a matching bracelet and diamond pinky ring, signifying his wealth on the block. Cross was the epitome of a well-groomed, get-money thug.

As Apple sat and watched him, she heard the announcement of the upcoming Summer Jam concert. She, Ayesha, and Mesha had their tickets in advance. It was the much-needed break she sought from Harlem and her family. Excited, she rushed over to the radio and turned up the volume to hear the 2010 Summer Jam lineup that would include Drake, Trey Songz, Ludacris, Juelz Santana, Usher, Gucci Mane, Nicki Minaj, and a few more. Apple screamed because she yearned to see her favorite artists, Drake, Trey Songz, and Ludacris, perform. It was her first concert, and she couldn't wait to go with her best friends.

She rushed back to the window and continued to look down at Cross and his goons. She only wished Cross was the one taking her to the concert. She pictured herself riding in his truck, styling in the passenger seat, being his woman and the envy of all the other bitches chasing after her boo.

"One day, you're gonna be mines," she said to herself in an assuring whisper.

The door abruptly flew open, and Apple's mother came rushing into the bedroom, disturbing Apple from her fantasy.

"Apple, run to the store and pick me up a pack of Newports."

"I'm busy," Apple snapped back.

"Busy doin' what?" her mother barked. "Bitch, you're seventeen, and you ain't doin' nothin' but blasting music in my muthafuckin' house."

Looking over at her mother, Apple sucked her teeth and rolled her eyes. She couldn't wait until she had a place of her own, away from her disruptive mother. Apple tried to ignore her mother and turned her attention back to Cross on the block.

Her mother shouted, "Apple, you hear me talkin' to you?"

"Yeah. And? I said I'm busy!" Apple snapped back.

"What the fuck is so interesting that got you lookin' out that fuckin' window?"

Apple continued to ignore her mother, but became unsettled when Denise walked up to the window and looked outside with her daughter.

"You sittin' here lookin' at these nappy-head niggas on the corner, tryin' to get your pussy wet. Bitch, I ain't tryin' to become a fuckin' grandmother because your fuckin' ass is in heat."

Apple sighed. "You need to preach that to Kola."

"Don't get fuckin' smart wit' me."

"Why don't you ask Kola or Nichols to go?"

"'Cause I asked ya fuckin' ass."

Apple sighed and sucked her teeth again. "I fuckin' hate it here."

"Then leave! You and ya sister seventeen. Get the fuck out my crib if you feel you're woman enough to handle your own!"

"I will too. Real soon!"

Apple snatched the twenty-dollar bill her mother had in her hand and stormed out the bedroom. She knew the only way out her mother's crib was money, and unfortunately, she didn't have any. She had no job, no stable boyfriend, and was barely making her grades in school. She had beauty like her sister, and men yearned for her like she was Helen of Troy. Still, her looks weren't providing her with any money, which she needed.

Denise Evans was impossible to deal with most times. She had been on Section 8 for the longest. She and her mother had received welfare and government checks all their lives and knew how to work the system. Now, she was teaching her three daughters the tricks-of-the-trade in benefiting from the system—if not a weak man.

Thirty-five years young, Denise wasn't only unemployed, she'd never had a job, and the only money she ever earned was what she tricked off men.

She'd gotten pregnant with Apple and Kola when she was only seventeen. The twins' father, Ronald, was a construction worker with a good heart and a great-paying job. He and Denise had met at a mutual friend's party one night, where Denise lured the twenty-five-year-old from Trinidad with her tight dress and long legs. The two hit it off instantly, and four months later, they got married after Denise found out she was pregnant.

Ronald wanted to be in the girls' lives after they were born, but their mother was so busy whoring in the streets and carrying on, he couldn't tolerate it any longer. He thought she was a good woman, but grew tired of the drinking and cursing over time. He felt ignored.

Then Denise became pregnant by another man a year later with Nichols. That's when Ronald left to find better, but not before Denise hit him with child support and alimony payments. She wanted to drain him of everything he had, and for years, Ronald suffered from depression. Almost everything he worked hard for went to Denise and the kids. But Denise could care less, splurging his hard-earned money on mostly herself.

Denise had years of hood experience, so she knew how to manipulate the system to make the majority of the court's judgments go her way. Ronald soon became tired of fighting Denise and the courts, and on the twins' thirteenth birthday, he blew his brains out with a .357. They found his body two days later.

Nichols' father, Dominique, was a different breed of

man, though. Denise had met him on the block. She was attracted to his style and the money. She got pregnant by him a month after they met, but she soon found out he had eight kids and she would become his ninth baby mama.

On top of his many women and children, he was a violent man. Dominique used to beat on Denise, and even slapped around her twin girls until they were ten years old. One time, Denise fought him back, and he beat her so severely, she had to spend a week in the hospital. Dominique was charged with her abuse, and then soon after, he caught a drug charge and was sentenced to fifteen years to life.

Apple never understood her mother and missed her father a great deal. She only had a few pictures of him and some memories. Her mother was a beautiful woman, but she was a ghetto tragedy who never had anything to call her own, except heartache, the bottle she clung to every night, a beat-up pussy, a box of Newports, and the projects they grew up in. Denise would whore herself out for a good time and a few dollars, and Apple loathed how her mother treated a man with a big dick and some cash better than her own daughters.

Apple knew she was totally opposite from her mother and had dreams of being somebody. She wanted to be rich, marry Cross, move from the projects, and have her own, something her mother never had. She was determined to be different from her family. She wanted to be that chick that everyone looked up to and respected. She wanted to be the woman in Cross's life. She wanted to be noticed. She wanted to be known and loved.

Chapter 2

Apple strutted across the busy Harlem street and walked toward the bodega where Cross and his friends were hanging out. The sun was shining brightly like a jewel in the sky, and the warm weather made it feel more like summer than spring. Apple's heart pumped rapidly as she came closer to Cross. Just being a few feet from him got her excited and nervous. She tried not to look directly at him while she walked his way, but she couldn't help stealing a glance from the corner of her eyes.

They all were gambling, playing dice on the side of the bodega. Cross clutched a knot of money in his hand and was talking shit. He was hunched over, shaking the dice in his grip and swiftly letting them roll to the ground with the anticipation of winning the cash displayed in front of him—$500.

Soon, there was yelling and excitement. Having won the pot, Cross rose up and shouted, "Yeah, muthafuckas! Give me my fuckin' money. Ya'll niggas don't fuckin' know? I'm Vegas out this bitch, sendin' ya'll niggas home broke wit' ya pockets turned inside out."

Apple smiled, hearing him rant in excitement. The men were so into their dice game, and Cross was so busy collecting his winnings, they didn't notice her pass and enter the store. Apple wished she could share in Cross's winning moment.

However, she came back to her senses, went up to the bodega owner, and said, "Fernando, let me get a pack of Newports."

"Twelve dollars."

"Damn, Fernando! Why you keep raising the price and shit?" Apple complained.

"You and your mother stop smoking, then it be cheaper," Fernando joked.

"Oh, so I see you got jokes, huh? Shit, I'ma stop, but fuck it. It's my mother's money anyway."

Fernando passed her the pack, but Apple wanted to get a few other things from the store while she had the chance. She knew she needed some tampons because her "friend" was almost coming, and she didn't want to get caught out there. She hated sharing with her sister because Kola always wanted to bitch about everything. Apple sighed, debating whether she should get the pack of tampons from Rite Aid or something to eat, since she was starving. She knew there wasn't anything to eat at the apartment, and she felt the urge for one of Fernando's turkey and cheese hero with mustard, mayo, onions, and lettuce.

"Fuck it. Fernando, make me a turkey and cheese. You know how I like it," Apple said.

Fernando smiled. "I got you."

Apple felt her stomach growling, and she hated walking around on an empty stomach. If her friend came, she would beef with Kola or Nichols about borrowing one of their tampons, but right then, she was hungry.

She waited around the front entrance, reading the *Daily News* and trying to pass time. Two of Cross's goons walked into the store, and they were loud. Apple glanced at them. They were cute, but none of them could hold her interest like Cross did.

"Damn, ma, what you gettin' from here? I got you," one of them offered.

Apple smiled. "I'm a'ight."

"C'mon, ma, my treat. You lookin' too sexy to come out ya pockets," he continued. "Yo, Fernando, what she gettin'? I got her." The man placed a fifty on the countertop.

Apple knew Edge was Cross's right-hand man. He was hot-tempered and volatile, while Cross was calm and a calculated hustler. But they were close like brothers.

"Really, you ain't gotta pay. I got my own," Apple lied.

"Fo' real, ma? A'ight, I hear that shit, but I'ma still be nice and treat you, and next time, you got me. A'ight."

"Maybe."

Edge locked eyes with her. Apple knew he was flirting, and she knew he probably wanted much more from her than a conversation and a smile. In fact, she knew he wanted to hit it. Every nigga wanted to fuck sex her and her sisters, but Apple didn't want her name to carry around the hood recklessly and have word get back to Cross that she was a ho. So, she rarely fucked with dudes from around her way because she knew niggas talked more than bitches—especially when it came to pussy.

"Yo, Edge, you riding out to Summer Jam wit' us, right?" the second man asked. "Cross said he was goin' to roll wit' us."

Apple's ears perked up when she heard Cross would be at Summer Jam too. She started to listen more closely to their conversation. She heard the man tell Edge that they were leaving out in three trucks to show a presence, and that they knew a few dudes backstage and would have VIP access.

Apple wished she could ride with them. She wanted to profile and be up close with the celebrities. But she, Ayesha, and Mesha were taking public transportation to the New Jersey arena, and getting there from Harlem would take them a year and a day. Apple was excited about the concert, but she dreaded the bus and train ride there. Also, since their tickets were almost nosebleed seats, she knew that Drake, Trey Songz, and the others would look like ants because they would be seated the farthest away. She wanted to witness the sweat pour off of Trey Songz's abs and see Drake up close at his finest.

After Edge paid for her sandwich, he tried to get her number. Apple was grateful, but turned him down gently.

"I'm seventeen," she stated.

"And ya eighteen when?"

"In two months."

"A'ight, I'ma take that rain check until your eighteenth birthday then treat you to somethin' nice."

Apple smiled. She wished it was Cross coming at her the way Edge was. She exited the bodega and noticed that her boo, Cross, was gone. She wanted to look at him again, but she knew he was a busy man and didn't keep too long at one location. She walked back to her building with her sandwich, cigarettes, and the twenty dollars her mother had given her.

Becoming even more excited about Summer Jam, Apple knew she needed to look spectacular that night because it was going to be a star-packed event. And with all the ballers and shot-callers that would be in Giants Stadium, she wanted her outfit to be tight and sexy enough to stop traffic.

Apple walked into the lobby as her sister Kola was exiting the elevator. Kola was clad in a pair of tight white coochie-cutting cotton shorts, a striped metallic halter top, and stiletto heels with the red bottoms. She sported expensive gold bangles and hoop earrings, with her long black hair styled into a ponytail. She looked like she was about to work a corner. Apple looked at her sister, and their eyes met. They thought the same thing. Aside from the difference in style and mannerism, they were identical—from head to toe.

"Where you goin'?" Apple asked.

"Out."

"Like that?"

"And? I got places to be," Kola replied with attitude.

Apple sucked her teeth. "Whatever."

"You went to the store for Mommy?" Kola asked.

"Yeah."

"Let me get a cigarette," Kola said.

"No. Go buy your own. Besides, you know how Mommy gets when she got cigarettes missing."

"It ain't like you didn't already take one, Apple. Shit, I'm just asking for only one. I need a smoke right now. You know she stressin' a bitch," Kola told her.

Apple hesitated and then passed Kola the pack of cigarettes, knowing Denise was going to rage when she found out cigarettes were missing from her pack before she could even smoke one. But Apple was used to her mother's loud and abusive ways, which was a normal thing in her household.

Kola took two from the pack and thanked Apple. "I heard you goin' to Summer Jam with Ayesha and Mesha. Y'all got an extra ticket?"

"No," Apple replied shortly.

"Damn! Why you gotta say it like that?" Kola asked. "Y'all probably ain't got good seats anyway."

"Stop hatin', Kola."

"I'm not. I'm just sayin . . . I probably can do better."

Apple stared at her sister with disgust and wanted to smack her. Kola was selfish and always thought she was the better twin, always trying to outdo everybody.

Keeping her cool, Apple replied, "Then do better and stay out my shit."

"Whateva, Apple. I'm out. Have fun." Kola strutted out the lobby, switching her petite backside and catching eyes from the young boys around.

Apple watched her sister get into a burgundy Benz with chrome wheels and knew Kola had probably snatched up some local drug dealer. She shrugged off her sister's annoying comment and continued upstairs to the apartment. Once she was inside, her mother was frantic about her missing cigarettes and cursed Apple out.

"Apple, you owe me money! Why you let your sister go into my pack like that?"

"She just did."

"And where the fuck is my change?"

"Gone."

"Apple, don't fuckin' play wit' me! I need my fuckin' money!" Denise shouted.

"Well, I was hungry and got me a sandwich. You ain't buyin' or cookin' shit," Apple exclaimed.

"Y'all some ungrateful kids. I fuckin' swear, I shoulda aborted y'all when I had the chance." Denise lit up a Newport and heatedly walked into her bedroom.

Apple just smirked and said under her breath, "Next time, go to the store your damn self." She clutched the twenty-dollar bill in her hand and knew it would be put to better use.

Apple walked into the bedroom to see her younger sister, Nichols, lying on her bed and reading the latest issue of *Vibe* magazine. Nichols smiled upon seeing her big sister. She was sixteen, full of energy, and developing a body like a porn star, thick in all the right places—hips, thighs, and ass—and slim where it mattered—the waist. Like her twin sisters, Nichols had many young men in the projects vying for her, but she was into her books and still in school on the regular. She was an A student and looked up to her twin sisters like role models. While Kola was teaching her about boys, clothes, and sex, Apple wanted Nichols to stay in school and not get caught up in a wayward lifestyle.

"I heard you're going to Summer Jam with Mesha and Ayesha. Ooh, can I come, Apple?" Nichols asked with gleam in her eyes.

"We ain't got any more tickets."

Nichols sucked her teeth. "I wanna go."

"I'm sorry, Nichols. We could only get three tickets."

"I never get to do shit wit' y'all. All I do is lie around here and do nothin'. It ain't fair." Nichols had a sad stare. Being more of an introvert, Nichols spent most of her time studying and with her only close friend.

Apple took a seat next to her. "Nichols, I promise next time we gonna do somethin' together. I'm gonna look out for you this summer."

"You promise?" Nichols asked with a smile.

"I promise. C'mon, girl, you my baby sister. I got you."

"Kola said she was goin' to get me into the clubs this summer," Nichols informed her.

"Nichols, you don't need to be in the club."

"You and Kola go all the time, and y'all only a year older than me. I'm grown too."

"You need to stop tryin' to grow up so fast."

Nichols rolled her neck and snapped her fingers. "Look who's talking."

"We still older and wiser."

"Apple, all I do is go to school, study, and read. I wanna have some fun like y'all. I'm tired of being cooped up in this crib with Mommy always yelling at somebody."

"That's because you're smart, Nichols, and you got potential to be better. Forget Mommy. She just hating 'cause we better than her, and we got something going for ourselves. We divas, and she ain't."

Nichols laughed. "Don't let Mommy hear you say that."

Apple stared at Nichols' young figure in her jean skirt, which displayed her meaty thighs and smooth brown skin, and knew that, if she didn't already, she was going to have problems in the future. Grown men looked at Nichols like she was prey—a sweet, young piece of meat. She wasn't street savvy like her twin sisters, so Apple and Kola always felt they needed to keep a keen eye on her because the men in the projects were thirsty for a taste of her.

Nichols was growing fast and becoming more influenced by her sisters and their ways. She wanted to get out of the nest and learn how to fly on her own.

Apple noticed Nichols' clothing was becoming tighter and more revealing. She noticed the look in Nichols' eyes when Kola's young hustler friends would come by the crib. Apple knew that look all too well—lust. She began to wonder if Nichols was still a virgin.

"So what you gonna wear to Summer Jam?" Nichols asked.

"I don't even know. I ain't got shit to wear," Apple returned with a discouraged sigh.

"You know there's gonna be many cuties up in there. Damn, I hate you, Apple!" Nichols joked.

"Next year, we go together. I promise, because I'm gonna be paid," Apple said, trying to assure her little sister.

Nichols smiled, leaping from the bed and rushing to the closet. She swung open the door and went leafing through all of Apple's clothing. Apple's wardrobe wasn't extensive like Kola's. She did have some nice things, but they were all outdated, and Apple had grown tired of the style.

"You need to go shopping," Nichols told her.

"With what money?"

"Then borrow some clothes from Kola. You know she got a bunch of gear she ain't wearing in her closet."

"You know how she is wit' her shit," Apple reminded her sister.

"Yeah, I know. That's why I don't ask and just sneak her outfits back into her closet when she ain't looking," Nichols informed Apple with a devilish smile.

"Oooh, you a sneak."

"Hey, her clothes be lookin' too good on me."

Apple and Nichols both laughed.

Apple's mood turned serious, as she thought about what to wear to the Summer Jam concert. She knew it would be a bad look for her to go in something outdated.

Every bitch at that concert was going to try and outdo each other, and Apple felt she needed to step up her game or probably not go at all—especially after finding out that Cross was going to be there.

She sat next to Nichols and began pondering her options. She needed some cash, and she needed it fast. She remembered a nice, sexy outfit she saw on 125th Street the other day when she was hanging out with Ayesha. The price tag was $200, which was way out of her budget for clothes. However, Apple knew once she was seen in it, heads would turn, and dudes would drool over the way her body fit into the skintight shorts and trendy shirt.

Apple even thought about getting Kola and her crew to shoplift the outfit for her. Kola's girls had the means, the nerves, and the attitude to boost from any store and get away with it. But she hated to owe Kola any favors. It was very frustrating for Apple to know what she wanted to wear to the concert but not be able to afford it.

"What's on your mind, Apple?" Nichols inquired with concern.

"Nothin'," she replied. Apple then looked at her sister and smiled. "I'll be back."

"Where you going?"

"Out for a minute."

"Can I come?" Nichols asked.

"No," Apple shouted.

Nichols sucked her teeth and caught an attitude; she hated being the little sister.

Apple snatched a cigarette from off the dresser and

walked out the apartment. She needed a smoke and a walk. She marched down the pissy-smelling stairway and stepped into the lobby, only to see Supreme and Guy Tony conducting business with a young male stranger. Apple was aware of Supreme's loan-sharking reputation. He was a bully, a pervert, and, most importantly, feared in the neighborhood.

Supreme turned to see Apple standing close by, trying to exit. He took a pull from the burning Black & Mild, eyed Apple's luscious body from head to toe, and said, "You tryin' to pass, Apple?"

"Yeah," she uttered.

"How's ya moms doin'? She good, right?" Supreme asked, his tone dirty.

"She fine." Apple tried to be short.

Supreme nodded with a smile, his eyes dancing all over Apple's petite, curvy figure. He had a craving for young girls like Apple. She was the one he desired the most, but she always kept her distance from him. In her eyes, Supreme was nothing but a goofball.

Guy Tony, Supreme's young worker and underling, stood silently next to his boss. He looked at Apple with a deadpan stare, the .45 peeking from underneath his shirt. He was nineteen with a secret crush on Apple.

She knew Guy Tony by his government name, Anthony. They went to grade school together and used to be cool until high school, when he started running with Supreme. It was at that time he turned into "Guy Gooney." He had gotten sucked into the loan-sharking business with Supreme, and the two remained close ever since.

Apple noticed the nervous, young stranger by the door. She wanted to mind her business. She didn't care for any of the men or their shady business tactics. However, she did notice the large roll of twenties and fifties that Supreme had clutched in his hand. It sparked a gleam in her eyes.

"You need somethin', Apple?" Supreme asked.

"I just need to pass," she said.

"You sure that's all you need?" Supreme had a hint of persuasion in his voice as he counted his large knot.

"Yeah, now move," she spat.

Supreme smiled. He was six-one with a broad build to him. He sported little jewelry and a denim jacket with a switchblade in the pocket, which he was known to use on deadbeats, sticking his victims in the hands, eye, knee, or wherever he was able to cause agonizing pain, as a warning for them to pay up soon.

Slowly, Supreme stepped out of Apple's way with an unruly smile. He couldn't keep his eyes off her body. "If you need somethin', Apple, you can always come to me."

"Whatever," Apple said before exiting the building.

As she walked out into the street, the only thing on her mind was Supreme's bankroll. She figured he had to have about five grand in his pockets, and she knew she could do wonders with that money. First, she would get herself the bomb outfit for Summer Jam, and second, she would leave the projects for something better. But those were only dreams. Supreme was a snake—a first-class jerk. Still, he had money, which was something she truly needed.

Apple took a seat on top of the bench, took a few pulls from her cigarette, and thought about doing the unthinkable. That bankroll in Supreme's hand had excited her. In Apple's mind, it was easy money. Summer Jam was next week, and she needed an outfit, her hair done, money for transportation, and maybe a little extra something for food and activities with her girls.

"Just this one time, you gotta look right for Cross," she convinced herself.

She took a few more pulls from her cigarette, sighed heavily, jumped from off the bench, and hurried back to see Supreme. After walking into the lobby, she noticed the stranger had left, but Supreme and Guy Tony had lingered around, talking.

Supreme immediately saw Apple re-enter the building. He turned with a smile. "You came back for somethin'?" he asked with a smirk.

Apple looked up at him, wondering if she was doing the right thing by asking him for a loan. "Can we talk?"

Supreme looked at the young beauty for a moment. Then he exhaled the smoke from the Black & Mild he puffed on and gestured for Apple to follow him into the stairwell for privacy. "Give me a minute, Guy," he said.

Guy Tony nodded.

As Apple followed behind him, Supreme asked, "What you need?"

"I need a favor."

"How much?" Supreme asked, already knowing she wanted money. It was always about money with him. Supreme towered over Apple's five-three frame and waited for her to answer.

"Two hundred," Apple replied, afraid that if she asked for more he would shut her down.

"Two hundred, huh?"

"I'll pay you back," she told him.

"I know you will. It ain't a choice. But you know I'm about my business, Apple. I take it seriously. I'm nothin' to play with in these streets."

"I know."

"What you need this paper for anyway?"

"I'd rather not say."

Supreme chuckled and licked his lips. He was known to have females fuck or suck him repeatedly to free themselves from their debts. He had the same plan for Apple. If she couldn't pay him back, he would have her sleep off her debt.

"You know what? Since I like you, I'ma hook you up." Supreme reached into his pocket, peeled off five crisp C-notes, and passed them to Apple. "Take five hundred and have yourself a good time."

"But I only need two," Apple contested meekly.

"I know you're good for it. I'll get my money back one way or another, Apple. You remember that. I don't like to be fucked wit'," Supreme stated in a cold tone.

Apple wasn't intimidated by his subtle threats, though. For some inexplicable reason she felt that the most he would do to her is try to bark on her in front of her peoples, which she could handle. She had been around men scarier than him, and she knew how to handle herself. She thought Supreme was a clown-ass dude, and in her mind he was a dumb ass for loaning her the money knowing she didn't work.

She smiled and responded, "Thanks."

"You got three weeks to pay that back to me wit' three points added to that, Apple. After that, I might become a problem."

"It won't be a problem, Supreme," she assured him.

"As long as we got that understanding then."

Apple rushed up the concrete stairway, while Supreme watched her in her form-fitting skirt, leeringly. This loan was motivated by pure lust. He massaged his crotch and thought about her young pussy. It was a loan he was eager to get paid back in sex. He didn't want the money; he wanted her.

Chapter 3

K ola stepped into the seedy and dimly lit strip club
on Amsterdam Avenue, where the young women
walked around butt naked with either a drink or cash
in their hands. It was pure underground, where weed
smoke lingered in the air, cheap liquor was served from
a makeshift bar, and for the right amount of cash, one of
the ghetto-style women would fuck anyone in the back
rooms.

Drake's "Best I Ever Had" blared throughout the
spot, while the male customers fondled the women with
lustful attention, sucked tits, and squeezed asses. Coochies
were wet, and dicks were hard from the surrounding
temptation.

Kola followed behind Mike-Mike, strutting through
the crowd. Clad in a revealing short skirt, a tight shirt,
and her long, defined light-brown legs standing erect
in some clear stiletto heels, her chandelier earrings and
diamond bracelet gleamed magnificently in the place. She
quickly caught the attention of a few men in the room.

They thought she was a dancer. They eyed her like she was the prize to go after. Kola smiled and flirted with a few of them, but she wasn't about to take her clothes off, especially for free. She just came to enjoy the scene and the ladies with her friend Mike-Mike.

"You want a drink, Kola?" Mike-Mike asked.

"Yeah, get me some Grey Goose."

"A'ight, I got you, luv," Mike-Mike said with a smile.

Mike-Mike was Kola's friend from the building, and the two occasionally fucked each other for fun. They both liked to get into different shit, it being either sex or getting money, and the two sometimes did it together, even having a threesome from time to time. But they still did their thang with other people without any feelings of jealousy in the mix.

Kola and Mike-Mike had a mutual respect for each other that went back to grade school. They understood each other, and no one could break their special bond. Mike-Mike was a go-getter and a brawler who hustled the block under Cross, and if Kola had any beef, he had her back and vice versa.

Mike-Mike moved through the crowd with a strong confidence. He was like a pit bull, with his wide build and strong arms, and weighed close to three hundred pounds. He was only six-two, but his appearance alone was intimidating to many. He rocked a shaved head and a thick beard, and was sometimes mistaken for a Muslim. His forearm was covered in tattoos, his ears sported diamonds, and he was a beast on the streets and in the bedroom. Kola loved him, but they weren't in love. They were just cool with each other.

Kola stood by the stage and was fixated on a sweaty, young female working hard for a few dollars. The stripper was short, but thick all over. She was butt naked, her shoes laid on one side of the stage and her clothing to the opposite. With her legs spread, she was playing with her clit to the sound of Drake. She worked the stage with such zeal; she looked like she was born to be a freak.

Kola smiled, admiring the girl. She was somewhat into women. For her, it felt good to try new things, and tonight she wanted to experiment with her third threesome. Bored, she was ready to indulge in some sexual excitement.

Kola began tipping the dancer. She spread a few dollars onto the girl and had her work her body for a few twenties in singles. The dancer rotated, made her ass cheeks clap like applause, and spread herself all around, showing Kola every inch of her body—ass crack and all. Her kitty-cat was shaved, her thighs were thick like a tree trunk, and her nipples were dark like Hershey's chocolate. The girl put on such a show; Kola gave her an extra twenty.

"What's ya name?" Kola asked.

"Kandy."

"I like you, Kandy," Kola said.

"Thanks."

Kola felt up her tits, grabbed her thighs. "I wanna talk to you later."

"A'ight," Kandy replied with a smile.

Mike-Mike returned with Kola's drink. He looked over at Kandy then asked Kola, "You like that?"

"Yeah, she's cute and sexy."

"Fuck it. You wanna do her?" he asked.

"Let me look around first," Kola said.

Mike-Mike nodded and took a sip from his Corona. He looked around the room to see who was who, made some quick observations, and then focused his attention back to Kola and the girl on stage.

The place was buzzing with naked, willing women and constantly flowing with alcohol. Men and women were disappearing in and out of the back rooms for VIP all night. Money was being made, while fantasies were being fulfilled.

Kola watched some lesbian action being performed on stage, where two girls were contorted in the 69 position, tits pressed against flesh; legs spread wide.

The men howled and tossed dollar bills at the lewd action. One dude even went as far as to pour his beer down one girl's back and then between the other girl's legs. Still, the girls didn't miss a beat pleasing each other.

Fixated on the action just like the men, Kola continually tossed money at them. An hour had passed, and she was on her third drink. Feeling tipsy and horny, she looked around for Kandy and spotted the thick, bootylicious, brown-skinned shorty giving someone a lap dance in a nearby corner. Kola kept her eyes keenly on Kandy, admiring her thick physique and sexy swag.

Kola was loose like her mother, having quickly adopted her promiscuous ways. She loved action. She'd lost her virginity to Mike-Mike at thirteen, and from there on, sex was her playground. It was her world to explore and enjoy—mostly with men, but sprinkled with a few women if they were cute and sexy like her. She and Mike-Mike would frequent certain strip clubs looking for the right ladies to get up with. They had an agenda and wanted to get things in motion before summer's end.

Kola wanted out of her mother's place and was willing to do whatever it took. Even though she and her mother were alike in many respects, sometimes they bumped heads. She couldn't understand why her mom was always tripping. She thought it was hate, coming from her moms. Kola had her youth, and her mother didn't. Her mother still possessed her beauty, but Denise didn't have that hustle like Kola, who knew those welfare schemes were getting old. There wasn't any real money behind a government check, and Kola wasn't about to get pregnant by some nigga and lose her dynamite shape just to hit a nigga up for child support. It wasn't happening.

Though she and Apple were cool sometimes, Kola felt that Apple was just too chill, reserved, and maybe even looked down on her. Kola was a freak, but she was about herself and ready to make it happen in any way possible. In Kola's mind, Apple was lazy. She was one step away from getting knocked up by some loser and living off welfare checks just like Denise. Kola wanted more. She and Mike-Mike had devised a scheme to get money, and they were ready to put their plan in motion as soon as they chose the right girls to participate.

Kola tapped Mike-Mike on his shoulder and whispered in his ear, "I'm ready to do this. I wanna fuck wit' her." She pointed over to Kandy.

Mike-Mike smiled. "Nice." He downed his shot of Henny and said, "Whenever you ready."

Kola got up and walked over to Kandy. She watched Kandy grind against the young man's hard-on, her legs spread across his lap. She loved the way Kandy leaned back into the dude, her back pushed against his chest as he cupped her tits, and her arm wrapped around him for control, her fat ass parked in his lap like a root.

Kandy was naked in his grip, feeling the guy's hard dick pushing through his jeans. When she looked up and noticed Kola staring at her, she displayed a lustful smile. Kandy licked her lips and continued to toy with the young client.

The feel of her soft buttery skin and juicy pussy had him wide open. He moaned in her ear, "Damn, ma! You got a nigga wanting to fuck right now."

"You gotta pay to play," she replied.

Kola enjoyed the show that Kandy had put on and felt the urges between her legs. When the two women locked eyes, Kandy immediately knew what the look was about. It was one she was familiar with. She quickly finished up her lap dance; making him grunt and moan then collected her money after rising up from the rigid dick that was pushing against her butt while pleasing him.

Kandy excited the young dude to the point where he had to get up and rush to the bathroom. She smiled at her effect on him.

"That was nice," Kola stated.

"You like that?" Kandy teased.

"I did. But, me and my friend, we're ready to pay to play wit' you," Kola told her. "How much?"

Kandy stared at Kola's beauty, admiring the stunning young girl from head to toe, and uttered, "Two hundred."

"Cool, let's go," Kola said.

Kandy smiled and picked up her things. Sweaty and naked in her clear six-inch stilettos, she followed behind Kola. Mike-Mike met the girls at the entrance to the long hallway that led to one of the four VIP rooms. He slipped the security a fifty-dollar bill for the room and followed behind the two women.

Kandy led them into a dimmed room, which was sparsely decorated with a long leather couch and a folding chair. The room was a reasonable size for sex or other pleasures, with the burning incense masking any bad smell from previous use of the room.

Mike-Mike closed the door behind him, ready to fuck and get some head.

Kandy waited for her payment, which came from Mike-Mike. He pulled out a wad of bills and passed Kandy two hundred dollars in twenties. Liking the attraction, Kandy smiled, and the trio wasted no time.

"How you want it?" Kandy asked.

"Us first; he can watch," Kola instructed.

Again, Kandy smiled. She walked up to Kola and placed her hands on her hips. She neared her face toward Kola's and then glanced over at Mike-Mike, who was seated in the folding chair and watching the two intensely.

Kandy slowly began to lift Kola's short skirt up, exposing the pink-and-white panties she had on. Kandy then removed them with a smile and care, having Kola step out of them and show off her trimmed pussy hairs. Kola's rich light-brown skin was soft like silk, and Kandy touched her in admiration. Kandy gradually moved her hand up Kola's smooth thighs, grabbed her throbbing pussy, and began finger-fucking her slowly and deliberately.

Kola let out a pleasing moan and clenched her walls around Kandy's fingers, and as the two kissed excitedly, she felt Kandy's finger pushing deeper into her.

Mike-Mike sat with patience, admiring the action and growing harder by the minute, as Kola and Kandy moved their action over to the leather couch, where Kandy made Kola lie on her back. Kola arched upwards and spread her legs.

When Kola was in position, waiting with anticipation for her kitty to be licked, Kandy moved between her legs and buried her face into her throbbing pussy. Her tongue wrestled with Kola's sensitive clit. Kola gasped and clasped her legs around Kandy, who dug her tongue deep inside Kola's pussy and slipped a wet finger in her ass.

As Kandy busied herself with Kola, Kola looked over at Mike-Mike with an inviting smile. She panted, feeling

Kandy's tongue skillfully digging into her, and then gestured for him to join in on the fun.

Mike-Mike stood up and pulled off his shirt, revealing his hairy, tattooed chest. He moved closer to the ladies, unbuttoning his jeans, and removing his Timberlands. After taking a long pull from a cigarette, he put it out before taking a seat on the couch and removing his boxers.

Kandy paused to gaze at Mike-Mike's package. She wanted to see what he was working with and was really impressed.

Mike-Mike leaned back with his arms across the couch in a dignified manner, his dick hard like a rock. He was big and long, and ready to fuck.

Kandy leaned in for the action. She engulfed him whole, showing Mike-Mike her skill in sucking dick, deep-throating him while coiling the tip with her tongue and massaging his nuts. Kola joined in on the action, tea-bagging him from below.

Mike-Mike had both ladies slobbering him down, as he closed his eyes, enjoying the treat. Soon, a Magnum was ripped open and rolled onto his thick size, and Kandy quickly straddled him. She jerked, clinging to his thick frame, gasping, and he fucked her like the beast he was.

He then changed the condom and switched to Kola. He fucked her from the back, squeezing her neck and slapping her ass.

The three went at it intensely. Kandy rode Mike-Mike like he was a stallion in a race, while Kola sat on his face and had her pussy eaten out.

Kola squirmed and exhaled, clawing at his chest, feeling his tongue wiggle inside of her. She was about to come, and she let it be known. "Oh shit! Baby, I'm comin'," she exclaimed, feeling her ass squeezed like it was a juicy fruit.

Kandy rode his dick, feeling every inch of it travel farther inside her. Her legs quivered, and she bit down on her tongue as Mike-Mike thrust deep into her.

"Oh! Oh! Oh! Oh shit! Oh, big daddy! Oh shit!" Kandy cried out, feeling the urge to come all over his big, working dick.

Mike worked Kola's pussy deep like a coal miner and then felt her come all over his face. Spent, Kola rolled off his face like she was limp and hit the floor.

Kandy was next. She twisted and turned and buried her manicured nails into Mike-Mike's skin, feeling herself explode from the constant pounding he put her insides through.

"Aaahhhh shit! Oh shit! Fuck!" Kandy screamed out as her body tensed up from the action, his dick roughing her pussy up.

Kandy closed her eyes and came like she never had before. She felt the pulsation of Mike-Mike's orgasm quaking inside of her like he was Mount St. Helens erupting. She collapsed on his chest and knew it was the best sex she'd ever had. The trio had gone at it for a half-hour.

Before Kandy exited, Kola hit her up with a business proposition. "How would you like to have sex like that all the time?" she asked.

"Shit. Y'all wicked wit' it," Kandy replied. "I might be down."

Kola smiled. "We gonna talk."

Kola saved Kandy's number in her phone and promised to call her again when the time was right. She liked Kandy because she was a freak and down for whatever.

Kandy was so satisfied and in awe of Mike-Mike's performance, she was ready to pay him. But it was all part of Kola's plan. Kola knew Mike-Mike was a beast in the pussy, and she didn't mind sharing the dick for a profitable gain later on.

Chapter 4

Apple was excited about Summer Jam. She had money for an outfit and to get her hair done, with enough spending money left over. She wasn't thinking about Supreme or paying back the loan anytime soon. As far as she was concerned, Summer Jam and Cross were her main priorities. The money was in her hands, and she was going to have a good time with it. In her naïve mind it was an investment. Cross would see her looking hot at Summer Jam, wife her, and as her man he'd either step to Supreme for her or he'd give her enough dough to pay him back. Either way, she told herself not to worry.

Mesha convinced Apple to save a hundred dollars on her outfit. She knew of a local booster who had the same outfit for cheaper. Apple was down. A hundred dollars less was a steal for her.

The girls met Jay-Ray at his Harlem apartment on Seventh Avenue. His place was littered with stolen clothing and other items, some with the store tags still on them. Apple was wide-eyed at the range of clothing

Jay-Ray had in his place—Donna Karan, Gucci, Prada, Tommy Hilfiger, Dolce & Gabbana. He had it all.

Mesha and Apple looked around the apartment like two kids in a candy store.

"Damn, Jay-Ray! Where you get all this shit?" Apple asked.

"I got the hookup," he said. Jay-Ray was the flamboyant type, sporting tight, skinny jeans, jewelry, colorful shirts, and he wore his hair long in curls like Ice-T.

"I see."

"See, I told you, girl," Mesha said. "Jay-Ray be havin' the best shit."

Apple browsed through some of the things that she knew would take months for her to afford. She picked up a pair of black Manolo Blahnik shoes with a price tag of $700. "How much for these?" she asked.

Jay-Ray looked at the shoes and replied, "For you, three hundred."

It was a bargain, but the shoes were still out of Apple's budget range. She put the shoes down and decided to go cheaper. As Apple looked through a ton of clothes in the bedroom, she knew, if she was able to take even a few items home, Kola would envy her.

Mesha picked up a pair of Apple Bottom jeans, smiled, and looked over at Apple. "See, here you go, Apple, wit' ya name on it and everything—*Apple* Bottom."

Apple laughed. "Nah, not my style."

"Girl, you better get you a pair of these. They would kill on you, wit' ya shape, and they for fifty dollars too.

Niggas gonna love seein' your ass in these."

Apple laughed again. "Mesha, you crazy, girl."

Mesha sucked her teeth playfully and replied, "Well, I'm gettin' them. They my size too."

Apple smiled and continued searching. She needed to find the right attire for the concert, something that would catch Cross's attention. She wanted to be a diva. She wanted to be noticed by her love, and the right wardrobe said a lot about a bitch.

The girls spent an hour in Jay-Ray's place looking and buying. He was cool with the length of time they spent there because he was making money. He had a team of teenagers under his wing, and shady employees he paid off in the department stores to get whatever he wanted. In the business of stealing since he was a kid, Jay-Ray had graduated to a professional booster by the time he reached puberty.

Apple smiled at the right thing to wear to the concert. She spent a total of three hundred dollars with Jay-Ray, who was pleased to have her business. She bought an assortment of things for her cash and knew that the money she'd spent at Jay-Ray's apartment was a bargain, because the stuff she walked out with would have totaled up to a thousand dollars in a department store.

Apple and Mesha exited the building with smiles on their faces. They were like two kids on a merry-go-round. They joked and laughed and strutted down 125th Street joyfully.

"I'm hungry."

"Me too," Apple replied.

"McDonald's dollar menu," Mesha suggested.

"Girl, you read my mind."

Being on a budget after having spent money on their clothes and shoes, the two rushed to the nearest McDonald's and strutted into the packed fast-food restaurant on 125th Street.

"What you want, Apple? Just get us a table. It's lookin' crazy in here," Mesha said.

Apple looked up at the dollar menu and said, "Get me that McDouble with two apple pies and a sweet tea." She then slipped Mesha five dollars and went looking for a table to sit at. Apple had noticed the fellows in the place gawking at her and Mesha the minute they'd stepped in, but she ignored them.

Apple got a window seat, and while waiting for Mesha with the food, she looked through her bags of clothing, smiling with excitement. She couldn't wait to be seen in her new outfits. She had the body and curves to fill out everything she bought. If Cross didn't notice her at Summer Jam, then he had to be blind, because Apple knew she had it going on.

She looked around the restaurant and shook her head at all the hungry black people in the place. Most were overweight and out of shape, but not Apple. She was always watching her figure and knew that obesity wasn't coming her way anytime soon.

Mesha came to the table with a tray of food and sat opposite Apple. The two began tearing into their burgers and downing the sweet teas that they loved, especially on a hot spring day.

"Oooh, I needed this. This tea going down my throat is better than sex right now," Mesha joked.

Apple laughed. "Shit, you crazy, girl. I don't know about that. It's a'ight."

"Whateva. You know it's hot, and ya pussy probably sweating like a runaway slave."

"My shit a'ight," Apple said. "See, she cooling. You're the one in the skintight jeans who got these niggas lookin' and breaking their necks at you."

"Girl, and like you don't, wit' them shorts you got on, legs showing and teasing muthafuckas. You a mess, Apple."

"I'm a mess that's gonna be lookin' fly at Summer Jam."

"I hear that shit. You and me both, bitch," Mesha chimed, slapping Apple five.

They continued eating their meals and feeling the eyes of men watching them from all over the room.

Mesha noticed two cuties in the place that she wouldn't have minded getting with, but she was content with her boo, Naquin. The couple had been together since freshman year in high school, and he was Mesha's first.

Mesha was a sultry, long-legged, ravishing beauty with light skin, hazel eyes, and shoulder-length black hair. When it came to beauty, she and Apple were running neck and neck. Still, they never hated on each other and had been friends since junior high school.

Apple was petite and curvy. Mesha was too, but she had thicker hips and more butt for the men to stare at. Both girls were able to stir up a man's heart without even a thought. The two couldn't even eat their food in peace without several men trying to approach them for conversation and a minute of their time. But the two girls, used to being hit on and approached, sometimes with good manners or just plain rudely, turned the eager men down.

"Ill . . . not," Mesha commented about one of the guys that tried to come on to her.

He was tall and shapeless, with a scruffy beard, and had hopes of getting her number.

"Stop being picky," Apple said with a smile.

"You fuck him then."

Apple chuckled. "Never that."

"A'ight then. Besides, when was the last time you got some dick? Or are you still tryin' to save it for Cross?"

"I'm good. You know I get mines," Apple replied.

"And when was that? The last nigga I know you fucked was Terrance. What? His ten-year sentence got you dried up now?"

Apple sucked her teeth and remembered Terrance as being only a fling, a substitute until the real thing came along.

"Then before him, Jason. Oh, and I can't forget Ramee. Yeah, he fucked you *and* your sister."

"And?"

"I'm just sayin', girl . . . I ain't tryin' to get at you, but you need to stop waiting for Cross, and get booed up soon. You ain't gettin' any younger. You done passed up on some fine niggas that wanted to holla at you. Besides, when have you ever known Cross to wife up some chick? Shit, that nigga's too busy treatin' his dick like it's some fuckin' passport, traveling up in all them hoes, like he JetBlue or somethin."

Apple sighed.

"I'm just sayin', do you and stop waitin' around daydreaming about this dude."

Apple heard her out, but she was still determined to pursue Cross. He was the one who made her heart skip beats and her panties wet like she had dipped them in a river.

The two finished up their meal and left the chain food spot, only to be approached by two young thugs waiting by the exit.

"Yo, ma, let me holla at you for a minute," one of the young thugs called out.

"Yo, shawty, let me holla at you," the second said, chasing after Apple.

The ladies laughed and replied in unison, "We good."

"I'm sayin, ma, y'all lookin' good as shit. What's ya name?"

Mesha and Apple continued smiling while walking away. They didn't even bother looking back.

"Yo, ma, why y'all actin' like that? I'm sayin', what's good wit' y'all?"

When they were far enough away, they heard one of the thugs yell out, "Yo, fuck y'all stuck-up bitches then! Wit' ya stank pussies!"

Mesha turned, flipped him the middle finger, and shouted, "Fuck you too!"

They laughed it off and headed for Mesha's apartment.

When the girls entered the lobby, they bumped into Supreme, who was exiting the building. Apple looked at Supreme indifferently as she walked beside Mesha.

Supreme smirked. "I hope you didn't forget about me, Apple," he said, as he kept it moving.

Confused, Mesha looked at Apple. "What's he talkin' about, Apple?"

"He's a creep."

"I don't like him. You ain't fuckin' wit' him, right, Apple? I mean, you ain't borrowed money from him or nothin'?" Mesha asked with concern.

"No, Mesha," Apple lied. "You know that nigga's a pervert."

"Yeah, he is."

The girls made it up to Mesha's apartment, where she lived with her seventy-year-old grandmother. They rushed into her room and began trying on the clothes they had bought from Jay-Ray. They modeled in front of Mesha's easel floor mirror while listening to Hot 97.

Apple gazed at herself in the mirror, wearing one of the skirts. As she turned around in the outfit, she looked out the bedroom window and noticed Supreme and Guy Tony getting into a black Escalade. She exhaled noisily, thinking about her debt to him. She knew there was no way she was going to pay back Supreme's money unless she got with Cross.

Apple didn't have a job or a hustle like Kola. Suddenly, the happiness she once displayed earlier quickly turned into a troubling frown. She thought about she and Kola being twins, both having natural beauty like Queen Nefertiti, yet she was a broke bitch, and Kola was seeing crazy dough, being a hustla. She hated to be compared to her sister, but the truth was, some days she wished she was her sister.

As Apple watched the Escalade pull off, she thought about the wealth Supreme had and wondered why he would bitch over a few hundred dollars when he had probably thousands to his name. She shrugged off her debt. She knew she was probably a small fry, compared to niggas that owed him much more, so she wasn't going to stress herself.

Mesha noticed the change in Apple's mood. "Are you OK?"

Apple turned with a forged smile and replied, "Yeah, I'm good. I was just thinking about how we gonna do it up at the concert. Maybe I might snatch me up a baller."

"Girl, wit' that skirt and your fuckin' legs, you might snatch you up a rapper, or maybe an athlete, to sweep you off your feet."

The girls laughed and continued trying on different clothing in the bedroom. Apple twirled herself around in the mirror, loving how her backside looked in the skirt. She smiled, knowing she looked good.

Chapter Five

It was a balmy Sunday afternoon, and Apple was in her room getting ready for the concert. She had the bedroom to herself. Nichols was in the living room watching cable, her mother was out in the streets, and Kola was in the third bedroom, with the door shut.

Apple was excited about this evening. She had her outfit displayed on the bed, and the stereo was playing her favorite song by Nicki Minaj. She was in the mirror doing her hair and singing to "Your Love."

Apple sang the lyrics with feeling, thinking about Cross. She was glowing in the mirror, thinking about love.

She, Ayesha, and Mesha had planned to take a cab to Penn Station and get on the New Jersey Transit to Jersey. Since the concert was starting at six o'clock, they had less than three hours to arrive before the first performance, and Apple didn't want to be late.

Apple swayed, bobbed to the tune, and continued singing. When the song ended, she repeated the track from the beginning, knowing she could listen to it all day while thinking about Cross.

After touching up her hair, she realized she was out of eyeliner. She sucked her teeth, knowing she had to ask Kola. Wanting to look good, she swallowed her pride, walked over to Kola's room, and knocked hard on the door.

"What?" Kola shouted.

"It's Apple. Why you got the door locked?"

"'Cause I'm busy!" Kola yelled.

"I need to borrow your eyeliner. Open the damn door!" Apple shouted back.

"Apple, I'm fuckin' busy!"

"Well, I'ma keep on knocking until you ain't busy," she snapped back.

Kola snatched open the bedroom door and glared at Apple. "You and Nichols already be borrowing my shit wit'out fuckin' asking."

"I don't touch your shit, Kola. That's Nichols."

Looking past her twin, Apple noticed Kola had a guy in the room. Kola was in her usual tight white shorts, which were unfastened, and her nipples showed through a tight T-shirt.

"Why you in my fuckin' business, Apple? Damn!" Kola closed the door to her room a little.

"I don't give a fuck who you fuckin'. I just wanna borrow your eyeliner."

"What? So you can look like a hooker for Summer Jam and hope that maybe you'll run into your baby, Cross?" Kola teased.

Apple sighed. "Look, you gonna let me use it or not?

I can buy my own; I just ain't got time to run to the store."

Kola sucked her teeth. "Whatever. Hold on." She closed the door on Apple and went to get the eyeliner.

Apple stood in the narrow hallway of their apartment, hands on her hip and an annoyed look across her face. She thought Kola had some nerve fucking a guy in their mother's place.

Kola's door flew open, and she tossed Apple the eyeliner that she needed.

"Thank you," Apple said.

"Don't lose my shit."

Apple retreated to the bedroom to finish dressing. She wasn't going to let Kola's attitude ruin the night she had planned with her girls. Apple looked at the time. It was already a quarter to four, and she wasn't dressed yet. She quickly donned her outfit and put on the makeup needed to make her look older than she really was. She checked herself in the mirror and loved what she saw. She'd managed to make herself look five years older, and with the body she walked around with, she knew dudes would be sweating her and her girls.

At a quarter past four, the apartment buzzer sounded. Apple ran to answer the door with her shoes in hand. "I got it!" she yelled out. She swung open the apartment door and greeted Mesha and Ayesha.

Mesha looked at Apple with a frown and barked, "You ain't finished dressin' yet?"

"I'm done, Mesha. Damn. I just gotta get my shit."

"Hurry up, girl. You know I ain't tryin' to be late."

Apple ran back into her bedroom, while Mesha and Ayesha walked into the apartment, saying hello to Nichols, who was on the couch watching MTV.

Nichols turned around and noticed the girls' attire. "Damn! Y'all is lookin' right."

Mesha smiled. "You know it."

"I'm goin' next year wit' y'all," Nichols said with an eager smile.

"I hear that," Ayesha said.

Mesha had on a pair of tight, drop-waist, double-button Seven jeans that highlighted every curve, a pair of white open-toe Fendi heels, and a liquid-gold mesh halter top that draped over her body and accented her breasts.

Ayesha wore a belted Lurex herringbone DKNY mini-skirt that exposed her thick legs and phat ass, with a pair of wraparound heels that made her look like an Amazon, and a tight sexy top that showed the outline of her nipples. Both women looked like divas.

They talked to Nichols while waiting for Apple, and the three focused on MTV's *The Real World*, admiring some of the cuties on the show.

Ten minutes later, Apple stepped out of her bedroom looking fabulous in her Marc Jacobs drop-waist skirt, her thick legs looking like they were stretching to the heavens in her favorite six-inch red-and-white stilettos, and wearing a white one-shoulder top that laced up the back and made her tits look immaculate. And her long, sensuous hair fell gracefully down to her shoulders, making her look like one of the cover models for a men's magazine.

"Chick, you tryin' to outdo us," Mesha joked.

Apple chuckled and replied, "Look at y'all bitches . . . fuckin' divas and shit." Mesha and Ayesha laughed.

"Damn, Apple, you lookin' like you thirty and shit," Nichols commented.

"I do, right?" Apple said with an exciting smile. She clutched her small knockoff Louis Vuitton bag and was ready to paint the city red. She hugged and kissed her sister good-bye then strutted out the doorway with her friends.

The girls made it down to the lobby and rushed to get a cab, since they were running late. It was a change of plan. The girls didn't want to be one minute late for the concert. They strutted to the cabstand to catcalls, pick-up lines, and compliments from block to block, but they walked close together and ignored the attention.

They reached the cabstand on the busy Harlem street and asked the driver how much it would cost them for a ride to Giants Stadium.

"Eighty-five dollars," the driver informed them.

"Damn! Why you lying?" Mesha barked.

"It's eighty-five dollars. That's gas, tolls, and bridges," the driver said.

It was already a quarter to five, and the girls didn't want to be late for the opening act.

Mesha sucked her teeth and looked at her girls. "Yo, what y'all wanna do? I mean, it's already almost five, and to keep it real, I look too fuckin' cute to be gettin' on a train or bus and be worrying about these thirsty-ass niggas dirtying me up."

"I'm sayin', that fare is a little too steep, Mesha," Apple let it be known.

"Apple, look at us. I'm sayin', how much you got to put up?" Mesha asked.

"I got twenty-five," Ayesha chimed.

"A'ight, I got forty then."

Both girls looked at Apple to fill in the gap.

Mesha said, "Apple, all you gotta do is put up twenty, and we good."

After spending money on clothes, her hair, and a few other expenses, Apple only had eighty dollars left. Though the bus and train were cheaper, she didn't want to be late for the concert either. Reluctantly, she agreed, and the girls jumped into the cab and were soon headed toward the George Washington Bridge into New Jersey.

With Sunday traffic, it was a forty-minute ride to Giants Stadium. The girls jumped out of the cab excitedly and were overwhelmed by the hordes of people and cars surrounding the stadium. It was Apple's first trip outside of Harlem, and by the look in her eyes, Giants Stadium could have been Europe. Even though it was only a few miles from the city, it was something different for her.

The girls hurried to the entrance. They didn't want to miss a single thing. It was like they were in Hollywood, with high-end cars in the parking lot and celebrity buses and trailers parked not too far from the event. The diversity of people attending Summer Jam was something Apple didn't expect. She noticed Asians, a few Indians, and even some Russians and Mexicans entering the building. There were also quite a few ladies dressed more provocatively than her and her crew. She knew what they came for—to catch a baller or maybe fuck a star.

The groupies were lined up outside of the stadium for miles, with a candid thirst in their eyes. Apple couldn't blame them, though, because she looked around and noticed the fine men in attendance, different races, and different sizes. She smiled and gawked at a few. She was in cutie heaven with the ballers and shot-callers all around her.

"Damn! Niggas is fuckin' fine out here," Apple commented with a smile.

"I know, right."

"But they ain't finer than my boo, Ludacris," Mesha stated.

"You mean *my* boo," Ayesha corrected her.

"Uh-uh, my baby comin' home to me tonight," Mesha joked.

"Well, as long as no one ain't touchin' my husband Drake, we good," Apple chimed in.

"Whateva, Apple," Mesha teased.

The trio soon made it past security into the vast arena and looked around for their seats. In the distance Apple could see her friend, Cartier from Brooklyn, heading down toward the Orchestra seats. It looked like she was with Bam and Lil' Momma.

"Cartier!" Apple screamed and caught hateful looks from the concert goers. "Cartier!" she yelled once again, ignoring the hard stares.

"Who you callin'?" Mesha asked the obvious.

"What it sound like? I just saw Cartier and her crew inching toward the floor seats. I was hoping to get a hook up."

"You can't just leave us," Mesha stated. "We came together we leave together."

Apple ignored her. She hated being seated so high, where it was hard to see anything, but happy to be out of Harlem for once, she made the best of it. Once the girls made it to their seats, Apple looked around wide-eyed at the thousands of fans who came to support their favorite artists.

The concert opened up with Drake singing "I'm Goin' In" with Cash Money's Birdman. The crowd went crazy. Apple jumped up and down, roaring with excitement with the screaming crowd. As she sang along, she kept her eyes on every single detail, like she would be quizzed on it later. It was an intense experience, with the lights, the blaring music, the colossal projector screens all over, and the screaming fans.

Drake closed the set with his big hit, "Over." Nicki Minaj performed the summer dancehall anthem, "Hold You" with Gyptian. She then sang "My Chick Bad" with Ludacris. Ayesha and Mesha went crazy, screaming out, "We love you, Ludacris!" The noise in the stadium was almost deafening, louder than any Jets or Giants game.

As the night continued, the crowd's screams never died down. Gucci Mane and Waka Flocka Flame represented for their state by performing "Wasted," "Lemonade," and "O, Let's Do It."

Apple was enjoying herself, dancing and singing. Soon, she didn't care where she was seated, as long as she was at Summer Jam having a good time with her friends.

The show ended with Usher on stage, and his performance was stellar. He closed out the show with a smash, performing "U Remind Me" and "Yeah!" with Ludacris.

Though it was getting late and they had a long ride home, Apple didn't want to leave. She wanted to linger around to look for Cross, so the girls decided to chill in the parking lot. They followed behind the thick crowd toward the exit. It was madness. Security guided the fans out like a herd. There was shouting, laughing, and a few incidents that got defused quickly.

They exited into the parking lot, where the after-party continued near a few high-end cars and trucks. The ballers and show-offs wanted to impress the ladies walking by with their tricked-out rides and bling. A few ladies mingled with the men, while Apple and her crew continued on their hunt. The girls strutted through the crowd, eyes on them from every direction and the men trying to get at them.

"Yo, ma, let me holla at you."

"Yo, shawty in that skirt, I'm feelin' them thighs. What's good?"

"Damn! Y'all lookin' fuckin' right!"

"Yo, love, let me holla at you and your girls, fo' real."

The catcalls came from every direction, but Apple and her crew just smiled and kept it moving. They were looking for the right dudes to fuck with, and a ride back to Harlem. It was late, and they dreaded the long train and bus ride back into the city.

"Oh shit! Ain't that Cross and his friends over there?" Mesha asked.

Hearing Cross's name made Apple's heart beat rapidly. She looked around and saw him posted up by his polished black Range Rover, encircled by his bejeweled crew of thugs.

The men came in three flashy trucks, all chromed out with tinted windows and blaring systems. They were the eye-candy in the parking lot, as ladies surrounded the Harlem crew, who had liquor and weed. They joked around and mingled with their admirers like they were celebrities themselves.

"C'mon, let's go over there and say what's up. Shit, maybe we can catch a ride back to the block," Mesha suggested.

Apple was a bit nervous. Seeing Cross so close made her heart flutter. Cross stood tall and fine in a brown Völkl jacket, crisp denim MEK jeans, and sporting a pair of white Uptowns, his jewelry shining nicely. He had a cup of liquor in his hand and was conversing with one of his homies.

"C'mon, Apple, let's see what's up," Mesha called out.

BAD APPLE THE BADDEST CHICK

Apple followed behind Mesha and Ayesha. When they got close, Mesha smiled, recognizing a couple of faces. She hollered, "What up, Trey? What up, Dink?"

"Mesha, what's good?" Dink replied with a smile.

"Y'all tell me. I wanna get my drink on too."

"Ain't you too young?" Trey said.

"Nigga, you only nineteen, two years older than me. Anyways, where my cup at?"

Trey and Dink laughed.

"You a wild girl, Mesha," Dink responded.

Trey hollered, "Ayesha, what's up?"

"Chillin'."

Trey and Dink looked over at Apple, and the lust in their eyes said it all.

"Yo, that ain't Kola, right? She too quiet right now," Dink said.

"You know her twin, Apple?" Mesha replied.

"Yeah, I see her around. Why you so quiet, ma?" Dink asked with coolness to his voice.

"'Cause I'm her," Apple replied casually.

Dink laughed. "Damn! You fine like your sister. But all y'all is lookin' so fuckin' right. Damn, let me get that ass, Mesha."

Mesha responded with, "Let me get a cup."

The men laughed, and Dink quickly poured Mesha a shot of Henny.

"You wanna mix that wit' somethin', ma?" Trey asked.

Mesha sucked her teeth, looked at them like they were crazy, and downed the liquor like the best of them.

NISA SANTIAGO

In her youth she was showing off. She wanted attention, and she got it. Trey and Dink were quickly impressed.

"Y'all want a shot too?" Dink asked.

Ayesha answered yes and was already reaching for her cup, but Apple was too busy staring at Cross, who stood just a few feet away from her.

"Yo, Apple, you want some of this?" Dink raised the half empty bottle of Hennessy.

"Yeah, I'm down."

Dink smiled while pouring her a shot.

Following behind her girls, Apple took it to the head. The liquor left a burning sensation down her throat, as it trickled easily into her system.

Dink poured the three girls another shot, which they downed quickly as well.

It was getting late, and the police started forcing everyone out of the parking lot. They even made arrests for disorderly conduct and other illegal activities that came into play after the concert ended.

Apple, Ayesha, and Mesha were having a good time with Dink and Trey, while Cross mingled with a few ladies. That made Apple jealous, but she kept her cool and continued drinking and chilling with her friends. Apple stared at the bitches holding Cross's attention and knew she was ten times better-looking than any of them. She bit her tongue, wanting to snatch every bitch away from her man. In her mind, he was hers.

When Cross finally headed in their direction, Apple immediately got excited. He strode their way with a cup in his hand, his eyes focused on the group. He walked up to Dink and Trey, while Apple stood right next to them, and said, "Yo, we 'bout to be out. Five-O's actin' up out here and shit."

"A'ight," Trey said.

Cross looked at Apple and her friends. "Y'all ridin' wit' us?"

"Of course," Mesha chimed.

Apple asked Cross, "Why? You drivin'?"

Cross chuckled. "You want me to?"

"It's whateva. I'll ride wit' you."

Cross smiled and then uttered, "You're cute."

Apple couldn't contain her smile. He had spoken to her, and it made Summer Jam the best for her. She wanted to follow Cross and ride with him, but his Range was already packed with his people and a few girls. Apple hated it, but she was fortunate to get a ride back with Trey and Dink in their Escalade that was sitting on 22-inch chrome rims.

As they jumped on the New Jersey Turnpike, following behind Cross, the liquor continued to flow. Soon, the men became a little horny and frisky. Dink was behind the wheel, with Apple riding shotgun.

Trey started to feel up Ayesha's smooth thighs in the backseat as she sat in the middle. Feeling tipsy, Ayesha and Mesha giggled and laughed, and before long, Trey had unzipped his jeans and pulled out his hard dick to impress the girls. Ayesha leaned in for the kill and slowly began sucking his dick while the truck did seventy miles per hour on the freeway.

"Ayesha is buggin'," Mesha slurred.

"Damn, nigga! I should've let you drive," Dink uttered, glancing at the action from his rearview mirror.

Apple just shook her head, knowing she wasn't about to tag along with Ayesha. When Dink looked at her with a hint in his eyes, she gave him the screw face and said, "I ain't my homegirl or my sister!"

With a look of disappointment, Dink replied, "Then maybe ya ass need to ride in the backseat and ya girl need to be up front."

"Whateva," Apple shot back.

Ayesha continued to suck Trey's dick, feeling the hard flesh going in and out of her mouth.

With his hand tangled in her hair, Trey moaned and closed his eyes, loving the way her glossy lips were taking care of him.

Mesha felt that wild urge between her thighs too. Liquor always made her horny, and the four cups of Henny that she'd downed had her feeling like she was ready to be a porn star—despite having a man at home.

"Yo, y'all wanna get a room?" Dink mentioned.

Dink was horny and wanted in on the action too. Ayesha and Mesha looked down for whatever, so he was ready to take full advantage of the young, liquored-up teens and fuck them till dawn came.

"Y'all do whateva. Just take me home," Apple stated.

"Yo, ma, why you actin' like that?" Dink asked.

"'Cause I'm tired, a'ight?" Apple was annoyed and

slightly embarrassed by the hood-rat behavior of Ayesha.

"Shit, you may look like your sister, but you ain't fuckin' fun like her. I mean, is ya pussy gold-plated?" Dink smirked.

Apple cut her eyes at him. "You'll never find out."

Dink laughed. "Whateva!"

A half-hour later, the truck pulled up to the projects, and Apple jumped out, ready to depart ways with everyone. She looked at her friends and asked, "Y'all comin'?"

Ayesha and Mesha hesitated. Trey had his hand between Ayesha's thighs, fingering her pussy, and Mesha was ready to jump in the front seat and keep Dink company.

"Nah, ma, they wanna have a good time tonight," Dink replied.

"A'ight, whatever," Apple said.

Mesha jumped into the front seat with Dink, and before the truck pulled off, she hollered out the window, "Call me, girl!"

Apple just kept walking into her building. When she reached the elevator, she ran into Supreme coming out of the stairway. He was alone and eyed Apple with a stare that sent chills down her spine.

"You gettin' my money, right?" he asked.

"I got ya money," Apple snapped back with attitude.

Supreme smiled. "Just checkin' up on you, but you lookin' nice tonight. I like that."

When he reached out to gently rub the small of her back, Apple moved away from him. The elevator doors opened, and she quickly got in. As the doors closed, she stood there with Supreme watching her from the lobby with an eerie smile. She shook her head and knew he might be a problem soon.

Chapter 6

K ola got into the backseat of the waiting cab, wearing a brown tight-fitting khaki dress and a pair of stilettos. She oozed with sex appeal and beauty, with all her curves showing perfectly. The men on the corner couldn't take their eyes off of her as they watched her get in the cab.

"Damn!" one male shouted.

Kola smiled, knowing she had those thirsty-ass wannabes drooling. They could look, but they couldn't touch.

It was late night, with midnight creeping up on the hour, and Kola had business to attend to. She was off to a strip club in Brooklyn to check out a dancer that was supposed to be so sexy and fine, she was packing the club to capacity any night she worked.

Kola was willing to travel into Brooklyn alone and talk business. She was from the streets and knew how to handle herself very well. Mike-Mike, usually her backup, was making an out-of-town run for Cross, but Kola felt secure enough to travel alone. She was used to it. Her name was known in Harlem, and nobody fucked with her. She was an uptown girl—a Harlem chick—and her name had weight because of the dudes she rolled with. But Brooklyn was a different story. Out there, she was just an average pretty bitch with an attitude.

She told the driver, "Take me to Sunset Park."

Without traffic, it was a thirty-minute drive through any of the bridges or tunnels that traveled into Brooklyn. Once Kola reached her destination, she handed the driver a crisp hundred-dollar bill to cover the fifty-dollar fare, leaving a generous tip.

The strip club, located off Fourth Avenue on a back street in Brooklyn, was in a second-floor loft, with tight security at the entrance. Kola strutted to the place in all her glory, looking twice her age and feeling confident about the night.

She approached the two beefy security guards and asked, "What's the cover charge?"

The men looked at her, knowing she was a new face.

"You dancing?" one of them asked.

"Why you askin'?"

"Tip in is twenty-five," the other stated.

Kola reached into her bag and gave the man two twenties. "You can keep that," she said with a smirk.

"Oh, you a baller, huh?"

"I get mines."

He chuckled and said, "A'ight, just watch your back out here."

Kola smiled as he waved the wand across her body and searched through her purse for any illegal weapons.

He said, "You good. Just go upstairs, second floor."

Kola walked up the stairway in her steep heels and entered the dimmed room with rap music blaring and a crowd of patrons. She was impressed. The loft was huge and full of life, with a doorway that exited out into an open, elevated area that overlooked Brooklyn.

The raised stage had two naked big-booty strippers on it working hard for their dollars and was surrounded by men tossing money, that thirsty look on their faces. And the strippers had no shame in their game. They were working hard for their money.

Kola needed a drink. She looked around. The crowd and strippers were predominantly black, with a sprinkling of Puerto Ricans, Dominicans, and whites.

One dude gently grabbed her by the arm and asked, "You dancing, love? I never saw you here before."

Kola looked at him and wasn't impressed. She'd been feeling men watching her the minute she'd stepped into the place, but this one looked like he needed to pay to get pussy. Black and overweight, he had no style to him with his shapeless jeans and scruffy appearance, and his breath reeked. He had a Heineken in his hand and gazed at Kola as if longing for what he couldn't have.

"No, thank you," she politely replied, quickly moving herself away from him and walking closer to the stage.

Kola was looking around for a girl named Chyna Doll, who a male friend had put her up on. He let it be known to her that Chyna Doll was young and down for whatever, a freak, and a raving beauty with looks that many would kill for.

"Yo, Kola, this chick is off the hook, fo' real," the young kid had told her. "I'm telling you, she sucked my dick like gravity was in her mouth."

Kola needed more than a freak. She needed an elite stable of young hoes like herself down for whatever. She had planned on putting together an event—a sex party where people would pay admission. With the right girls who had good pussy and great head game, the men she invited would pay to play, and Kola needed the best.

She had talked to Kandy a few days ago, convincing her to try out one of her parties, and Kandy was down, especially after the dick-down she got from Mike-Mike. So Kola was after the next female to fill her stable of professionals. She wanted the cream of the crop because she was going to hit muthafuckas with membership fees to join her party. She was about her money and business, and if you didn't know how to work what your momma gave you, then she couldn't use you.

Kola looked around the room and observed every naked or scantily clad ho in the place. Some were really nice and sexy with their swag, but a few girls struck her as washed up. She moved to the stage and took a seat in one of the soft leather chairs. She watched a big-booty girl clap her butt cheeks together and then bend over to expose her goodies. She began tipping the stripper with a few dollar bills.

The place was buzzing with activity from corner to corner—lap dances, wall dances, a lot of bumping and grinding, and tricks disappearing into the VIP rooms with their stripper of choice for the night.

Kola noticed a tall beauty with an erotic aura stepping out of the dressing room. Scantily clad in a black baby doll dress that had sheer mesh with a sequined lace hem, cut-out sides, and twin straps, her rich caramel skin seemed to glow with sexiness. Her knee-high leather stilettos seemed to make her almost touch the sky, and her two long pigtails gave her that naughty-schoolgirl look.

Kola kept her eyes fixated on the girl during her long stride from the dressing room to the stage. She walked with confidence, her exotic, chinky eyes scanning the crowd for potential tricks for the night. Kola already liked her style because the girl portrayed herself as that bitch in the room.

Kola knew that had to be Chyna Doll, because everything about her screamed "confident." She watched the girl work the stage to Usher's "There Goes My Baby." She had a presence about her that made almost every eye in the room stay glued on her.

The tips started flowing her way, but Kola was outdoing the guys by spreading money all over the dancer like a heavy rainfall. Kola watched the stripper move across the stage with style and admired the way she swung herself around the pole with steadiness like a cat.

"What's your name?" Kola asked the woman as she did a split in front of her and leaned her body forward, showing the crowd just how flexible she was.

"Chyna Doll," she answered, never missing a beat in her performance.

The men clapped with excitement, their eyes dancing all over her body. The crowd of onlookers grew thicker around the stage as Chyna Doll brought out her bag of goodies and prepared to perform something naughty. She stripped down until she was butt naked, showing the crowd her curves.

Chyna clutched an eight-inch dildo the color of night. Sprawled out on her back, she spread her legs and rammed the thick tool deep into her pussy and fucked herself, making the men yell out. She then released the dildo from her grip and allowed the muscles in her pussy to take over, making the dildo move with the contraction of her vagina. She played with her breasts, pinched her nipples, and allowed the action to go on for a few minutes.

"Oh my God! Shit, girl, I got next," one onlooker joked.

The crowd laughed over the loud music. The DJ had switched up Usher for a more appropriate song—2 Live Crew's "Pop That Coochie."

Chyna Doll rolled over on her stomach, the thick, long dildo still inside her, and continued her lewd act without missing a step. She moaned and pressed her ample breasts against the stage, her legs spread wide, pretending she was getting fucked from behind. She took hold of the love tool once more and fucked herself the way she loved to get fucked—fast and rough. Chyna Doll's flexibility amazed everyone, twisting herself into a pretzel and working the plastic dick into her like it was the real thing.

Kola kept the money flowing. Though she had a hundred dollars in singles, she was so impressed, she even tossed out a few twenties. Chyna Doll smiled and winked at Kola.

After the act with the dildo, Chyna sprayed whipped cream across her breasts and lit herself on fire. Both erotic and dangerous at the same time, it was a sight to see. It was something new to the pack and left everyone wide-eyed. The fire raged for a short while, and then she blew it out.

By this time the stage was littered with money, small and big bills. Chyna was making her ends and causing some jealousy among her coworkers. Her wild act lasted for the next ten minutes, and when she was done, she scooped up her money into one pile. It took her a moment to count it and stash everything in her bag. Still naked, she strutted off the stage, needing to regroup for a moment.

Kola moved quickly in her direction. She tapped Chyna Doll on the shoulder and made it be known that she wanted a VIP session with her.

Chyna Doll smiled and then made a beeline for one of the rooms. She didn't care. Men or women, money was money, no matter where it came from, and she could regroup anytime.

Kola followed Chyna Doll into one of the VIP rooms and was impressed with her body from head to toe. The woman was so sexy, Kola wanted a taste of her.

"What you lookin' for?" Chyna Doll asked.

"Your time," Kola replied.

Kola passed Chyna a C-note, and she took the cash and put it in a safe place. Kola took a seat on the mattress and stared at the sexy, long-legged diva with a devious smile.

Chyna straddled Kola, wrapped her arms around her like Saran Wrap, and slowly began grinding into the young girl's lap. "You like that?" she asked seductively.

"I do," Kola said, "but I got somethin' you might like better."

"And what's that?"

"You're sexy and pretty. Not many women genuinely have both. They only think they do." Kola paused, trying to read Chyna's face. "You like doing this shit?"

"I make my ends. Why?"

Kola cupped Chyna's breasts. "I know you don't know me, but I'm about business myself. I got somethin' happening, somethin' that's nice and safe, and you can make plenty of ends by the end of the night." Kola stared at Chyna's beautiful face and knew the men she had set up would fall in love with that face. She slipped her another twenty, just to show she was about that money.

"I'm listening."

Chyna Doll was somewhat impressed. She knew Kola was young. Like many of the girls she danced with, her age would show behind all the makeup and tight body. Most of the girls in the club were either sixteen or a little older. At twenty-two, Chyna Doll was considered an old G, and was one of the few girls over twenty-one in the club. She had been dancing since she was seventeen, knew the ins and outs of the business, and was always looking for the next come-up.

Chyna Doll knew by the tone of Kola's voice and the way she carried herself that the girl was smart, and had business and street savvy. She knew Kola didn't dance, because she would have seen her in one club or another. Chyna Doll got around from borough to borough. She'd been in all the underground spots that were jumping, and she never forgot faces.

"I love your swag, boo. You got that shit down right. Men are going to love you, and the shit I got poppin' off wit' a friend of mines, I guarantee that you can make a gee or better a night. And you ain't gotta worry about the bullshit," Kola assured her.

"You want me to do porn?" Chyna asked, a hint of unwillingness in her tone.

"Nah, I ain't into anything being recorded. I don't get down like that. What's done wit' us fuckin' stays wit' us. You feel me?" Kola spoke like a pimp.

Chyna Doll nodded and stopped grinding against Kola. She looked at the young teen, respecting her hustle.

Kola continued. "I'm 'bout to start throwing these sex parties. Some exclusive shit. If you ain't a member, then you ain't down. The people I got coming in are the best of the best. I'm talking about niggas so fuckin' fine, they make Denzel and Tyrese look like Steve Urkel."

Chyna laughed.

"But, fo' real, I'm putting together this elite stable of

women that know how to get down for that paper. I'm only 'bout makin' money."

"You a pimp or somethin'?"

"I hate pimps. That ain't my thang. You come in with me, do your business, and at the end of the night, you get your fair share of that gwap. But if you ain't happy wit' it, shit, you free to go your own way. This is your choice, baby. I just want you in for the ride. It's gonna be a safe thang, feel me?" Kola said with coolness.

Chyna Doll was in deep thought. Kola had her sold on it, and she needed to try something different. The men she did VIP with were cheap, sometimes nasty with their hygiene, and didn't appeal to her at all.

"You in, Chyna Doll?" Kola asked. "I got ya back on this. Promise you that."

"A'ight, I'll try it out, but if it ain't right, I'm walking. I've been doin' my own thang for a long time, but I'll see what you about."

Kola smiled. "Oh, it's right. Believe me. It's official like drug money."

Kola was happy. With Chyna Doll and Kandy in, her plans were coming together. She needed two more, and then it would be on.

Kola was on her way. She wanted out of her mother's place and wanted to be "the baddest chick" in Harlem. She didn't tolerate being a broke bitch and knew that using sex was the quickest way out of poverty.

Chapter 7

It was almost two weeks after Summer Jam, and Apple was reliving that brief encounter with Cross in her mind on the daily. It was a Thursday morning, and once again, she was penniless. She got out of bed to look outside the window, but there was no Cross or any of his goons lingering outside. The block had been quiet for a few days, and Apple missed looking at her eye-candy that would post up outside her bedroom window. She'd heard that police had done a sweep a few days earlier and was praying that Cross didn't get caught up in the raid. Sighing, she started to get ready for her day.

❧

Mesha and Ayesha had told Apple about their encounter with Dink and Trey. She listened half-heartedly about how well-endowed Trey was, while Dink really didn't have anything to work with. Apple laughed, thinking about how much shit-talking Dink did that evening. The girls admitted that they had major regrets sleeping with Trey and Dink, and they both blamed it on the alcohol. However, Mesha carried her regret more, knowing she had a boyfriend.

Apple walked to the bathroom, but it was already occupied. She banged on the door and shouted, "Hurry up! I gotta go!"

"Wait!" Kola shouted from the other side.

Apple sucked her teeth. She knew Kola was going to be in there for a while. Her sister had no consideration for anybody but herself, and it was getting on Apple's last nerve.

Apple walked into the kitchen, where Nichols was preparing breakfast. She smiled. Her little sister was a sweetheart.

"Kola's still in the bathroom?" Nichols asked.

"Yeah, that bitch is."

"That's why I got up early and went before her. You know how she is, Apple."

"Where's Ma?"

"Still 'sleep. I ain't tryin' to wake her up," Nichols replied.

Apple began doing the pee-pee dance, trying to hold her urine. "Shit. I'm 'bout to kick down that door if she don't hurry up."

"Go next door and use Ms. Terri's bathroom."

"Her fuckin' son's a pervert."

"He probably ain't home. But what you gonna do? Stand there and pee on yourself?"

Apple knew her sister was right, so she rushed out

the door to Ms. Terri's, a kind Caribbean woman in her late fifties. She was from St. Lucia and had migrated to America thirty years ago. She was like a second mother to the girls. When they were young, Ms. Terri didn't mind watching them while their mother was in the streets. She would feed them, clothe them, and talk to them sometimes, when needed.

Ms. Terri had four kids, two adult sons who lived on their own, a daughter just starting college, and a young son who was the twins' age. She had raised a respectable family and wanted to help bring up Denise's children, but there was always some conflict with the two women. So Ms. Terri thought it was best to mind her own business and stick to raising her own kids.

Apple anxiously knocked on Ms. Terri's door, still trying to hold her urine. "Ms. Terri, it's me, Apple. Please open the door. I have to use your bathroom," she cried out. She continued to bang until the five-four, medium-build woman with long locks and wrinkling brown skin answered the door.

She smiled at Apple. "Kola again?"

Apple nodded.

Ms. Terri moved to the side and invited Apple into her home, and Apple rushed past the woman and ran into her bathroom, where she quickly relieved herself. She spent a few minutes in the cherry-scented bathroom, which was clean and stocked with toiletries, unlike their own, which was always out of toilet paper, soap, and other items to keep a young woman fresh.

Sometimes Apple wondered how she kept her hygiene up to par, with her mother too lazy to shop, clean, cook, and do other things. Apple felt like she was living with Peg Bundy from *Married with Children*. She hated her home but loved Ms. Terri's place, and if it wasn't for her perverted son trying to fuck her every chance he got, then Apple would've spent more time there.

"Better?" Ms. Terri asked as Apple exited the bathroom.

"You're the best, Ms. Terri. Thank you."

"Anytime, chile. You can always come if you need somethin'," she said in a motherly way.

Apple was happy that Ms. Terri's son, Jerome, wasn't around. He was the worst. She remembered one time she was at the apartment talking to Ms. Terri, and behind his mother's back, Jerome flashed himself and grabbed his dick. It was only one of many incidents that she went through with him. Other times he would grab her ass, and Apple would quickly check him on it. Out of respect for Ms. Terri, she never really hurt the boy, though she had slapped and punched him a few times when he'd disrespected her.

"You hungry, Apple?" Ms. Terri asked.

"No, I'm OK, Ms. Terri. Nichols is cooking breakfast."

"How's your mother and the family?"

"They good," Apple lied.

Ms. Terri smiled. She missed having the girls over, but times had changed, and Apple and her sisters were growing older. They didn't have time anymore to sit around to sip tea, talk, and pretend to be what the girls seemed to long for—family. Apple wanted to see more of Ms. Terri too, but with Jerome constantly trying to get between her legs, she just stayed away altogether.

Apple hugged Ms. Terri and promised to visit her more often, but it was a promise she didn't intend to keep. She walked out of the apartment and went back into hers. Nichols had finished fixing breakfast, and Kola was still in the bathroom.

Apple stormed to the bathroom and started kicking and banging on the door wildly. "Kola, you a selfish fuckin' bitch! You got other people living here too!" she yelled.

Kola screamed back, "Just fuckin' wait! Damn!" Not caring about Apple's tantrum, she remained in the bathroom, taking her sweet time with her hair.

"Fuck you, bitch! Fo' real, fuck you!" Apple screamed.

"Fuck you too, Apple. Broke bitch!"

"What?"

The commotion had awakened their mother, who came walking out of her bedroom. Tying her robe, she said, "Would both y'all bitches just shut the fuck up! Damn it, I'm tryin' to sleep."

"Tell Kola to get her triflin' ass out the bathroom then."

Denise looked at Apple as if she didn't care. She didn't have to use it, so it didn't bother her none that Kola was taking her time in the bathroom. She looked at Apple and said, "Just go next door."

"I already did," Apple snapped back.

"So what you bitchin' for?"

"'Cause she gets on my fuckin' nerves!"

"Apple, kill that fuckin' noise, or else I'ma start makin' some noise of my own. You understand?"

Apple sucked her teeth, rolled her eyes, and sharply replied, "Whateva!" Then she stormed back into the kitchen, where Nichols had breakfast ready and on the table.

"At least you get to eat first," Nichols said to Apple with a smile.

Apple sat at the table and returned the smile. Nichols was her favorite. She cared for her baby sister more than anyone else in the house.

While pouring Apple what was left of the orange juice, Nichols said, "You snooze, you lose, right?"

Apple downed the juice and ate her breakfast. She and Nichols had their sisterly moment together, and Apple liked that. When breakfast was done, Apple made sure that whatever was leftover got thrown in the trash. She didn't want Kola to have anything Nichols had made. It was her way of revenge.

As Apple was exiting the kitchen, Kola entered the room wearing her usual tight shorts and shirt. Paying Apple no mind, she asked, "What y'all eating?"

"You mean, what *were* we eating?" Apple smirked then kept it moving.

Kola looked around the kitchen. The table was clear, and the dishes were piled up in the sink. Then she noticed her breakfast in the trash. Her face lit up with anger.

"Apple, why the fuck you throw my food out like that? You a straight-up bitch! Sometimes, I swear . . ."

"You ain't the one that cooked it," Apple replied with a look of satisfaction.

Nichols just stood on the sidelines and watched her twin sisters argue like they were strangers on the street. After about ten minutes of listening to one call the other a bitch one too many times, she left the apartment. Nichols always left out to find a friend when her sisters or her mother became too much for her to handle.

She escaped downstairs to the lower floor and went to chill with her friend from school, Benny, who lived with his grandmother and didn't mind having Nichols around for company. The fifteen-year-old let Nichols into his home with a welcoming smile.

"Who's actin' up now?" he asked, knowing the routine with her.

"Apple and Kola."

"Those two are like cats and dogs sometimes."

"Tell me about it," Nichols replied.

She went into his bedroom, and the two began playing the game Halo on his Xbox 360. They both were huge fans of the game, and it was Nichols' way of escaping the bullshit she had to endure in her dysfunctional home.

It was late afternoon when Apple exited her apartment. She moved down the pissy-smelling stairway in a rush and out into the lobby. However, before she could leave out her building, Supreme and one of his henchmen quickly confronted her. The two startled Apple, who was shocked to see them as they approached her from behind.

"Hey, Apple, where's my fuckin' money?" Supreme asked, a threatening chill in his voice.

"You told me three weeks. It's only been two so far."

"It's been two? Nah, not on my fuckin' calendar. Call it a leap week or somethin', but I need my fuckin' payment."

"What? Get the fuck outta here, Supreme! You told me three weeks. Don't think I'm some dumb bitch."

Supreme marched up to her and grabbed her by the arm. "Bitch, don't fuckin' play me! You fuckin' hear me? You borrowed five hundred from me, and with the interest added to that, you now owe me an extra one hundred and fifty dollars. So I want my fuckin' six hundred and fifty soon. You understand? You either pay me in cash or pussy, but either way, I'ma get mine back."

Apple returned his hard gaze and responded, "So that's your fuckin' tactic? Put a bitch in debt so you can get some ass? You fuckin' pathetic nigga!"

Supreme smiled. "Nah, not as pathetic as you're gonna be if I don't get either in return. I'm warning you, Apple. Don't fuckin' try me. I ain't a nigga to fuck wit'."

Supreme released his tight grip on Apple and took a step back. His henchman was behind him, ready for anything. It wasn't Guy Tony, but an older-looking man that Apple had never seen before.

"Tomorrow, Apple, you come up wit' my bread or else. By the way, you lookin' good in that dress." Supreme grinned as he and his goon started to exit the building.

Apple overheard him say, "That bitch ain't comin' up wit' my money no time soon. After I'm done wit' her, I might let you fuck her."

Supreme laughed while walking out the building, leaving Apple furious. She'd be damned if she let Supreme touch her in any type of way. She felt duped. Supreme was trying to strong-arm her, and she wanted to spit in his face.

Apple collected herself and exited the lobby, knowing if Supreme even tried to penetrate her with his dirty dick, she would go "Lorena Bobbitt" on his ass.

Chapter 8

A few days had passed since Apple's run-in with Supreme. She'd been keeping a low profile, knowing he had some issues and wanted to exploit her in so many ways. With Supreme, it wasn't about the debt, but the control he wanted to have over her. She knew he had his way with many women because of the money they owed him. For them, it was easier to fuck him a few times than to pay up their outstanding debts.

Apple felt trapped. She was embarrassed about borrowing money from a loan shark to buy an outfit for Summer Jam and having to pay him back with pussy. She didn't want the hood to know about her dealings with Supreme, and she especially didn't want word to reach Kola.

Apple devised a scheme that was sure to keep Supreme and his goons off her ass. Every day, she would look out her window and keep an eye out for him. When she thought he wasn't around, she would break out, making sure she didn't have any interference on her way to wherever.

One evening, she ran into Guy Tony at the corner bodega. When he pressured her about the money she owed, she lied, knowing he wasn't the brightest star in the galaxy. She said she had the money at home and promised, if he hung around, she would run to her place and get it. He believed her, and she ran off, leaving him waiting for her return.

Apple knew her constant lying and ducking Supreme wouldn't work forever. So she picked the lock to Kola's room while she wasn't home and went rummaging through her closet looking for clothes that she hardly wore anymore. She removed a few short skirts, some really short coochie-cutting shorts, and a few tops. Apple and Kola were exactly the same size, so she knew it would work. When she was satisfied with the stuff she snatched from Kola's closet, she put everything else back the way she found it and returned to her bedroom.

Apple felt Kola had so many clothes that she wouldn't realize a few pieces were missing. She laid out Kola's clothing on the bed and tried to figure out how she would work everything out.

Just then Nichols walked into the bedroom. "What you doin' wit' Kola's clothes all laying out on the bed?"

"Nothin', Nichols. It ain't your business."

"Kola's goin' to kill you when she sees her stuff out like that."

"She ain't gonna kill nobody, 'cause she ain't gonna know they missing. A'ight, Nichols?"

Nichols sucked her teeth. She knew it was best to stay out her sister's business, not wanting to get caught up in any sibling rivalry. "It's your funeral," she responded before exiting the bedroom.

Apple shut the door behind her sister and then quickly picked up the clothes and stashed them in the bottom of her closet. It was her only choice, since Supreme and his people were on her ass every day. She just needed time to get his money together without the continuous harassment.

"It's gonna work," she said to herself with a sure smile.

⁂

Two days later, Apple was walking out the apartment clad in some skimpy white coochie-cutting shorts and a shirt so tight, it pinched her nipples. Though it was a hot June afternoon, the wardrobe was out of character for her, but it was something she needed to do.

Apple hadn't seen Kola all morning and thought she was probably shacked up with some nigga. It was perfect. When she stepped out of the elevator, the first faces she saw were those of Supreme and Guy Tony.

Supreme glared at Apple and marched up to her with the quickness. He grabbed her by her arm the minute she stepped off the elevator and shouted, "Bitch, you tryin' to fuckin' duck me!"

Apple quickly went into character. "Nigga, get the fuck off me!" she screamed, yanking her arm free from Supreme.

Supreme and Guy Tony were shocked.

Apple glared at them and continued her verbal onslaught. "Don't you ever put your grimy hands on me!"

"Bitch, who the fuck you talkin' to?" Supreme yelled back.

"Nigga, you better fuckin' recognize! I ain't that bitch to fuck wit', ya heard? You better chill with the bitch remarks 'fore I sick my goons on you!"

A startled Supreme glanced at Guy Tony, who could only shrug. Supreme was confused. "Apple, right?" he asked incredulously.

"Nigga, I ain't my sister. I'm Kola. Get it right!" she barked.

Supreme looked at Apple, trying to figure out if he had the right sister, but Apple looked completely like her twin sister. He then studied her wardrobe. It was tight, provocative, and revealing, something he rarely saw Apple wearing. He took a step back and knew something was wrong.

Apple was relieved that her plan to fool Supreme was working. She wanted to laugh, but kept her gangster attitude up. "What the fuck you want wit' my sister anyway?"

"Nah, it was just a misunderstanding, that's all, Kola," Supreme said.

"It better be. That's my fuckin' sister. You know my fuckin' crowd, nigga. Now back the fuck up!"

"Yeah, I know. Ain't no beef wit' you, Kola."

Though Supreme was a rough-and-tumble dude who'd made a name for himself, he knew not to fuck with

Kola and her vicious crew of hustlers and killers, including Cross, Mike-Mike, and Johnny Mack. He was aware of their reputation, and the last thing he needed was a war to start in Harlem.

Apple loved it. She smiled inwardly and wanted to push the scheme further, but she didn't want to take any chances. She already had them believing she was her sister, and for once, she thanked God that she was a twin. "Move!" she exclaimed.

Supreme, his face twisted with upset and wonder, quickly moved out of Apple's way and allowed her to pass. He had his doubts, but he didn't want to chance pressing Kola, if it was actually her, because Kola had a fierce reputation in the hood. Hustlers knew her and respected her, while Apple was just her twin sister.

Apple quickly exited the lobby with such a cool stride and serious attitude that she actually started to believe she was her sister. She exhaled with relief, leaving Supreme looking stupid in the lobby.

When she was gone, Guy Tony looked at his boss. "Yo, I think somebody tryin' to play you."

"Yeah, I'ma be on it, Guy. If the bitch thinks her sister is gonna be her fuckin' messiah, she got another fuckin' thang comin'."

Apple quickly headed to the 135th Street train station. She just wanted to spend the day out of Harlem. She met up with Ayesha and Mesha in the city, where she went to change her clothes in a public bathroom, and the girls spent the day out and about in the city. They had lunch in

Times Square, where Mesha picked up the bill, and then they met a couple of cute guys, who tricked on them for the day.

By late evening, Apple was on the subway back to Harlem with Ayesha and Mesha. Fearing she would run into Supreme on her way home, she lied to her friends, telling them she had to get off a stop early and meet someone. When Mesha pressured Apple about who it was, she told them it was a boy. Mesha was ecstatic and started bombarding her with questions. Apple promised that they would talk later and then rushed out of the subway car to change clothes in the nearest bathroom.

She moved through the projects with a watchful eye on everything. Again, she was looking like Kola in her tight, revealing shorts, and with her sassy attitude. Once Apple reached her building and entered the apartment, she quickly stripped out of Kola's clothing, wanting to enjoy the comfort of her bedroom. Nichols was already sleeping in her own bed, and Apple wanted to do the same.

Apple sat by the window and wondered how long she would be able to keep up the charade of being Kola, especially with Kola always being in Harlem. She felt that one day her cover might be blown and Kola would catch her in the act, or Supreme would finally pull her card. Still, she knew it was the only way she could duck Supreme.

Chapter 9

A week had passed, and as far as Apple could tell, her gimmick of pretending to be Kola was still holding up. Most of the time, though, she remained home, enduring her mother's rants and malicious ways, only going out if she couldn't help it. But she was growing tired of ducking Supreme and his goons, and whenever she ran into him, she would always pretend to be her sister. Apple noticed the frustration on Supreme's face when he couldn't tell the difference between the two.

Supreme, fearing that striking the wrong sister would cause a serious beef with Cross and Mike-Mike, played it cool. His time would come. He had Guy Tony stake out the building. He wanted to know which sister exited the building first. He made it be known to Guy Tony that he was to confront both sisters and call him when he did.

Guy Tony, now parked outside of the twins' building in a black Escalade, was watching the doorway with a keen eye. It was late afternoon, and he'd been staking out the building for three hours.

Around five o'clock that afternoon, one of the sisters exited the lobby. He got on the cell phone and dialed Supreme's number.

"Yeah. What you got?" Supreme asked.

"I got one comin' out the building now, but I don't know which one," Guy Tony informed him.

"Watch her."

"A'ight."

Kola strutted out the building in her tight-fitting mini-skirt and cut-off T-shirt that exposed her pierced belly button. She was so sexy and walked with such confidence, it made Guy Tony hard. He licked his lips and thought about doing the nasty with her, but he knew fucking a woman like Kola was only possible in his dreams. He kept his eyes stuck on her lustrous legs and slim waist, loving the way her skirt rode up her ass while she walked.

"Damn! You's a sexy lady, ma. I know that pussy is good," Guy Tony said to himself, watching her from head to toe. He slowly massaged his crotch and felt the need to masturbate as he watched Kola from a distance. He was also aware it could be Apple pretending to be her sister.

Just then Guy Tony observed the silver Lexus IS come to a stop in front of Kola, and he watched the long-legged twin in six-inch stilettos get into the passenger side of the car. He got a quick glimpse of the driver and confirmed it was Mike-Mike behind the wheel. He smiled and nodded, knowing it was Kola who had exited the building first. After watching the Lexus drive off, he dialed up Supreme again.

"What up?" Supreme asked.

"I got you, 'Preme. Yeah, it was Kola that left out the building first. She just got into a Lexus with Mike-Mike."

"You my muthafucka, Guy! Apple wanna play fuckin' games wit' me? A'ight. I'll be that way in twenty minutes. If she comes out before then, you follow her, a'ight?"

"I got you."

Guy Tony continued to wait, parked outside the building. After about fifteen minutes, he noticed Apple coming out dressed like her sister. She was in a tight, short jean skirt, a skimpy halter top, a pair of pumps, and carrying a bag.

Guy glared at Apple nearing the street and uttered to himself, "It ain't gonna work this time." He made another call to Supreme, who instructed him to follow her. Guy Tony was on it. He followed Apple down the street, where she quickly became the center of attention in her whorish outfit.

Unaware she was being followed, Apple strutted to the nearest fast-food restaurant on the corner of Lenox Avenue, where she went into the restroom to change her clothes. She spent fifteen minutes in the stall, making sure she looked right from top to bottom, and then stuffed Kola's clothes into the bottom of her bag. While customers entered and exited, she stared at herself in the bathroom mirror, making sure she looked OK.

When she was satisfied, she exhaled and walked out the bathroom into a crowded McDonald's. She clutched her bag and made sure she wasn't being gawked at, because it was obvious she went into the bathroom dressed completely different. Now she had on a pair of tight Capri pants, a pair of white Nike, and a T-shirt. Apple felt much more comfortable and wondered how Kola could be so at ease looking like a whore every day. Since no one seemed to notice her change of attire, Apple felt relieved. She walked out the McDonald's and headed south toward 125th Street.

Guy Tony smiled at himself, catching Apple red-handed in her act. "You sneaky fuckin' bitch!" He followed her in the truck, slowly creeping with traffic, the tinted windows low, and a keen eye on his mark, as he tried to avoid being spotted.

Apple walked a few blocks and then dipped into another project building off Seventh Avenue. Guy knew he couldn't follow her into the building without arousing suspicion, so he fell back and waited, but she never came back out.

Guy's phone rang, and it was Supreme.

"Where you at?" Supreme inquired.

"I'm on Seventh Avenue. She dipped into a building and never came back out. I been waiting on her for a fuckin' hour."

"A'ight. You remember what she had on, right?"

"Yeah, she came out the building in a tight jean skirt and halter top but now she got on some short pants and white Nikes. Also, I noticed Kola got her belly button pierced, but Apple don't."

"Good lookin' out, Guy. Just meet me. We'll catch up

wit' Apple on the rebound. She gotta come home some time."

Guy Tony nodded and drove off.

Hours had passed, and it was late in the evening. The sun was drifting from the clear sky, making night gradually ascend over the bustling Harlem neighborhood. The streets were full of traffic. Some folks were going in and out of the projects looking like they were in a steady rush, while other locals just lingered around. The night owls of the town were emerging from their places of rest and ready to take in the city's nightlife.

Guy Tony and Supreme sat parked in front of Apple's building. Supreme wanted to confront Apple and beat the shit out of her. He hated to be played and disrespected, and Apple's disrespect to him was like a slap and spit in his face. Supreme sat in the passenger seat, seething with anger, his .45 on his lap. He had a strong urge to just blow her brains out. He had killed people for less, and the way Apple lied when he challenged her about pretending to be Kola made him almost become a raging lunatic.

"This bitch better hurry the fuck up and give me my money! She thinks this is a fuckin' game wit' me," Supreme said, anger pouring from his voice.

Guy Tony, aware of Supreme's deadly temper, sat quietly. He knew there was no calming him, so he just sat listening to him rant about the violence he would do to her. And the things he heard made him almost feel sorry for her.

It was nearing nine o'clock, and the two had sat for almost two hours waiting impatiently, knowing that Apple would arrive soon. They scanned the area, making sure they weren't so easily seen and also keeping an eye out for her.

∽∾∽

Apple strutted to her building looking like Kola again. The hood was blaring with rap music, and blinged-out guys with their pants low were lingering about on the balmy Thursday night. She had just come from Ayesha's place, where the two just chilled, reminisced, and talked about a variety of things, from men to friends, as she braided her friend's hair. Apple was ready to confess to Ayesha about her problem with Supreme, but the embarrassment of anyone knowing about her borrowing money from the vile loan shark stopped her from saying a mumbling word.

She walked into the lobby, thinking it was clear of any danger, and believing she once again had deceived Supreme, if he was watching her from a distance. She smiled as she approached the elevator. She just wanted to strip away her clothing and take a nice, soothing shower, with the summer heat sticking to her skin.

"Hurry the fuck up!" Apple exclaimed, looking up at the display and seeing that the elevator had been stuck on the sixth floor for the longest. She didn't want to take the pissy stairway, especially with the shoes she had on.

Apple looked around; it was quiet, and no thugs were around. She liked it that way. She continued to look up at the illuminated display, which changed from six to five. *Finally*, she thought.

The quietness of the lobby was suddenly disrupted by a booming voice that startled her.

"Yo, Apple!" Supreme shouted.

It was like he appeared out of thin air, his size and height towering over Apple like a skyscraper. He looked fiercely at her and approached her with his quick step.

Apple threw her game face on and said, "Didn't I fuckin' tell you—"

Before Apple could say another word, Supreme quickly grabbed the petite twin by her throat and forced her into the stairway.

Apple struggled with him, fighting, kicking, and trying to shout, "Get the fuck off me!" But Supreme's strength was so overwhelming, it felt like she had a pair of large vise grips wrapped around her neck. Apple struggled to breathe. She tried to kick him in his genitalia, but Supreme didn't budge.

"You tryin' to play me, bitch!" he screamed. He thrust her against the solid wall, keeping his strong grip around her. The two tussled, but Supreme was winning the battle.

Guy Tony suddenly appeared in the stairway and looked at Apple. He had a deadpan gaze as he stood behind his boss. He didn't dare interfere with Supreme's business.

"Get the fuck off me, muthafucka!" Apple shouted, still trying to fight back.

"You playin' me, bitch!"

"You wanna fuck wit'—"

"Bitch, cut the fuckin' charades!" he said, cutting her off. "I know you ain't her. We seen your tramp sister ride off with Mike-Mike earlier."

The light and fire in Apple's eyes slowly began to diminish when she heard that. The jig was up.

"Now, where's my fuckin' money? Or do I gotta rape you in this stairway to get what's mine?"

Supreme was so close to Apple, her breasts were pressed into his chest, and she could smell every bit of his breath.

Supreme forced her legs open and moved his hand up her smooth light-brown thigh, resting it near her pussy and feeling the warmth between her legs. "I want what's owed to me, you fuckin' bitch! You think you can take from me and play me? Huh, bitch?" he shouted.

"Fuck you!" Apple spat back.

"Oh, you got balls now, huh. Let's see then." Supreme grabbed himself a handful of her pussy and molested her with a fiendish smile.

Apple squirmed in his tight hold, but she couldn't break free. She felt his long, thin fingers pry into her panties and try to penetrate her. She cringed and cried out as Supreme violated her. "Stop it!"

"Nah, I don't feel any balls, but I feel somethin' much nicer," Supreme mocked. He pushed against her more vigorously and began pulling up her skirt, exposing her panties. He was ready to rip Apple's panties off and bend her over for a forceful fuck, but she fought back, biting him on the side of his neck and drawing blood.

After pushing him away, she dropped her skirt and prepared to fight back some more.

"You fuckin' bitch!" he shouted.

"Fuck you!"

Supreme was ready to hurt Apple but stopped when the door flew open and Kola charged into the stairway, shouting, "What the fuck you doin' to my sister?"

Supreme glared at Kola and shouted, "Stay the fuck out my business! This shit don't concern you."

"Muthafucka, like hell it don't! That's my sister you fuckin' wit'! Nigga, you musta lost ya fuckin' mind!"

"I ain't got no beef wit' you, Kola."

"You do now. You think shit is sweet? Or do I gotta call my niggas to ride on ya bitch ass? You know my circle, nigga. Don't fuck wit' me!"

Supreme looked at both sisters. He was furious and wanted to kill them both, but he knew his limits with Kola. She was both bark and bite.

Guy Tony had his boss' back, but he wasn't ready to war with Cross and Mike-Mike, so he stood in the background quietly, hoping Supreme would step off.

Apple was somewhat relieved that her sister came to her aid. It was the only time she felt happy to have her around.

Supreme smiled mockingly. "You a bad bitch, huh?"

"Try me, muthafucka!" Kola locked eyes with him.

"Nah, we cool. Y'all ladies have a good night," Supreme replied casually. He then looked at Apple and said, "I'll see you around, Apple." He stepped out of the stairway, Guy Tony following closely behind.

Kola kept her eyes on him until he was out of the lobby. She then looked at her sister and barked, "What the fuck business you got wit' that nigga?"

Apple looked back at her sister with contempt. "It's nothin'!"

"What you mean, nothin'? I hear you screaming from the lobby, and I walk in to see this nigga got his fuckin' hands on you. Are you crazy or stupid?!"

"Kola, stay out my business. I can handle it."

"You in trouble wit' this nigga? You took money from him?"

"No, a'ight!"

"Apple, if you got some kinda beef wit' Supreme let me know. I can get my peoples on it and handle him."

Apple didn't need her sister prying into her business and protecting her like she was some charity case. She didn't need Kola holding her hand. Kola had more love and respect in the hood than Apple ever had, and Apple was also jealous of her sister.

"I'm fuckin' OK. Just step off!" Apple screamed.

Kola looked at her sister up and down. "Yo, I don't know what your fuckin' game is or what really is your fuckin' problem, but you lookin' stupid wit' my fuckin' clothes on. Fo' real, you need to take my shit off and wash it. Then check your fuckin' self. What? You tryin' to be me now, huh?"

"Fuck you, Kola!" Apple shouted then raced upstairs in her heels.

Kola followed behind her, and the two continued their argument inside the apartment. Nichols was on the couch watching TV when she heard the shouting and the door slam.

"Why you in my shit, Apple?"

"Kola, step the fuck off!" Apple screamed, snatching off the shirt and unbuttoning the skirt.

"No. You tell me why that nigga was pressed up on you like that! Huh, Apple? What the fuck business you got wit' him? He a fuckin' creep. You fuckin' that nigga?"

Apple turned. "I ain't a fuckin' whore, like you, bitch!"

"'Bitch'? Remember, I'm the one that saved your fuckin' ass!"

Apple tossed Kola's shirt at her and then kicked off the shoes.

Nichols was dumbfounded by her sisters' argument and wanted them to stop. She stood up and watched her two sisters up in each other's face like they were boxers in the ring.

"You's a disrespectful bitch, Apple!"

"I'll be disrespectful. Just get the fuck out my face!"

"So, what you tryin' to do? Fight me now? Huh, Apple? What's good then, punk!"

Nichols was fed up with the nonsense between her sisters. Tears trickling down her face, she burst out, "Stop it! Stop it! Why y'all always gotta be fighting? I'm tired of this shit! Damn it!" She stormed out of the room and hurried into her mother's bedroom, leaving the twins astounded by her outburst.

Kola took a step back from Apple, regaining her composure. "You know what? I don't need this shit. You can keep my fuckin' clothes. You seem to need them more than me. I'll just buy some new shit." She walked out the door and slammed it shut behind her.

Apple sucked her teeth. She stepped out of the skirt and left everything scattered about in the living room. Dressed in only her panties and bra, she went into the bathroom, turned on the water, and filled the dirty tub up until she was able to jump in and submerge herself from her reality.

She cried underwater, wishing she was able to drown herself. She needed a change in her life, wanted something different, but it felt like she was living through the same bullshit every day.

Chapter Ten

A few weeks into summer, Harlem had become a hot town. A drug dealer had been murdered, found shot to death on 139th Street and Lenox, and the hood was buzzing with police activity. Word on the streets was, it was a rival of Cross, a man named Donny B. He was found sprawled out on the hard concrete with two shots to his head at two o'clock in the morning. Donny B had been hanging out with some friends near the bodega when a dark Chevy crept up while they were drinking and mingling. A hooded shooter leaped from the car and fired at him at point-blank range, dropping him where he stood as his friends ran off.

The crime scene had been taped off, and bystanders hung around talking about the cold-blooded shooting. Police were trying to take statements from them, but nobody wanted to get involved, fearing retaliation for snitching.

The body had been transported to the morgue, while the half-dozen cops still canvassed the neighborhood, trying to collect evidence and statements. Hours had passed since the killing, but the police still didn't have any clues. Morning soon became afternoon, and gradually, the block was littered with foot traffic and nosy neighbors still inquiring about the shooting.

Nichols walked down Lenox Avenue with her friend Dina. It was a beautiful afternoon, and the two young girls wanted to enjoy the summer day by looking at boys, window-shopping, and maybe, from the right store, shoplift a few items.

Nichols was clad in a short skirt, exposing her young, meaty thighs, and a loose T-shirt that hid her developing breasts.

Dina teased her, saying, "Yo, you gonna mess around and get us raped out here, looking like that. I wish I had your legs."

"Please. Niggas is lookin', but they know not to touch." Nichols chuckled. "Besides, if he's cute enough, maybe I'll let him touch."

Dina laughed. "Uh-huh, look at you. You talkin' like Kola now."

"Kola be doin' her thang. She be gettin' money and running these dudes out here."

"And you wanna be next in line, right?" Dina asked.

"Maybe," Nichols replied slowly.

"Now, you know you're too much of a square to be like your sister, Nichols. That ain't you. You're too smart for that."

Nichols changed her expression. She hated when her sisters and friends treated her like a bookworm who didn't know any better. Though she was ignorant of the street life, she wanted to have her fun too. She wanted to be noticed and gawked at by the fellows and treated like she was a top model. Nichols knew she was pretty; in fact, it was the one good thing her mother had passed down to her and her sisters.

The summer was young and hot, and both girls just wanted to meet cute boys and run through Harlem like it was their personal playground. Nichols also wanted to party and experience the things she'd heard her sisters talk about. She wanted to lose her virginity, and she wanted to get out of her mother's home and experience new things. She felt trapped in that filthy apartment.

Always stuck in Harlem, all Nichols knew was her projects and 125th Street. She was always cleaning and cooking, while her sisters ran the streets and their mother was getting fucked by every Tom, Dick, and Harry. Taking the A train to Queens or riding the No. 6 train into the Bronx was something foreign to her.

Nichols and Dina slowly made their way toward the scene of the crime that took place early that morning. They were both stunned by the tangled yellow tape and bloodstained ground.

Walking up to a stranger, Nichols asked, "Yo, what happened?"

A thin, frail-looking man with rotten teeth turned to look at the young girls, a bagged bottle of whisky clutched in his fist. "Some nigga got shot."

"Wow! Who?" Nichols asked with wide eyes.

"Don't know. He dead, though," the stranger stated.

Nichols looked around. Even though death had occurred in her neighborhood before, and she would always hear gunshots outside her bedroom window, she was still astounded that a murder had happened not too far from her home.

"That's crazy," Dina said.

The two looked at the scene for a short moment and then moved on. They wished they had seen the body, but with summer just starting, there was going to be more shootings and more killings.

The afternoon sun was beating down on them like it was hitched to them personally. Nichols wanted to hit up 125th Street and linger about, hoping to see something she liked and get a friend to steal it for her when the chance came. It was such a nice day, she didn't want to see her home for hours. She planned on hanging out with Dina all day and probably even into the night.

Evening came fast for Nichols, though. She and Dina were in Hue-Man Bookstore on Eighth Avenue looking at books and magazines. They sipped on cold milkshakes and sat in the lounging area of the café inside the bookstore talking about the articles they were reading, admiring the cute guys entering and exiting the store.

"Ooh, he's cute. I like that chocolate. He got that Tyrese thing goin' on," Nichols said with a smile.

Dina quickly agreed.

Nichols was having a great time with her friend at the Hue-Man Bookstore, where she was able to escape the harshness of her home and free her mind from any trouble. Not only did she not have to worry about her mother going upside her head, or her two sisters arguing over nonsense, but she had books to read and a place to chill.

Dina was getting tired, and she needed to head back home to help her mother with some cleaning. She stood up. "You coming? It's getting late."

Nichols looked at the time and realized it was almost eight. She sighed. "Nah, I'm going to chill. You go ahead. I'll call you later." She was reading an article about Trey Songz and admiring his physique with a pleased smile. She wanted to stay until the place closed.

"You sure, girl? That's a long walk home by yourself."

"Dina, I'm gonna be all right. Shit, I grew up out here. They know me."

Dina was skeptical about leaving Nichols by herself, but she had promised her mother that she would be home before nine o'clock. She gathered up her things and left Nichols seated at the table, her face buried in the latest issue of *Vibe* magazine.

Nichols lost track of the time, until informed by one of the workers that the place was closing. After gathering her things, she walked out of the store and into the evening, where the city was still bustling and loud. The weather remained hot as the night took over the day.

Nichols began her walk on 125th Street, not rushing to get home. When she reached the corner of Seventh

Avenue and 125th Street, she noticed a cute, young thug seated in the passenger seat of a dark blue Tahoe with spinning, chrome wheels and rap music blaring. The truck had stopped at a red light. She locked eyes with the young man, who had smooth brown skin and stylish long braids. He smiled at Nichols as he nodded to the music, and Nichols couldn't help but smile back. The thug's pearly white teeth glistened, his eyes penetrating Nichols' like he was a hypnotist.

She thought he was the finest thing she had laid eyes on. The two had this unspoken attraction between them, and she wanted to know his name. But the light suddenly changed to green, and the Tahoe made its way down 125th, the rap music slowly fading out. She sighed, wishing they had time to introduce themselves. Nichols hated that they'd met so briefly, but she realized there wasn't anything she could have done about it.

She continued her walk toward home, hoping her apartment would be free from drama. As she made her way down the street, she was hounded with looks and catcalls from a variety of men, some of which made her extremely uncomfortable. They looked at her as if she was a sheep trapped in a lion's den.

When Nichols made it to Lenox Avenue, she noticed the same truck parked in front of Sylvia's Restaurant. A whirl of excitement hit her like a rapid storm. She smiled while walking closer to the truck. She was hoping her cutie from the intersection was still seated in the passenger seat. She didn't want to be too obvious by staring at the truck, so she kept her eyes straight ahead and slowly walked by the vehicle, pretending it didn't exist. Out of her peripheral vision, she noticed a figure seated in the passenger seat, and a slow smile formed on her face.

As Nichols walked by, she heard someone say, "Ay, shawty, I know you, right?"

She turned to see who called out to her and was flattered that it was the same cutie in the front passenger seat. "Say what?" she replied, trying to look unconcerned.

"I saw you watching me at that light."

Nichols sucked her teeth. "Please. You know you was watching me."

He laughed. "A'ight, yeah, I was, but you fine, shawty. You Kola's sister, right?" he asked with the warmest smile.

"Yeah. And?"

"Nah, I'm cool wit' ya sister. She my peoples, but damn, her sister is so much finer. What's your name, beautiful?" he asked with politeness.

As Nichols approached the truck, she was unable to contain her smile any longer. She fixed her eyes on the young thug with the Colgate smile and Jim Jones swag. "Nichols."

"Yeah, I like that name," he said. "I could get used to saying that."

"And what's your name?"

"Delray."

"It's cute."

"Thanks. So where you on ya way to?"

"Home."

"Damn! So early? Shit, the sun ain't even set fully yet. What? Ya moms got you on curfew this summer?"

"No. Ain't nothing to do right now," Nichols snapped back, offended by his remark.

"So we can find somethin' to do. Yo, my man in there gettin' us somethin' to eat right now. You hungry? I can hit him on the jack and tell him to get you a plate too. It ain't no thang."

"Nah, I'm good."

"You sure? 'Cause I swear I just heard your stomach growling like a muthafucka. It sounded like you got a grizzly bear or somethin' in there," Delray joked.

Nichols laughed. "No. Why you tryin' to play me?"

"It's all love. But you're so pretty. I like you." Delray reached out to grab Nichols by her hand gently and pulled her closer to the truck. He looked her in the face. "So what's up? Let's chill for the night. Let me take you out somewhere. It's a nice night, and I ain't got nothin' to do right now. We can get to know each other better, you feel me?"

"What about your boy?" she asked.

"He good. I'll drop him off, take the keys to the truck, and we can roll out."

Nichols quickly mulled over the idea of spending time with Delray, and it sounded so sweet to her. It was her opportunity to stay out longer. She knew her mother was probably too busy shacked up with some man to even care what time she came home, and her twin sisters were always out doing their own thing. Nichols felt this was her chance to stray away from the nest and do her. She had a fine young man willing to spend time with her, and maybe he was a potential boyfriend, because she liked everything about him from head to toe.

Delray's True Religion designer jeans hung low off his ass, and his wife-beater hugged his chiseled frame, with his defined muscular arms and strapping chest. She loved a man with braids, and the bling around his neck and wrist told her he was balling.

Nichols batted her eyes, trying to look sexy and flirty. "Where are we going to go?" she asked.

"I know a place you'll like."

"Really?"

"It ain't far from here."

The two talked for about ten minutes, and the more time Nichols spent with Delray, the more she was ready to leave with him. She loved the way he touched her lightly, making her feel wanted. He made her laugh and smile a lot and she'd only just met him. His confidence was appealing.

Delray's friend came walking out of Sylvia's holding two plastic bags of food. He was tall and lean, older in the face, and his eyes showed a lot of experience. He looked aloof to Nichols.

He walked up to Delray, noticing Nichols, and asked, "Who this?"

"My new shawty," Delray joked.

He passed Delray the bags of food and walked around to the driver's side.

"Jah, she comin' wit' us," Delray said.

Jah just looked at him then looked at her. "Well, she better hurry up then. I got some place to be." He got into the truck and started the ignition.

"You comin', right, baby?"

Nichols was a little hesitant, but Delray sealed the deal by saying, "It'll be fun. I got you, Nichols. My treat. You never know, maybe sparks might fly between us."

He smiled, causing Nichols to smile after him, and she jumped into the backseat and tried to relax as they pulled off.

❦

An hour later, the two were parked on Riverside Drive, where they'd shared a plate of hot soul food from Sylvia's and enjoyed an illuminated view of the George Washington Bridge in the distance.

Delray held Nichols in his arms like they were a loving couple. He felt her soft, round bottom rub against him like a cushion, and he loved the way his arms slipped into her womanly curves. Though she was only sixteen, her body was built like a mature woman's, and he loved the feel of her every inch.

"This is nice," Nichols said, her eyes wide with joy.

"It is, right?" Delray replied with ease.

The two acted like they had known each other for years. Nichols felt as if she had found the man who'd make her world right. She didn't want to leave his hold; time seemed to have slowed down when she was with him. He had shared his meal with her, they had wonderful conversation, and even though Delray was nineteen, Nichols felt he understood her. She talked, and he would listen. Nichols easily opened up to him about her problems at home, and Delray listened like he was a paid therapist.

He agreed with what Nichols said. She should be treated more like an adult. Her family did take her for granted. He nodded and put in his two cents when Nichols complained about her two sisters arguing, and he consoled her when she beefed about not being loved or wanted.

Delray kissed Nichols on her neck tenderly, holding her tighter. "I got your back, baby. You wit' me now, so you ain't got to worry."

Nichols smiled at his words. Her heart had found comfort; she had found love so quickly, right around the corner. She was happy she just didn't walk on by. They had known each other only for a couple hours, but she felt like Delray understood her completely. He was easy to talk to, he made her laugh, and he made her feel so secure, she wanted to stay forever in his arms. Nichols didn't believe she was naïve. She was sixteen, smart, and knew about boys.

Delray continued planting sweet, pleasing kisses against her neck, squeezing her waist tighter, and Nichols savored the moment. His touch was so inviting, the inside of her thighs felt like cream. She closed her eyes, relishing his strength and alluring scent. And though it was getting late, she wasn't in any rush.

Delray slowly turned in her direction, and his eyes met hers. He smiled. "You're beautiful. You know that, right?"

Nichols smiled and replied with a meek, "Thank you."

Soon their lips touched, and their tongues became entwined. The taste of his fresh breath and the way his hands touched her skin made her purr with stimulation.

After they kissed for a moment, Delray slowly pulled himself away from her, eyes locked with the young teen. He smiled proudly and said, "Come back to my place and chill. I'm not too far from here."

Nichols didn't answer him. Instead, she stared into his tempting brown eyes, her eyes smiling back. She was hot and bothered, and was itching to feel the touch of a man inside her. She had witnessed her sisters' promiscuous actions many times and had heard them and their friends boast about how great it was being in love, and being dicked down so good that their legs quivered when they came and their bodies felt stuck to wherever they lay after making love. Nichols was yearning for that feeling. She wanted to feel what her sisters and friends felt. She assumed she had found love with Delray, though she'd only been with him for a few hours, since her pussy was throbbing uncontrollably.

"You down, baby?" Delray asked.

"Yeah, I'm down."

Chapter 11

The small room in the two-bedroom apartment on the Upper West Side reeked of weed and was cluttered with rumpled clothes, kicked-off sneakers, plates containing food remnants, and video games scattered across the squeaky Shaw hardwood floor. The walls were covered with posters of rappers, athletes, and voluptuous women, oiled and wearing next to nothing, and with the only piece of furniture in the room being an unmade wood platform bed positioned in the center, it resembled the typical bachelor's crib.

Nichols looked around the cramped bedroom. The place reminded her of home, so she wasn't taken aback by the mess. Delray moved farther into the bedroom and removed his tank top, tossing it on the untidy bed and exposing his rock-hard abs. He was like a perfectly designed sculpture, his brown skin impeccably wrapped around tightly developed flesh that gleamed with sex appeal.

Delray cleared the bed, tossing everything on the floor, and picked up the remote to the television. He then took a seat at the end of the bed, turned on the TV, and gestured for Nichols to join him. Nichols walked forward and sat closely to him, knowing what he wanted—sex. Feeling his hand slowly glide up her thigh and under her skirt, she knew she was making it too easy for him.

He slowly leaned her back and cupped her breasts, positioning her for sex. "You like me?" he asked with a smile.

"Yeah, I do."

"'Cause I really like you."

Nichols smiled and then felt him tugging at her panties. He gripped the sides tightly and tried to yank them off. At first, she tried to close her legs to prevent them from being pulled off, but between Delray's soft look, his light kisses to the inside of her bellybutton, and his kind, soothing words, within five minutes, her panties came sliding off.

Delray began fondling Nichols. He gently pushed his index and middle finger into her, and recognized she was a virgin. That excited him and made him want her even more, knowing he would be the first to pop her cherry with his thick dick.

Nichols lay on her back, her panties lost in the debris on the floor, and her bra unsnapped and almost completely off.

Delray pulled up her skirt and played with her pubic hair. He had the innocent sixteen-year-old in the palm of his hand and was taking his sweet time with her. He had all night to toy with her.

As he sucked on Nichols' hard nipples, he unzipped his pants and slid out of them. He then positioned himself between her shapely thighs. Delray wanted to find his rhythm and fuck her correctly without it hurting her, but the strong urge to penetrate her had quickly taken over. He just wanted to take her virginity and come inside her.

Before Nichols could protest and mention anything about a condom, Delray had the tip of his dick breaking through her walls. He held her down on the mattress firmly and thrust himself into her, causing her to scream out in pain.

"Ouch! Ouch!" she cried out, dragging her nails down the center of his back and bracing herself for the worst of it.

Delray didn't care about her cries of pain. He wanted to fuck, and he wanted to be rough. Nichols gritted her teeth and wanted to pull herself from underneath him, but the weight of his body kept her pinned between him and the mattress. She felt her vagina being torn open from his girth, and since this was her first time, she was experiencing more pain than pleasure.

Delray pounded into Nichols with little sympathy for her virgin state. He squeezed her thighs and breasts, grunted in her ear as he felt his nut brewing, and didn't notice the tears developing in her young eyes as the blood ran down her thighs.

"Ouch! Slow . . . please, slow," Nichols pleaded.

Ignoring her, Delray continued, his fist clutching the sheets soiled from previous use, and sweat pouring from his brow.

The room had no fan or air conditioning, and the summer heat was the only thing that circulated in the bedroom. Nichols' breasts were sweaty against Delray's chest, and the pounding inside of her seemed unrelenting. She closed her eyes, bit down on her bottom lip, and endured the pain, realizing he didn't plan to stop anytime soon. He seemed transfixed by the pain he was causing her. Nichols hadn't imagined losing her virginity this way. She'd always fantasized about a man like Delray, but always thought he would be more gentle and caring, that the sex would be easygoing and loving.

Nichols swore she saw someone watching them from the doorway, but his penis going in and out of her like a freight train kept her distracted.

"Oh shit! I'm comin'!" Delray grunted. He danced on top of her, feeling his nut coming soon. He bit Nichols' nipple, causing her to scream out, and then wrapped his hand around her neck tightly as he came inside of her.

Nichols gasped, feeling Delray's penis going deeper. He shook like he was having a seizure. When he was done, he got up, shook his penis, exhaled, and looked for his stuff. It felt like he had just gone to the bathroom on her. Nichols lay there in tears. Between her thighs was red with blood. Delray didn't even offer her a towel to clean herself with.

Before she could get up and reach for her belongings, three men suddenly appeared in the room, startling her. She knew something was wrong, but before she could react, she found herself pinned down by her arms and screaming for help, while a second man rushed between her legs, thrusting into her for a quick and forceful fuck.

"Relax, girl. We just tryin' to have some fun wit' you, and then we'll get down to business," Delray proclaimed with a devious smile.

A few hours later, Nichols found herself bonded with handcuffs to a steel radiator, butt naked, bleeding, and scared. She was at another location and didn't remember how she'd arrived there. The ground was cold and the place haunting, with its rusty exposed pipes overhead, and the barren concrete walls made the dingy basement look like a dark dungeon. Three men stood around her, gawking at her, delighted to see her captive like some zoo animal.

Nichols cried out, her eyes swollen from crying and her face panic-stricken. She searched the room for any sight of Delray. She wanted an explanation from him. Her pussy was so sore, she couldn't even sit in a correct posture. And she didn't know how many men had raped her, because she had passed out from the abuse.

The men waited around, obviously for the alpha male to show up, and he soon arrived. Supreme walked into the basement with his number one guy right behind him, Guy Tony. He looked at Nichols with amusement. He went up to the scared Nichols, hunched down, and stroked her face like a concerned parent.

Nichols flinched, moving away from him, but she was restricted. The handcuffs cut into her wrist, and she ached from the pain.

"You're here 'cause of your sisters, Nichols. They fuck wit' me, I fuck wit' them. But don't worry, when I get my money, you get let go. Until then, get comfortable," Supreme said.

Nichols cried out, "No!"

Supreme stood over the naked girl and admired her body. He loved the way her curves rounded every inch of her and how succulent her tits looked. Her skin looked so soft and she was just so innocent. He knew Delray and his goons already had their way with her. They were vicious like that—a group of bloodthirsty hounds that would, for the right price, do anything he asked.

Supreme knew Delray would be the right man for the job. He needed a smooth-talking pimp to convince Nichols into leaving with him, one that she'd even trust, waiting for the right opportunity to strike. He didn't want to force the girl off the street and draw attention to himself, so he and Delray had watched Nichols and Dina the entire day as they walked up and down 125th Street, going in and out of stores, and then waited as the two were inside Hue-Man Bookstore.

When they saw Dina exit the store without Nichols, Delray knew it was perfect. They followed Nichols from the store, and Delray made sure they stopped at the red light where she was about to cross the street, so he could make eye contact with her. Everything had worked out as planned. Nichols was too gullible; she wasn't like her sisters. And with the right game, he had her eating out of his hand.

Nichols curled up and continued to cry. She was so scared, she wanted to pee on herself, but she figured the worst was over. She was being held for ransom, and she figured Kola would pay up for her release, so for the time being, she closed her eyes and tried to think positively.

Supreme left his two goons to watch her closely, but once the doors were shut behind him, the violation and abuse began again. Both men stripped from their jeans, swollen dicks in hand, and raped and sodomized a defenseless Nichols, whose screams couldn't penetrate the thick concrete walls and locked doors.

Chapter 12

I t was nearing afternoon, when Apple was suddenly awakened by her mother charging into the bedroom and shouting, "Apple, where the fuck is Nichols? She ain't come home last night!"

Apple stirred from her bed, the mention of Nichols not coming home last night making her rise quickly. "Ma, what are you talking about?"

She looked over at Nichol's bed, which was still made, and worry sunk into her like the Titanic. She sprung to her feet. It wasn't like Nichols to hang out all night and not let anyone know. She rushed toward Kola's bedroom and banged on the door, but there was no answer.

Fuck it! Apple thought. She picked the bedroom lock, and when she and her mother entered Kola's bedroom, it was empty.

Then it dawned on Denise. "That bitch probably got my daughter hanging out all night with her."

Apple thought the same thing. She tried to call Kola, but her call went straight to voice mail. The two decided to chill, and wait until Kola came home.

Late afternoon came, and Denise and Apple were watching TV, their nerves on edge. Apple kept calling Kola on her phone, but again her calls when straight to voice mail.

Apple went to the store, hoping she would run into one of her sisters, but the blocks were empty and quiet. With two murders in the past three days, the cops were on steady patrol and locking up hustlers left and right.

Kola finally walked through the front door around six in the evening.

"Kola, where's Nichols?" Denise asked.

"I don't know," Kola returned with a hint of sarcasm.

"Nichols ain't come home last night, Kola," Apple told her.

Upon hearing that, Kola's expression went from that of a bad girl to a worried sister. She looked at her family and spat, "What you mean, she ain't come home last night? Where the fuck is she?"

"We tryin' to find that out now," Apple said.

All of a sudden, Kola had the look of a lost soul. She immediately began to think the worst. She knew she had enemies, and wondered if someone got to Nichols in retaliation for something she'd done in her past.

She got on her phone and began making calls. The first person she called was Dina. After three rings, Dina picked up.

"Dina, where's Nichols?" she asked frantically.

"I don't know. The last time I saw her was yesterday

evening. I left her sitting in Hue-Man on Eighth Avenue. Why? What happened?'

"She ain't come home last night," Kola said.

"What!"

"You sure that was the last time you saw her?" Kola asked.

"Yes. She wanted to stay, but I had to leave," Dina said. "I'm coming over there."

After Dina hung up, Kola made a few more phone calls. She called up a few thugs and put the word out that her little sister was missing.

Denise wanted to call the police, but Kola was against having pigs in her business, knowing her people would be on it. But Denise was adamant about getting law enforcement involved. Nichols was her baby girl, and no matter how harsh she was toward her girls, she still loved them and knew the cops were probably better at finding a missing young girl than anyone else.

"Ma, I got this!" Kola yelled.

"I'm calling them, Kola. She's my fuckin' daughter!" Denise screamed out.

"I'll find her my damn self, and whoever disrespects her or do somethin' to her, God help them, 'cause they gonna have to deal wit' me." Kola charged out the apartment and slammed the door shut, leaving Apple and Denise wondering and worried.

Twenty-four hours after Nichols' disappearance, two detectives entered the untidy apartment, where Denise sat on the couch worrying about her missing daughter. Apple sat next to her and had the same concern.

The two suit-and-tie detectives looked around the apartment and noticed the tattered furniture, ragged carpeting, and soiled walls, and quickly passed judgment on the mother, figuring the daughter was more of a runaway than a kidnap victim. Still, they had to carry out their job, minus their opinion. They stood over the family, trying to look concerned, but it wasn't easy for them to reserve judgment. From their experience, many missing young girls sixteen and under were either trying to escape from something at home—abuse, rape, molestation—or in other cases, leaving home in pursuit of love or a dream.

Detective Miles was tall, young in the face, easy on the eyes, and looked more caring than his partner. He said, "Miss, sometimes a young girl runs away in search of love. Did she have a boyfriend or someone?"

"My daughter ain't go chasing behind some fuckin' boy. She ain't like that. They took my baby!"

Detective Greggs was older, shorter, had a graying beard, and appeared to be the father of many. He knew Harlem like the back of his hand. He remembered being a rookie cop during the days when Nicky Barnes and Frank Lucas ran the show. He had watched Harlem change drastically over the years. Witnessed the birth of crack cocaine firsthand. He remembered Rich Porter and Alpo, young kingpins coming up after the older ones died out on the streets or in prison. His thirty-plus years on the force were met with good times, but also racism and neglect. He had seen his fair share of missing young runaways chasing after pimps and boyfriends, thinking they had found love. Years later, they'd be either turning tricks or dying slowly while chasing a high.

"Did she have any enemies at school or in the neighborhood?" Detective Greggs inquired.

"No, not my baby." Denise started sniffling.

Detective Greggs had seen many mothers heartbroken over their children's absence. Sometimes, it could have been prevented with good parenting, but other times the child left on their own volition. He remained unfazed by Denise's tears. Looking at the condition of the apartment, he wondered why Child Protective Services hadn't already intervened and taken her children away.

"Look, I'm going to be honest with you," Greggs told Denise. "She's young, and the chances are she's with a boyfriend that you are unaware of. She thinks she's found love and wants to chase it. Give it some time. She'll come back."

But Denise still wasn't buying it, so the detectives took down Nichols' description, and Denise gave them a small headshot Nichols had taken at school. Still, both detectives were reluctant to pursue the case.

Apple broke her silence. "She don't have a boyfriend, a'ight! My little sister tells me everything. If she was dealing wit' someone, then I damn sure woulda known about it."

"We'll look into it, ma'am, I promise," Detective Miles expressed half-heartedly.

They then exited the apartment, leaving Apple feeling like she couldn't trust them and that she would have to handle things on her own. She rushed into her room and quickly got dressed, sliding into a pair of jeans and a T-shirt. She rushed by her mother and bolted for the stairway. She left her building with an attitude and strolled through the projects, asking around for her little sister.

But everyone was giving her the same answer: "Didn't see her."

Apple rushed up to Lenox Avenue, where the bustling streets were filled with people and young teens. With the drive of a machine, she went into every establishment with a picture of Nichols and asked if she had been inside in the past twenty-four hours, but the replies were all negative.

Apple stood on the avenue, tears trickling down her face. She was fearing the worst, knowing that something had probably happened to her little sister already. She started walking up the block, her mind racing. Faces became a blur to her, and the sound of traffic was muted from her mind as she moved up and down the street with speed.

By nightfall, it seemed hopeless. After hitting every block and every corner, Apple was no closer to finding out what happened to Nichols. She slowly walked back to her home, praying that, when she walked through her front door, Nichols would be there waiting for her with a smile and a hug; that it was only a nightmare.

When she made it to the corner of Lenox Avenue and 139th Street, she spotted Guy Tony chilling out with a few friends. Something wild sparked inside of her, and then it dawned on her that Supreme was probably the one responsible for her sister's disappearance. He definitely had the motive and reputation to do something so vile and heartless.

She marched over to Guy Tony, her eyes beaming on him intensely. She bent down, picked up a beer bottle, and rushed up to him while he had his back turned to her.

Guy Tony noticed the look of expectation his friends had in their eyes, distracted by something or someone approaching from behind him. By the time he turned around, Apple had already struck him upside his head with a glass bottle, smashing it into pieces.

"Bitch, what the fuck is ya problem?" Guy Tony screamed out as he doubled over in pain, clutching his bleeding wound.

"Where the fuck is my sister?" Apple yelled.

Apple was poised and ready to strike again if needed, but Guy Tony's friend quickly intervened, knocking the jagged tool from her hand and restraining her from doing any more damage.

Apple fought and cursed, creating a scene. "Get the fuck off me! Get off me!"

Onlookers gathered to watch the activity from a distance, to see what would transpire next.

Guy Tony wiped the blood from his face while glaring at Apple. "You fuckin' bitch! What the fuck you talkin' about?"

"You took her! Give her back! She ain't got shit to do

wit' what's going on wit' Supreme and me!"

"We ain't take ya sister! You done fuckin' lost your mind," he shouted back.

Apple, squirming and fidgeting in her captor's arms, had tears streaming down her face as she looked at Guy Tony with hostility.

Meanwhile, as more people gathered around the dispute, Guy Tony started to get nervous. Even though he was the one assaulted, he knew the police would most likely be more sympathetic to Apple and see her as the victim. Not to mention he had his .45 tucked snugly in his waistband. He had a long rap sheet and didn't want to see Central Booking anytime soon.

He looked at his friend and said, "Let her go."

Everyone looked at him with confusion.

Guy Tony repeated himself. "I said, 'let her fuckin' go!'"

As soon as Guy Tony's friend released Apple, she went up to Guy Tony and spat in his face, which was rapidly followed by a hard right-hand smack. "Where is she?" she continued, rage and anger devouring her. She had no proof that Guy Tony or Supreme had anything to do with her sister's disappearance, but her gut wouldn't let it go.

Guy Tony knew to keep his cool. There were too many people around watching. Too many witnesses that didn't like him and would easily lie on him. He stepped back from Apple and said, "I don't know what you're talking about."

"Muthafucka, don't lie to me! You took her! You fuckin' took her!" Apple screamed, her accusations echoing off into the streets.

Guy Tony knew it was time for his exit. He ignored Apple and turned to get into his truck, but Apple wasn't through with him. She lunged at him, grabbing him by his T-shirt from the back and stretching it until it tore.

"Yo, someone get this crazy bitch off me!" Guy Tony shouted.

A few hands pulled Apple free from Guy Tony's torn shirt, and he kept it moving until he was in his truck and had the ignition started.

Apple screamed out, "He got my little sister! They kidnapped her! They took her!" She watched as the truck drove off, and her world slowly became a lot dimmer.

The police soon arrived, but the disturbance was already done with. Apple walked away feeling hopeless. *Maybe Nichols did run away,* she began to think. She moved through the projects slowly, vowing to continue her search no matter how late it got. Apple was determined to find out what happened to her little sister, and was hoping it wasn't something she'd done that caused Nichols to suffer.

An hour past midnight, Apple stood lingering in front of her building, still drying her tears. The hope of her sister being home was a bust when she'd walked through her front door earlier and there was no sign of Nichols or Kola around. Only her mother was there, staring out the living room window, smoking a Newport, clutching a half-empty glass of vodka, her face looking like it had aged ten more years.

The two looked at each other, but no words were exchanged. Their look said it all. It was hard to even think of the worst.

Unable to remain in the apartment any longer, Apple went back outside to breathe and think of places where Nichols could be. She hadn't heard or seen Kola in hours, but Apple was sure she was doing her part somewhere to help find Nichols.

Apple took a long pull from the cigarette as she looked around the projects. Paranoia had kicked in, so as far as she was concerned, everybody was a suspect. She thought about all of the jealous bitches that hated on her and her sisters for the longest time. She thought about the thirsty guys that wanted to sleep with her, those she'd turned down, sometimes in the worst way. She thought about her enemies from the past, the bitches she and Kola had jumped on, with the hair-pulling, face-scarring, skin-bruising, and clothes-tearing. They both were beasts on the streets when it came to having each other's backs, even though at times, they were each other's own worst enemy.

Apple took a few more drags and flicked the cigarette away. Then she noticed Kola stepping out of a burgundy Range Rover with fancy tires and rims. Kola exited the truck in her short skirt and sexy stilettos. Apple watched Kola come her way from a good distance, but she didn't move from her spot. She knew Kola had put the word out on the street about their missing sister, and she waited anxiously for any kind of news.

Kola stepped up to Apple with a straight gaze. "Let me holla at you."

Apple followed behind Kola, and the two met in the stairway of their building. Apple's heart pounded with worry, thinking Kola had some bad news to tell her. She tried to brace herself for anything.

"What's up?" she asked.

"What beef you got wit' Supreme? And don't fuckin' lie to me, Apple. I need to know."

"He took Nichols?"

"We don't know. But it's funny how all of a sudden he got you in the stairway roughing you up, and then a few days later, Nichols is missing. What's up wit' that?"

Apple didn't want to come clean, knowing how quickly things could spiral out of control, even though they already had. But she didn't want to believe Nichols was taken because of a meager debt she owed. It scared her to know that she could be responsible for her sister's kidnapping, and it was eating away at her conscience.

Kola stared at Apple, demanding an answer from her.

Apple shut her eyes for a moment, leaned her back against the wall, then looked at her younger sibling by only forty-six minutes. "I borrowed money from him, a'ight?"

"You dumb bitch!" Kola barked. "You know how grimy that nigga is! Why the fuck did you even get in bed wit' that nigga? What the fuck were you thinkin'?"

"I just needed it. It was important."

"And you couldn't come to me for it?"

Apple sucked her teeth and spit out a quick, "Please."

"So now you in debt to this stupid muthafucka for how much?"

"I borrowed five hundred, but he raised it to six-fifty."

"Six hundred and fifty dollars? Why? For a fuckin' outfit for that Summer Jam concert? You tell Supreme I'll give him his fuckin' money, but if he touches my sister, he's dead."

Apple was quiet. It was the first time in a long while that she let Kola talk without interfering. She knew Kola was right. She tried to hold back her tears and contain her guilt.

She now knew that she had grossly underestimated Supreme. Stupidly she thought she would take the money, he'd push up for sex, and she'd turn him down. Never in her wildest imagination did she think he would handle young girls as he did a dude on the street. Even though there was no solid proof that Supreme was responsible for Nichols' disappearance, she knew he had a hand in it somehow.

"I can't even look at you right now, Apple, but I swear, if anything happens to Nichols, I will never forgive you for this." Kola charged out the stairway exit and slammed the door behind her, leaving Apple slumped against the wall, knowing she had seriously fucked up.

Chapter 13

Two days after Nichols' kidnapping, she was still confined to the cold, dirty ground, handcuffed to the radiator, and being raped repeatedly. The abuse was starting to break her down. She would never be the same. She continued to sob, while her hope of being freed died out. Nichols trembled, her stomach growling with hunger, her naked body covered with bruises and welts. She couldn't move or stand up, and hadn't been allowed to shower since becoming captive.

Supreme and Guy Tony walked into the basement. Supreme, dressed in a Nike track suit and clutching a cigar in his hand, went over to Nichols and looked down at her with fake compassion. He then looked at his three goons and shouted, "This is what y'all do to her?"

"We got bored, man," one of the men replied, in an attempt at humor. "She was the only thing around to play with."

Supreme smiled at his men, knowing he didn't care how they treated her, but he wanted her to feel comfortable.

He looked at one of his goons and instructed, "Yo, take them handcuffs off. Let her free for a moment."

Nichols was quickly freed, and she hugged the cold floor with her naked breasts and sobbed.

Supreme stood over her and said, "Look, we gonna get through this, a'ight? You hungry?"

Nichols continued to sob, her body trembling from the chill and abuse.

Supreme looked over at his goons and said, "Yo, go get her somethin' to eat. Some chicken and rice from that bodega up the block. And bring her some water."

One took off, while the others were baffled as to what he was doing.

Supreme picked her up from the floor and carried her over to the couch and placed her gently on her side. Then he said to her, "Once your sister pays up, you get let go."

A confused Guy Tony looked at Supreme but kept his mouth shut.

Weak and frightened, Nichols looked up at Supreme with teary eyes and didn't say a word. Hearing him say that she would be let go was a relief to her. Somewhat. She curled up on the couch and lay there.

Supreme sat next to her, stroking her hair and admiring her beauty behind the battered face and constant tears. "It's not your fault that you're here. I just got some unfinished business wit' your sisters, and once that is taken care of, you're free to go," he told her.

He continued to stroke her. His touch went from her long hair to her slim neck, and then he touched the small of her back. "You know, you're beautiful just like your sisters. I always liked your sisters. They're somethin' else. Are you like your sisters, Nichols?"

Nichols looked at him, not understanding his question.

Supreme slowly massaged the small of her back and pulled her closer. "I'm sorry my peoples had to rough you up like that. It was uncalled for. They're like children; they just don't know how to treat certain toys. They get excited and then play too rough. Did they hurt you?"

Nichols body tensed up from Supreme's touch. Her insides hurt, her jaw was slightly swollen, and her anus felt raw and violated. She had endured one penetration after the other—no mercy had been shown to her in the past two days.

Supreme licked his lips as he slid his hand near her backside, which he was admiring. He lusted over how firm her breasts were. Even though she was a virgin just a few days ago, Supreme had no use for her pussy now. Not after his workers had run a train on her. He had a taste for something else.

While Nichols lay curled up near Supreme's lap, he slowly began toying with her breasts. He felt Nichols cringe as his fingertips slowly kneaded her soft flesh.

"Please, no," she uttered faintly.

"This is it for you, baby. I promise, after this, no more. They won't touch you anymore," he said.

He began unzipping his jeans while massaging Nichols' tender thighs. He found pleasure in seeing the distress in the young girl's face. He then whipped out his dick, which was a magnificent size—long, heavy, and with the width of a steel pipe—then he gripped a handful of Nichols' long hair and forced her face into his lap.

"Go ahead. Get yourself a taste."

Nichols tried to resist, but she was no match for Supreme. She was weak and lethargic and only wanted to go home. Slowly, she complied.

As she felt Supreme's immense penis stretch the muscles in her jaw, Nichols began to sob again.

Supreme gripped the back of her head and made her gag, forcing the tip of his dick down the back of her throat. He could feel her body shiver from fear.

"That's right. Suck on daddy's dick, baby," Supreme uttered with delight as he grunted.

Nichols tried to please him for what seemed like forever. When he felt his eruption coming, he gripped Nichols' hair tightly, held her face steady in place, and allowed his nut to brew as her lips were wrapped around the mushroom tip.

"I'm coming!"

He forced Nichols to deep-throat him again, gripping her neck securely, while his goons stood around idly. Each of them had already had their way with Nichols and was craving for one more turn with the sixteen-year-old. Once Supreme was done, they would be on her next like vultures on a rotten corpse.

Nichols burst into tears, gagging and vomiting up phlegm. Her jaw ached along with her whole body.

She felt the burning around her neck, her eyes red with anguish, and her insides on fire from the pain. Her mind thought about death. Two days felt like two years, and the fatigue and abuse engulfed her like she was drowning.

As Supreme stood, the man he sent out for food returned, carrying a greasy plastic bag. He looked around the room and knew something had gone on without him.

"Damn! What I miss?" he questioned.

Supreme looked down at Nichols' naked body. A smile loomed as he pictured Apple and Kola in her place. "Bitches wanna fuck wit' me. They gonna regret that they ever tried to play me."

"Supreme, you still want this for her?" his man asked, holding up the bag of food.

Supreme snatched the bag from his hand and glared down at Nichols. He then removed the Styrofoam container from the bag and opened it up. It was filled with greasy rice and chicken. The aroma of the meal hit him quickly and made his mouth water.

"You hungry, baby?" he asked Nichols.

She didn't respond.

"I know I promised you a meal. Well, here it is." Supreme laughed and began dumping the hot food out, and it poured down on her like a shower.

Guy Tony just looked on without saying one word. It was a fucked-up thing to see. Still, Supreme was his friend and mentor, so he minded his business and walked out the room, not being able to stomach any more.

"Eat up," Supreme said with a smirk. "Cunt bitch!"

Nichols sobbed loudly. "Please . . . let me go! I wanna go home. I just wanna go home," she cried out.

"Oh, you wanna go home, huh?" Supreme said. "Well, your sister gotta pay off her debt to me, bitch. You just interest, that's fuckin' all."

Nichols lay motionless with the food scattered all around her. She closed her eyes and readied herself for the worst. She knew her chances of leaving there alive were very slim. She had seen all of their faces, and if they were brought to some kind of justice for their brutal crimes— rape, abuse, and kidnapping all being felonies—there was a good chance they would receive a life sentence from her testimony alone. If she knew the punishment for the crimes, they definitely knew as well. Being a smart girl, Nichols knew in her heart it was a chance they wouldn't take.

Supreme crouched down near the whimpering Nichols, pulled back her matted hair from her face, and looked at her with his cold eyes. "Apple owes me, but now it goes deeper than a fuckin' debt. You see, your sisters, they fuckin' disrespectful bitches, and they need to be taught a fuckin' lesson. But, to let you know, there was never any ransom. Nah, word gets out and it might start a war that I ain't ready to get into. But I gotta be subtle wit' my payback. They took money from me and don't wanna pay it back, so now I'm gonna take somethin' personal from them. Unfortunately, it gotta be you, love." He nodded to his triggerman.

Nichols went into a hysterical panic. She cried out

wildly, scampering across the ground and shouting, "Please! Don't do this! I don't wanna die! I don't wanna die! No! No!"

Supreme's triggerman approached Nichols with a .45 ready in his grip. He walked up to her as she tried to crawl to safety. He hunched over her, pressed the gun to the back of her head, and quickly fired two shots into her skull. *Bang! Bang!*

Nichols lay sprawled out in death, crimson blood thickening around her skull. The room fell silent as each member in the room stared down at the dead sixteen-year-old girl. The triggerman looked at Supreme and nodded.

Guy Tony heard the two shots from outside the doorway where he stood. He closed his eyes and shook his head. He lit up a cigarette. There was no turning back now. He remembered the look in Apple's eyes when she'd confronted him on the street the other day. It was a look he couldn't forget. She was desperate, looking for any hope in his eyes, but he'd refused to show her any. He wondered how things had gotten out of hand so fast.

Supreme stepped out of the room and looked at Guy Tony. He lit up a cigarette and said to him, "Yo, go help them wit' that mess."

Reluctantly, Guy did as he was told. When he looked at the body, all he could do was shake his head. He knew killing Nichols would create a problem. Without a doubt, Kola wouldn't let her death go unpunished.

Chapter 14

It was early morning on another hot summer day. Apple had fallen asleep for a few short hours on the living room couch still wearing the same clothes from the night before. A good night's sleep was becoming a distant memory for her. She couldn't think clearly, and sometimes she couldn't sleep at all. If she wasn't up all night worrying about her little sister, she was wandering out into the streets, hoping to find some information.

Now day three of Nichols' disappearance, it seemed the police weren't making the missing person case their priority. And Kola hadn't made any progress at all. So the family's hope of finding Nichols alive was fading, leaving everyone distraught.

Apple woke to police sirens blaring outside the window. She got up from the couch and looked around. The apartment was quiet and empty. After walking from room to room, she saw her mother passed out naked on her bed with an empty bottle of vodka on the nightstand. Drinking herself to death was Denise's way of coping.

Apple sighed and closed the bedroom door. She went into the kitchen. It was messy as usual, with dishes piled up and roaches scampering around. She wiped the few tears from her eyes, thinking about how Nichols was the one always cleaning up and cooking. She realized that her family took Nichols for granted, and now with her gone, it was hurting Apple deeply.

When Apple heard more police sirens outside, she knew something had happened. She peered out the window and could see the strong police activity by the dumpster, located a few feet from where Cross and his crew hung out. She noticed they were sealing off the area with yellow tape. Her first thought was homicide— something common in her hood.

Apple watched the police in action. When they shut down the block, she knew it was something serious. She observed two detectives walking to the scene, and a small crowd began gathering behind the yellow tape and whispering among themselves.

Suddenly, Apple felt a sickness in the pit of her stomach, unexpectedly roused by a troubling thought. It was obvious they had found a body. She thought the worst, yet prayed that it wasn't Nichols. Rushing from the window, she ran into her room to slip into something decent.

The crime scene on 132nd Street, across the street from the projects, was disturbing for most of the officers. They'd found the naked, battered body of a young teenage girl stuffed in a trash dumpster in a small lot with two gunshot wounds to her head. The detectives knew straightaway that she was raped. Beaten almost beyond recognition, her face was contorted, and her fingers and ribs were broken.

Uniformed officers and CSI flooded the area, causing bystanders to become curious as to who had been murdered. Word had gotten out that it was a young girl in her teens, but they didn't know her name or exact age yet. However, some of the neighbors speculated but weren't saying anything until the victim's identity was confirmed.

The morning was overcome with death and the anguish on the detectives' faces as they held their breaths, knowing it wouldn't be easy relaying the news to the victim's family. The area was dusted for fingerprints, and then the body was processed, which included taking photos, before being carefully removed from the dumpster a few hours after it was found by a group of young kids while playing.

A few bystanders cried out when word started getting around that it was Nichols' body in the dumpster.

"Oh my God! Are you kidding me?" a young woman in her housecoat and slippers exclaimed when the news reached her. Her eyes welled up with tears. She had known little Nichols since she was in diapers.

Others were heartbroken about the news, stating she was a sweet, young girl, unlike her sisters, especially Kola. They all knew the family would be devastated, that there would be trouble in the hood when Kola found out about her sister's murder. The crowd of onlookers suddenly noticed Apple rushing from her building.

Clad in a pair of white-and-blue pajama pants, flip-flops, and a T-shirt, with her hair wrapped tightly underneath a multi-colored scarf, Apple ran to the location with a sense of urgency, her eyes on the crime scene, where she noticed a body covered by a white sheet and surrounded by detectives and crime scene investigators.

The closer she got, the faster her heart beat, and the more she felt her chest tightening up. She had a gut feeling that something was wrong. Her eyes watered, but she wasn't into full-blown tears yet. Not knowing the identity of the victim was eating her up inside. She needed to know who they'd found in the dumpster.

Apple was ready to rip through the crime scene tape and rush past the lone officer assigned to guard the scene, but he held her back.

"Miss, you can't pass."

She struggled with the officer, shouting, "Get off me! Get the fuck off me! Yo, who they find? Who is that? Is that my sister? Is that fuckin' her?"

Apple struggled with the officer, who realized that, from her strong outburst, she had to be close to the victim. Still, he had a responsibility to the victim and the crime scene. He strengthened his hold on Apple. Other officers came to aid him, but they stood around and watched Apple cry out hysterically, all sympathetic to her.

"Is it her? Just fuckin' tell me! Is it Nichols? Is it my little sister?" she ranted.

Two well-dressed detectives walked up to Apple and allowed her to pass through to where they stood near the covered body. From the missing person's report and picture given to them, they knew it was Nichols.

One quickly consoled Apple. "I'm sorry. It's her."

Apple let out a piercing scream that echoed throughout the projects and made the hair on everyone's skin rise. She collapsed into the detective's arms, hysterical with grief, and then dropped to her knees while still in his hold.

The detective held her for a short moment and then nodded to a uniformed officer for his help. "Take care of her," he said to the cop.

The cop nodded and took Apple into his grasp, relieving Detective Johnson of the grieving young woman. The onlookers stood close by and watched everything unfold. A few were teary-eyed, while others were outraged by the murder, but most were just lost and couldn't understand it. What kind of monster could do such a thing?

It was a long while before Apple stopped crying. Then the detectives decided to tell her mother the disturbing news that her youngest daughter was dead.

When the detectives came to her apartment door, Denise was awakened from her sleep by the loud knocking. She woke up with an empty vodka bottle lying next to her and a troubling attitude. She answered the door scantily clad in a long, soiled house robe that was untied and open, exposing her nakedness to the two men. Her bushy pussy hairs and perky tits were in full view, stunning the two detectives.

"Ma'am, do you mind putting some clothes on?" Detective Rice said politely.

"What the fuck ya'll want?"

"Can we come in?" Detective Johnson asked.

Denise stepped back from the doorway and allowed the two men inside. They walked into the cluttered room, where they stood in the center with a casual attitude. They knew the news of her daughter's death would be hard on her.

Denise walked into the room, tying her robe to satisfy the detectives, and waited to hear what they had to say.

Detective Rice looked her square in her eyes. There was never any easy way to relay the news to someone that a loved one was brutally murdered. "I'm sorry to say, but we found your daughter this morning. She was murdered. I know it's hard, but we will find the people that did this," he told her.

Denise just stood in the center of the room and didn't react to the news right away. Surprisingly, she chuckled, and the two detectives looked at her with confusion. But then, right after, the tears followed, and next came the violent outburst. Denise screamed out with such intensity, she almost startled the detectives. She then quickly trashed a few things in the living room and fell out into the tattered couch headfirst, where she coiled up—the news of her daughter's murder finally sinking in.

Detective Johnson went over to her and tried to calm her down a bit. He then gave her his card and told her to call his number if she needed him.

There wasn't anything more the two men could do. They let the mother grieve on her own and nonchalantly walked out of the apartment. When the door shut, they could still hear Denise sobbing loudly.

The news of Nichols' murder hit Kola like a ton of bricks. She raced home to where the chaos was happening and couldn't believe it was true.

From the passenger seat of a Chevy Tahoe, she told the driver, "Hurry the fuck up!"

The Tahoe raced north up the FDR Drive, swerving in and out of traffic like it was the police.

Kola had tried to fight back the tears when a close friend made the phone call about Nichols earlier that morning. She didn't want to believe it, but more calls came, and all of them were telling her the same thing: "Yo, someone murdered Nichols."

Kola wanted to get her crew together and turn Harlem out. She was ready to shoot her gun off and kill everyone responsible for her sister's death. The first person she called was Mike-Mike. She hit his phone and stated that she needed him, and Mike-Mike told her that he was on his way.

Kola felt a tightening in her chest, and her eyes were red and teary behind the dark shades she wore. She couldn't believe Nichols was dead. She couldn't believe someone had the audacity to disrespect her like that. She wanted to wake up from the nightmare, but she knew it was all too real. She stared out the passenger window, watching the cars pass by in a blur. She tried to hide her pain from the driver, Danny, who happened to be Mike-Mike's cousin. They had just come from Brooklyn, where she had stayed the night with a stripper.

Kola couldn't help but think that she should have done more once Apple told her that she'd borrowed money from Supreme. She and Mike-Mike tore Harlem upside down for two days looking for Supreme, but no one had seen him. He was ghost. *What else could I have done?* Kola temporarily shrugged off her feelings of guilt. If anyone was to blame, it was Apple.

It was late morning when Kola woke up with the young blonde-haired stripper in her arms. Both of them were naked and entwined under wrinkled white sheets, the four walls in the room being the only witness to their sin. Kola was still doing her business, in and out of different strip clubs every night, and linking up with the freakiest, sexiest chicks to get her parties popping before summer's end.

Kola had the gift of gab, and within a few short weeks, she had a nice-size stable of the baddest chicks to join her business. She talked about money, prosperity, and good dick to the young girls, who were willing to try whatever to come up.

She had met Jessica, aka the Bunny Rabbit, in a downtown Brooklyn strip club, and after convincing her to spend the night with her, the two left in a gypsy cab early in the morning, just before dawn.

The driver dropped the two young girls off at a brownstone in Fort Greene, where Bunny Rabbit rented a single bedroom weekly on the third floor.

The two didn't waste time once the bedroom door was shut. Kola moved her hands up Bunny Rabbit's skirt and removed her panties. She loved Bunny Rabbit's curves and the way her balloon-size tits jiggled up and down when she moved.

The girls changed positions as often as a racecar driver switches gears in a race. Their tryst continued until dawn broke through the windows of the bedroom.

Later, in the early afternoon, Kola was awakened by the ringing of her cell phone, but she ignored it.

Bunny Rabbit slowly turned to face Kola with a nice smile. "Good morning," Bunny Rabbit greeted.

"Let's make it a great morning." Kola cupped Bunny's breast and continued to kiss on her neck.

They were about to start another round of pleasing, when Kola's phone went off again. Annoyed, Kola looked at the caller ID and noticed it was Danny calling. Thinking it was probably about some business she needed to deal with, she decided to take the call. When she answered, Danny instantly hit her with the grim news about Nichols. She stood up and reacted with a quick tantrum, which startled Bunny Rabbit.

"Baby, is everything OK?" Bunny Rabbit asked with a nervous stare.

Kola ignored the innocent question. In full tears after she hung up, she quickly got dressed. Danny had mentioned that he would pick her up, and fifteen minutes after the phone call, he was outside the brownstone. Kola got into the Tahoe and wanted to hurry back into Harlem.

~~~

Kola arrived in Harlem an hour after her sister's body was placed into a body bag and taken to the city morgue, getting there just in time to see the end result of the police investigation. A small crowd was still gathered around the crime scene, and the whispers and speculation continued among the locals. Police tried to gather as much evidence and statements from those around, but many didn't know anything, and those who did, refused to cooperate.

Kola rushed from the truck and ran to the roped-off crime scene. Stunned with grief, she was unable to fight back the tears that trickled underneath her dark shades. The big bad wild side of her was quickly replaced with a crying teenager who didn't understand why her sister was dead. She stood in the middle of the street looking like a lost little girl, her eyes stuck on where they had found the body in the trash.

Kola had a fierce reputation in the hood, ran with a dangerous drug crew, but still someone had the balls to murder Nichols. She felt helpless that she wasn't able to protect her little sister from being tossed in the trash like garbage.

Danny stood next to the inconsolable Kola. He put his arm around her and vowed, "Yo, we gonna find out who did this. You know that, right? We gonna kill whoever was behind this."

Kola didn't answer him. She just continued to stare where her sister had fallen. One particular name wouldn't leave her mind—Supreme.

"Supreme did this! That muthafucka gotta die!"

Danny wanted to ask particulars, but thought against it for now. He didn't need to know the why's and how's. Not right now. Not while she was grieving. Instead, he replied, "I got your back, Kola."

She looked around for one of his associates but didn't see anyone. She went up to the local residents still lingering around the crime scene, and with weight in her tone, she asked, "Yo, any of y'all seen my sister Apple?"

The few men and women shook their head and replied with a no. But a thirteen-year-old girl said to Kola, "They took her down to the precinct."

Kola didn't even thank the young girl for the information. She just stormed away and headed to the apartment to see her mother. Danny followed behind her, trying to keep up.

Kola rushed up the stairway, stormed through the front door, and shouted out for her mother. But she didn't get an answer.

Danny entered seconds later and observed Kola moving down the hallway hastily.

She pushed open her mother's bedroom door and found her curled up in the corner between the unmade bed and weathered dresser, butt naked and holding a bottle of Johnny Walker in her hand.

Kola snatched the bottle out of her mother's grip and

smashed it against the wall, staining the walls with its contents. "What the fuck is you doin'?" she yelled. "Your daughter's dead, and you up here gettin' fuckin' drunk!"

Denise looked up at her daughter with cold eyes and replied, "Get the fuck out my room, Kola!"

"Fuck, no! Look at you! You're fuckin' pathetic, Ma. Nichols is dead, and you wanna sit here and drink yourself to death. You want me to feel sorry for you? Well, I fuckin' don't. You a dumb bitch."

Danny entered the bedroom to find Kola standing over her naked mother and raining down a barrage of insults at the woman. He stood near the doorway and minded his business. It was a family affair that he didn't want to get involved with. He figured Kola was grieving over the death, and he believed her way with dealing with the pain was through anger and violence.

Denise slowly stood to her feet, her face twisted in anguish, and her speech back to her daughter was slurred.

Kola glared at her mother with contempt and was ready to knock her back down where she stood.

But it was Apple who Kola had the actual problem with. Her mother was just the scapegoat, until she confronted her sister. Kola felt it was Apple's fault that their sister was dead. Apple was the one who got into debt with Supreme and didn't pay back what she owed. She hated her sister and had the urge to brutally beat her down once they were face to face.

Kola was so enraged, she didn't notice her right hand was bleeding. She had cut it when she'd snatched away the bottle and tossed it into the wall. The small cut on the inside of her palm turned her hand red, but she didn't fuss about it. She exited the bedroom and went into the bathroom.

"Kola, you a'ight?" Danny asked.

"I'm fuckin' fine," she responded heatedly. She turned on the faucet and ran cold water over her cut.

With the shades off and the water running, she looked at herself in the mirror. Her eyes quickly became flooded with tears, and her breathing shallow. Her hands quivered as she gripped the sink. It felt like she was having a panic attack.

The death of her little sister once again overcame her, and she broke down with grief and remorse. The thought of her failing to protect Nichols was too much for her to handle. She surrendered to the weakness grief was bringing her body.

She suddenly fell to her knees and continued to sob, her wail echoing in the hallway.

No one bothered to disturb her from sobbing. Danny felt she needed to get it out of her system. With a straight-faced look, he lightly gripped the butt of the 9mm tucked in his jeans as he stood outside the bathroom door.

Chapter 15

Apple stepped off the city bus on Lenox Avenue and slowly made her way back home. It had been twenty-four hours since they'd found her sister's body. After leaving the precinct, she couldn't go straight home. She couldn't bear walking into that apartment so soon, knowing she wouldn't see Nichols alive in it anymore. She needed to escape somewhere far.

After she'd walked out the precinct early that evening, she got on the A train and rode it aimlessly until it reached the last stop, Mott Avenue in Far Rockaway, Queens. She then made her way to Rockaway Beach, where she sat in the sand and stared at the ocean for hours. She watched the sky gradually alter as the sun fell below the horizon and made way for the evening stars and the full moon that shimmered off the ocean. She sat close to the sea and listened to the waves crashing against the shore and let her tears fall. Though she was far from home, the pain was still close. She couldn't believe Nichols was dead.

Apple curled against the sand as the night went on.

She tried to find comfort with her body against the earth, hearing the ocean in the background, and fell asleep on the beach.

She woke several hours later to an orange sky and the soothing sound of the water. She lifted herself to her feet, dusted the sand from her clothes, and straightened her wrinkled clothing. Though it was a new day, she was still haunted by the previous day's pain. She walked off the beach in a trance-like state and trekked back to the train station for her long ride back into Harlem. There she called the only Brooklyn friend she had, only she didn't pick up.

"Yo, Cartier, I wanted to come through. This Apple. Nichols is dead. Gone. I fucked up…call me when you get this. One."

Apple walked through the front door of her apartment, and before she could step farther inside, Kola came lunging at her from the hallway, screaming out, "You stupid fuckin' bitch!" and tackled her to the floor.

The sisters fought pound for pound, until Danny pulled them apart. "Yo, fuckin' chill!" he exclaimed.

"No! Fuck that bitch!" Kola shouted. "She got Nichols killed!"

Danny held Kola back, allowing Apple to collect herself as she got off the floor. Apple didn't charge or fight back. Kola's words had cut into her deeper than the sharpest samurai sword. She looked at her sister and then just walked right back out of the apartment, not bothering to dry her tears as she rushed down the stairway and out the lobby. She darted into the street and turned the corner, headed to the nearest train station. She wanted the nightmarish day to fast-forward.

The anger that resided in Apple needed to be released, and the only one she wanted to confront was Supreme. She was determined to hunt him down and take out her revenge. She walked every block in her Harlem neighborhood, searching for either him or Guy Tony, but they were nowhere to be found. It seemed like Supreme and everyone associated with him had just up and disappeared. It was odd. Apple figured Supreme knew the heat was on and probably left town for a few.

She ended up wandering around Harlem most of the day and late into the evening, not knowing what to do with herself, because she didn't feel comfortable going home and fighting with Kola.

The night continued without any success, and Apple was exhausted from walking block after block. So she decided to take her chances going home. If Kola was still around, then she would knuckle up and fight her, if needed.

Apple walked into the lobby and pressed the button for the elevator. She waited around in silence, until she saw Lil' Meek walk into the lobby clad in a tattered black jacket and old jeans that were clearly too big for him. She ignored the crackhead, knowing he was probably begging on the streets to get his next high.

Apple wished the elevator would hurry up. She didn't

have the patience for Lil' Meek's begging. As she felt him come closer, she prepared herself to curse him out and push him away. Lil' Meek staggered toward Apple with a week's smell on him.

Lil' Meek, aka Dominquez, was in his late twenties and known throughout the hood as the one who knew everybody's business. He'd attended NYU for a few semesters, but after his fourth semester, he started a relationship with a bad girlfriend. He soon started partying all night then going to class late. Slowly but surely, he stopped showing up for his classes' altogether. He was arrested a few times for public drunkenness, and then came the drugs—weed laced with cocaine in the beginning—compliments of his girlfriend.

A year later, Lil' Meek, with his slim five-six frame and ashy, pale, bronze skin, was hooked on crack cocaine, his life withered away to nothing. He'd become a has-been who'd thrown away his future chasing pussy and a high.

Despite Lil' Meek's shabby appearance, he still was smart and sometimes easy to talk to. But with his foul odor, he was known to clear out rooms and make people retch. Apple, wanting to avoid his stench, was ready to rush for the stairway.

"Hey, Apple, can I borrow a dollar?"

Apple was almost into the stairway when she heard him shout out, "I heard you lookin' for Supreme! I know where he's at."

She stopped and turned to face Meek. "What you talking about?" she asked with a quizzical look.

Meek approached her, and Apple cringed from his smell. Yet, she was ready to endure it for the information he was about to give her.

"I heard what happened to your sister, Apple. I'm sorry to hear that, but you got a dollar? I just need to hold somethin' real fast. I need a trip, but I got you, Apple." Lil' Meek fidgeted with himself, glancing around the lobby nervously as he waited for Apple to loan him what he needed.

Apple sucked her teeth as she reached into her pocket and passed him a wrinkled dollar bill. She then stepped back from him, her stomach churning just by the sight and smell of him. She had known Lil' Meek since she was a child in her early days of grade school, and actually used to think of him as being cute. It somewhat troubled her to see the drastic change in him.

"A'ight, tell me what you know," Apple demanded.

Lil' Meek smiled. "Yeah, like I was saying, Supreme still in Harlem, but I be everywhere in this town and watch everything. He chillin' up on the West Side, Apple, keeping low and shit over by Riverside Drive."

"How do I know this shit is accurate?"

"'Cause, Apple . . . I cop from his cousin out there all the time. I travel blocks to get some of the best shit his cousin be selling out the apartment. I copped yesterday and seen Supreme chillin' in his cut. He don't know me, but I know him."

Meek gave more information, and Apple took mental notes. Lil' Meek nodded and walked out the back exit.

Apple went into her apartment, which was quiet. Kola was gone, and her mother was in her room. She went straight into her bedroom and refused to turn on the lights. She undressed in the dark and slid under the covers. She peered at the bed her sister used to lie in and closed her eyes. It was hard to look at the empty bed without thoughts of Nichols rushing to her mind. She remembered her sister looking to her for advice many times, and the many late-night talks they'd had.

Apple sighed heavily, turned over, and tried to block out the memories, which were bringing tears to her eyes. She cried most of the night and couldn't wait to confront Supreme the next day. She wanted to see him suffer greatly.

The next morning, Apple took the bus to the location Lil' Meek had given her. She looked stunning in her short denim skirt and high heels. She wore a tight camisole top, and her beautiful black hair was styled into one long ponytail. She walked down 149th Street and got a lot of unwanted attention from male passersby and drivers blowing their horns. They must've been admiring her gleaming, long, defined legs, and beauty that could take your breath away. But Apple, focused only on finding Supreme and confronting him, ignored the catcalls.

She approached a slate gray, seven-story brick building right off 149th Street and Riverside Drive. The quiet location offered the residents a fantastic view of New Jersey across the Hudson. She wondered how Lil' Meek even entered the building without drawing attention to himself. It wasn't the projects, where crackheads were always about. She thought he had to be lying. Though he'd said that Supreme's cousin was running drugs out of his apartment, the surrounding streets were clean, the place had security cameras, and it looked like doctors and lawyers lived there.

Still, she was willing to take the chance to investigate. She'd concealed a small blade in the lining of her panties, wanting to walk up close to Supreme and cut his throat open when she got the chance.

She walked into the building's atrium and glanced around. It was a magnificent structure, with its aging but elegant concrete construction, gray marble flooring, and glass wall that lined the lobby. Apple rarely came to the West Side, where classy stone buildings and tree-lined streets were the norm.

Since there wasn't a doorman or security on hand at the moment, Apple just proceeded toward the elevators. Lil' Meek had told her that Supreme could be found on the fourth floor, Apartment 4B. She entered the elevator, pressed 4, and waited in the silence, her heart beating like African drums.

The elevator soon reached the fourth floor, and she moved down the pristine hallway searching for the apartment, adjusting the blade in the lining of her panties when she found Apartment 4B. She hesitated to knock. Not having a plan, she just looked at the door.

Supreme was a strong and powerful man, outweighing Apple by a hundred-plus pounds and towering over her by almost a foot. She knew he could easily snap her neck and toss her body to the side, but she was so fueled with rage, she felt like she had the power of Superman.

Apple continued to look at the door of Apartment 4B right in front of her. She began to wonder why she was hesitating. Had it been Kola in her place, it would have been on and popping. With a few thugs backing her, Kola would have kicked down the door with her crew and shot up everyone in the place.

Wiping the few tears that trickled down her cheeks, she felt like her heart was trying to rip through her chest. She felt her adrenaline kicking in and wanted to take full advantage of the situation. She clenched her fist and bit down on her bottom lip, knowing that those responsible for killing Nichols were almost certainly behind the door. It would be easier to just call up Kola and have her handle things, but she wasn't speaking to her sister at all, especially after Kola had attacked her and put the full blame on her. She thought it was best to keep her twin sister out the mix for now and keep her distance, since things were getting really ugly between the two of them.

Apple began psyching herself up by thinking about Nichols, knowing her body was rotting away in some morgue while Supreme was chilling and still breathing.

"Fuck this shit!" she said to herself. She banged on the door like she was police and then stood there firmly with a livid stare, ready for anything.

Becoming impatient, she banged on the door again. It took a while for someone to answer, but eventually, she heard the locks turning, and the door slowly opened. A tall, slender man answered with an unpleasant look, wearing a wife-beater, his upper body swathed with tattoos, and braids twisted down to his back.

He looked at Apple, his face warped from irritation. "Yo, who the fuck is you? And why you bangin' on my fuckin' door like you police?"

"Supreme here?" she asked sternly, ready to push him out her way and look for herself.

"What, bitch? Who the fuck is you?" he barked.

"I'm lookin' for Supreme," she repeated unwaveringly.

The man looked her up and down. "Yo, you one of his side chicks?"

Apple was tired of his questions and rushed forward, ready to fight him.

"Yo, you better step the fuck back!" he said, blocking the entrance to the apartment. "You don't fuckin' know me!"

But Apple didn't scare easily, especially not now with fire and rage running through her blood. "I'm not leaving until I see that muthafucka!" she exclaimed.

The stranger sighed heavily. The last thing he needed was his nosy neighbors calling the cops because of a dispute in front of his doorway. He frowned at Apple then turned into the apartment and shouted, "Yo, 'Preme, you got some crazy broad out here lookin' for ya ass! Come check her before I do!"

Apple heard Supreme shout back, "Who that, Don?"

"I don't know, nigga, but she finer than a muthafucka."

Don looked at Apple with a corrupt smile. "Whoever she is, she looks like she wants to scratch your eyes out."

Apple wasn't intimidated. She held her ground and waited for Supreme to appear.

Don stepped back from the doorway, and Supreme walked up. When he saw Apple standing in the hallway, a smile crept up on his face.

"Oh shit! Look who we got here. How the fuck did you find me?" Supreme asked, with some weight in his tone.

"I got resources," she spat.

Supreme chuckled. "What you want? You ready to pay back what you owe wit' fuckin' interest?"

"Muthafucka, are you fuckin' serious?"

Supreme casually replied, "Yeah, I'm fuckin' serious."

"Fuck you, muthafucka!" Apple shouted. "I ain't payin' you shit! How dare you!"

"Yo, yo, y'all gotta take this shit from in front of my door. I got fuckin' neighbors that be all in my business."

"Yo, Apple, step inside. Let's talk."

Apple hesitated for a moment. She tried to hold back her tears, but with Supreme standing there with a smirk on his face and still asking about her debt, she was ready to reach for her concealed blade and cut him open.

Don said to her, "Yo, shawty, you in or out? You can't be causing this drama in the hallway. This ain't that kind of building."

Apple went into the apartment, and Don closed the door. She was quickly overwhelmed by the décor of the place, with its marble flooring and modern furniture that had to be worth about fifty thousand. She was surprised to see the assortment of artwork that lined the eggshell-colored walls, which included a few framed photographs of Al Pacino lifted from various scenes in *Scarface* and two photos of the Gambino mob boss, John Gotti. There was a 60-inch plasma screen mounted on the wall and a high-end sound system with speakers scattered throughout the room, and a collection of movies and CDs all over.

Apple was taken aback by the place. For a moment, her mind was somewhere else. This was the way she'd always dreamed of living. It was like she'd stepped into a different world. The layout of the place was phenomenal— Italian décor in the living room, and marble floors and countertops in the foyer and kitchen area, which changed to parquet flooring in the living room. She didn't know niggas could live like this in Harlem.

Supreme stepped in front of her, snapping her back to reality. Then she remembered what she'd come for.

He looked at her with a cool stare and asked, "Like what you see?"

Apple ignored him and continued with her beefing. "I ain't payin' you shit back, you foul muthafucka! You had my sister murdered!"

"I don't know what you're talkin' about, Apple," Supreme shot back. "Look, I had a problem wit' you, not your sister. I heard about that, though. My condolences to you and your family. How are they holding up after such a tragedy? My hands are clean from that, but our business is still our business."

"What? Are you fuckin' kiddin' me?" Apple screamed.

She lunged for Supreme, but he quickly subdued her and tossed her into the couch like she was nothing. His cousin Don just stood on the sideline and watched, warning Supreme to be careful in the apartment.

"Relax, shawty. Ain't no need for that shit here," he told her coolly.

"Fuck you!"

Supreme let out a sinister chuckle. "Yeah, that would be nice, but unfortunately, you ain't on that level right now. But I tell you this—That shit wit' your sister, that's on you, love, not me. You probably could have prevented it, hypothetically . . . if I had some shit to do wit' it. But I don't rock like that."

"What?" she asked, confused by his statement.

Supreme smiled. "I'm just saying, you already lost one sister. Damn! It would be a shame if you was to lose another. Especially so soon."

"Are you threatening my twin?"

"Nah, I'm just saying, shit happens. You feel me, Apple? I know you and Kola ain't tight like that, but she's still kin. And ya moms . . . damn, she must be a fuckin' wreck right now, losing her youngest like that. But, look, shit happens, right? That's life. What can we do about it? We can't take time back, but we can make our future brighter by just doin' what's right. Ya feel me, Apple?"

Apple just looked at Supreme. In her heart, she knew

he was a devious muthafucka. "You hate me right now, huh?" Supreme asked with a smile.

"Go to fuckin' hell!" she shouted.

"Maybe. But, look, I can put the word out on the street, find out who's responsible for that shit. Get you the shooter. You want justice for Nichols, Apple? You want that nigga that pulled the trigger to pay? I can find him for you. You think you got resources; I got more."

Supreme stared at Apple for an answer. He then added, "I rather have you work wit' me than against me. You understand? You don't need any more bloodshed within your family. I'm just saying, it'll be a better situation for you and me."

Apple looked at Supreme, and realizing how dangerous he really was, she began to wonder what she had gotten herself into. His composed tone made him the devil she didn't need to know. She reluctantly surrendered her attitude and listened to what he had to say. She figured she couldn't get her revenge through the front door, so she decided to go around the back. She wanted to get close to him. To hurt him like he had hurt her family. Apple decided to be cunning like her mother and use the one thing that was golden to her—pussy.

"You do two things for me, and I'll make sure you turn out a'ight. You feel me, Apple? I'll make sure the nigga that hurt you will pay."

Supreme moved closer to Apple, seeing he had her somewhat relaxed and listening. He took a seat next to her and slowly placed his arm around her. He then softly said,

"First, tell me who told you I was here."

Don, standing behind Supreme, just smiled at the way he pimped his game on the young girl.

Apple was reluctant to tell Supreme, but the way he looked at her, she knew he wouldn't accept anything but the truth. She sighed deeply. "Lil' Meek."

"A'ight. And, second, you take care of me, and I'll take care of you. I promise you, nothin' will happen to you or your family. You understand? But you still owe me somethin'," he said coolly, a gleam in his eyes.

Apple couldn't believe she was about to do the unthinkable. Even though she was beefing with Kola and wasn't on good terms with her mother, she didn't want anything to happen to them, because they were still the only family she had left.

Supreme turned around and nodded to his cousin and then gestured for her to follow him into the bedroom. Apple slowly stood, her stomach in knots, her nerves frayed. She walked behind Supreme into the bedroom, and he slowly closed the door behind them.

Inside the lavish room, the king-size bed had a raised headboard displayed above polished hardwood floors, artwork hung on the walls, and the ceiling fan turned slowly.

Apple felt Supreme grab her from behind with such intensity, she flinched. She closed her eyes and felt his touch on her. *What the fuck am I doing?* She'd never thought she would be sleeping off her debt—and sleeping with the enemy.

Supreme slowly lifted her skirt and touched between her legs. He then ripped her panties off and noticed the small blade that fell to the floor. He looked down at it and knew what the sharp tool was meant for. He smiled, knowing that things had turned in a different direction.

With Apple's torn panties in his hand and her denim skirt raised to her hips, exposing her shaved vagina, Supreme pushed her forward, bent her over face down into the cushioned bed, and began unzipping his jeans. He pulled out his thick dick and readied it for entry.

Apple remained frozen in his hold, preparing herself to do the unimaginable. She felt his hand against her thigh, his fingers molesting her insides. She closed her eyes and waited for him to enter her.

Supreme gripped Apple by her hips and thrust his massive size into her, causing her to shriek briefly and gasp from the raw entry. Then he grabbed her by her neck, trying to keep her stable as he fucked her vigorously. He gripped her waist snugly, pounded his hard dick into her wet walls, and quickly took authority over her like NYPD on a Brooklyn back street.

Supreme fucked Apple so good, she couldn't resist the loud moan and quick burst of gasping, as he regulated every inch of her body, cupping her tits and stimulating her clit as he fucked her from the back.

As Supreme tore her pussy open like a Christmas gift, she clenched the bed sheets and closed her eyes, panting like a marathon runner. "Oh shit!" she cried out. "Ummm, oh shit!"

Supreme worked his strokes like he was in the porn business, and Apple's cries of pleasure echoed out into the other room, where Don could hear them. She squirmed and felt her nut brewing, as did Supreme, who was pulling her hair and smacking her ass.

Surprisingly, Apple loved it.

"Oh, yes, that pussy is tight, love. Shit, yes!" Supreme cried out, little beads of sweat glistening on his brow.

Supreme had always dreamed of having one of the twins in his bedroom, and Apple was the primary for him. He'd lusted after the young twin since she was thirteen. He didn't give a fuck about age.

Apple moaned as Supreme continued to fuck her doggy-style, her face and tits pressed into the wrinkled bed sheets, ass protruding, and her legs spread open into a downward V. Her eyes rolled to the back of her head as his wide, long, steel-pipe dick put her into a different frame of mind. He went in deep, hammering her G-spot with strength.

Apple's legs quivered uncontrollably, and she felt herself gasping. "Oh shit! I'm gonna come!" she cried out.

Supreme continued hammering into her pussy, while Apple's body constricted from busting her nut all over his dick. She was feeling it run down the inside of her legs. She was spent. It was so good, she felt the urge to climb up on the bed and take a nap.

But Supreme wasn't done yet. He held her by her slim, sweaty waist steadily and continued his onslaught, fucking her until he was about to erupt. Then he quickly pulled out and let it shoot across her back. His semen shot out of him like a Super Soaker, and his loud grunting and quaking during and after made it known that he'd enjoyed himself.

Supreme tossed Apple a towel to clean herself up. She then climbed onto the bed, and was so guilt-ridden by the deed she'd just committed, she curled herself into the fetal position and began crying, but he paid her no mind.

While putting back on his jeans, Supreme said to Apple, "Now that's how we work things out. But I keep my promises, love, so I'm gonna take care of you. You see this place? It's in my cousin's name, but it's all mine. You're welcome to stay if you want. I know things are hard, and you need to chill, escape that bullshit around the way. But I'ma go handle my business. You can chill, though."

Supreme walked out the bedroom shirtless and in his jeans, and met back up with his cousin in the kitchen.

Don winked at him, knowing he took care of business. He gave Supreme dap. "How was she?"

"It was somethin' worth the wait."

Don smiled.

"But, look, I need you to handle somethin' for me."

"Like what?"

"Put the word out on the streets about somethin'," Supreme replied.

"Important?"

"Yeah, it is."

Supreme told him what to put out on the streets, and Don replied, "I'm on it, cuz."

Supreme smiled and then returned to his business with Apple in the bedroom. He walked in to find her still lying naked in the fetal position.

By this time, Apple had dried her tears. She looked up at Supreme and asked, "Is this really your place?"

"For now, *mi casa, su casa*," he said with a welcoming smile.

When Apple smiled back, Supreme knew he had broken her. It was one of his greatest accomplishments—seeing one of the twins smiling in his bed.

Chapter 16

I t was late evening when a few squad cars went racing down Fifth Avenue, sirens blaring.

"Shots fired! Shots fired!" crackled over the police radio.

Two cop cars made a sharp right onto 132nd Street and came across the body of a male sprawled out across the hard concrete near the overpass on Park Avenue. The victim was suffering from three gunshot wounds that hit him center mass.

Three officers first arrived on the scene, and by the look of things, they knew the victim was critical. The homeless man, his eyes lifeless, was lying face up, and blood was spilling out from his back. It wasn't long before the man shot dead on the streets was identified by onlookers as Lil' Meek.

A small crowd gathered around, most showing little interest for the victim, but curious to see the police action in progress. They watched from a short distance as officers taped off the scene and detectives began investigating the murder. Lil' Meek wasn't known to have any enemies, and he didn't have much family around, except an elderly grandmother, who rarely left her apartment but kept in contact with her grandson.

The hood soon started buzzing about Lil' Meek's murder. A majority didn't care, and thought he was just another crackhead shot dead in the streets. The body was covered and transported to the morgue, while everyone else continued on with their evening activities, with little gossip about the murder after the police left the scene.

The sun had just set, and the balmy night was slowly developing over the projects. Kola sat in the passenger seat of the dark Tahoe listening to Danny inform her about news she needed to hear.

"Yo, Kola, from what I'm hearing on the streets, it was that nigga J-Dogg that bodied ya little sister," Danny said.

Kola was seething with anger and wanted to snap J-Dogg's neck. She knew he had just come home right before spring from doing an eighteen-month bid upstate. An independent thug with a violent attitude and a rap sheet longer than her arm, J-Dogg was always trouble. He was also known to be a gun-for-hire and would do anything for a few dollars.

Kola wanted him dead, but not before she got to torture him for more information. She wanted every breathing soul behind her sister's murder to suffer greatly. She wanted justice and knew she was the only one in the family capable of exacting it, since she thought Apple was just too weak and naïve at times, and her mother was just a stupid bitch.

✂∽∾⌇

Kola wasn't able to rest. She had met up with Mike-Mike at his crib a few hours earlier, needing his support. She wanted him to put as many guns as he could on the streets and do what they did best—Get information by brutal force and then murder everything that moved—but Mike-Mike was against it.

He had looked at Kola seriously and stated, "Nah, we can't do that right now, Kola. Shit is too hot out there."

"What the fuck you talkin''bout, Mike-Mike?"

"You heard me. We at war right now wit' this upcoming drug crew that's tryin' to step on our toes, make a name for themselves. Cross and me, we hot right now. Feds is on us, you hear me? We get involved wit' this shit wit' you, and we fuckin' ourselves."

With teary eyes, Kola returned with, "So, it's like that now, Mike-Mike? They body my little sister, and I'm supposed to let that shit ride like that?"

"Kola, you know it ain't nothin' personal. It's just too many bodies right now attracting fucked-up attention on our operation. It's just niggas is hot and need to chill from the body count. You know it ain't no disrespect wit' you. I got love for you, Kola, but you don't even know who did the shit yet. Niggas just talkin', that's all."

"Fuck you, Mike-Mike!" Kola barked.

Kola quickly stood from her chair, not believing what she'd heard. She never thought she would see the day when Mike-Mike and his peoples would turn away from her or act like some scared bitches. She'd been around them for years and witnessed the many murders and other violent acts they'd committed, and had proven time and time again that she was a ride-or-die bitch. She was the baddest chick around who always had their backs, and this was how they repaid her?

Mike-Mike remained seated in his cushioned La-Z-Boy recliner and looked up at Kola with cold eyes. He knew she was upset, but the streets were hot at the moment, and Cross had warned everyone to lay low and chill. He knew Kola was hurting over her sister's death deeply, and he wanted nothing more than to kill those behind it, but it was going to entail too great a risk, especially since the feds were investigating and watching them. Kola was emotional and not thinking rationally, seeing only revenge and not the aftermath.

Mike-Mike watched Kola storm out of his apartment ranting and cursing. After she slammed the door shut, he could still hear her mouth in the hallway. He lit up a Black & Mild and leaned back in his chair. Mike-Mike wanted to relax that morning and think about his chances on the streets. Donny B's murder a few days earlier had him a little spooked. Word on the streets was, he was an informant and working with the police.

Mike-Mike was the one who had snatched Donny B's life away violently. It was both personal and business, but now he had to lay low and allow things to smooth over.

But the abrupt kicking in of his front door an hour after Kola had left, and a dozen armed and suited tactical officers rushing in and screaming out, "Police! NYPD! NYPD!" made it clearly known that he had fucked up somewhere.

Mike-Mike rushed from his chair and tried to make his escape out the bedroom window, ready to leap from two floors up, but he was quickly subdued by a half-dozen officers, thrown forcefully to the floor, and pinned face down, where he was crushed against the floor by the boots and strong arms of several cops, and his arms forced behind his back.

He was read his rights and led out of the building shirtless, barefoot, and in his sagging jeans by the army of officers. It was a spectacle for everyone to see—the notorious drug dealer finally captured for Donny B's murder.

Kola was heartbroken when she received the news about Mike-Mike. It felt like her world was falling apart—her sister was dead, Apple was MIA, and now Mike-Mike, her longtime friend and lover, was incarcerated. Still, she was determined to get her revenge.

She plotted with Danny about going after J-Dogg and shooting him down like a dog. But then again, she wanted to kidnap him and put such a hurting on him, he would want to die. She tried to block out Mike-Mike's arrest from her mind. She knew he would do some time. Word was out on the streets that he was the one that killed Donny B, shooting him down in cold blood in front of his friends. Kola knew Mike-Mike was heartless like that, and his arrest was a great loss to her because, before the bullshit, he did anything she asked.

Kola gripped the .380 that Danny had given to her as the two rode around Harlem looking for J-Dogg with an obsession. They asked around for him relentlessly, but no one had seen their target. Danny pushed his truck up and down Fifth, Seventh, and Eighth Avenues from 110th Street to 145th Street, but there wasn't any sign of him. Kola was becoming frustrated but didn't want to give up the search. She ached in every part of her body to find him before the police or anyone else did.

However, as the evening progressed, and the search proved fruitless, the two grew tired. The frustration clearly showed on Kola's face. She didn't want to go home without someone paying for their sins against her family, but it seemed like J-Dogg had probably gotten wind that he was being hunted and skipped town. It was one in the morning when they finally called it quits and went their separate ways until the following day.

Kola walked into the apartment and went straight to her bedroom, closing her door. She removed the .380 from her Prada bag and placed it on the dresser. She looked at the gun for a moment, fantasizing about putting it to good use, spilling out the blood of her sister's killer and watching his life drain from him with pleasure. Every day since Nichols' murder, Kola found herself becoming angrier. She was becoming mad at herself and at the world, seething with disgust at the betrayal. She was ready to react, but it seemed like everyone was vanishing from her sights.

She hadn't seen Apple in a day or two, but she didn't care about her twin sister. In her eyes, Apple was the one responsible for Nichols' death also, and Kola wanted to make her sister pay for her stupidity too.

Kola slowly undressed and took a seat on her bed butt naked. She looked around her room and suddenly felt an uncontrollable rage. She started to destroy a few things in her bedroom, turning over her bed, shredding the bed sheets, and snatching the clothes out of her closet and tossing them wildly. She then smashed her mirror with the butt of the gun and kicked holes in the wall with the heel of her foot. Her frantic screams caused her mother to enter the bedroom to see what the commotion was about.

With a sharp glare, Kola turned toward her mother, gun still in her hand, and shouted, "Get the fuck outta my room!" She raised the .380 and pointed it at her mother's head.

Visibly startled, Denise stood there wide-eyed. She dared not challenge her daughter, because the look in Kola's eyes said that she was crazy. It was Denise's home, but at that moment, her daughter had the authority.

"Bitch, you done lost your fuckin' mind." Denise slowly turned toward the direction of her bedroom to get away from her daughter.

Kola stood there for a moment before finally lowering the gun. She then plopped down on the bed and felt the urge to just shoot off the .380. She wanted to empty the clip and release her aggravation on something close. She gripped the weapon tightly and looked down at it, and for that fraction of a second, thought about suicide. But she quickly rid her mind of such idiotic feelings and vowed to make things right.

Kola put the gun in the bottom of the drawer and then went to her bedroom window. She peered outside at the dark. Though it was quiet outside, her heart was raging and disturbed, and she couldn't sleep.

✵

J-Dogg sat behind the wheel of a dark blue Durango waiting for Supreme to return his phone call. Parked on the Bronx side of the 207th Street bridge near Fordham Road, close to the overpass on the Major Deegan Expressway that connected Washington Heights to the Bronx, he watched the light traffic pass by on the three-lane highway at two o'clock in the morning, his .45 within reach and a keen eye on his surroundings.

He had gotten word that Kola and a male stranger were looking for him and knew that someone probably had snitched on him about Nichols' murder. Now, the word was out on the streets that he was one of the men responsible for the murder. He was nervous and ready to leave town as soon as possible, knowing it wouldn't be long before the police started sniffing around for him. J-Dogg refused to go back to prison and would die before they put him back in a cell. This time, he knew he would be sentenced to life or put on death row for Nichols' murder.

J-Dogg sat impatiently in his ride, jumping at everything that moved in the dark. Earlier, he had hollered at Supreme, who'd promised him a ride out of town, a place to stay, and the much-needed cash that was owed to him. Things were too hot to stick around Harlem, and he knew someone could come gunning for him at anytime. J-Dogg felt if Supreme crossed him by not helping or paying the money he had asked for, he wasn't going to rest until Supreme got a bullet in his head, but Supreme had given J-Dogg his word.

J-Dogg trusted Supreme because he had worked for him before. Supreme had sounded really assuring over the phone that he would come through with the support. J-Dogg knew Supreme couldn't risk his capture, because he knew too much about everything on this high-profile rape and murder case, Nichols' death having been aired on every news station in the city.

J-Dogg's cell phone rang, and he picked up. "Yeah."

"You at the location?" Supreme asked.

J-Dogg was relieved to hear Supreme's voice. "Yeah, I been here for at least fifteen minutes. Where you at?"

"I'll be there in ten. Just hang tight. I got you."

"Just hurry the fuck up, Supreme. I ain't got all night."

The call ended, and J-Dogg continued to wait. Ten minutes later, he noticed headlights heading in his direction. He rose up and grabbed his gun, cocking it back and readying himself for anything. He kept an intense eye on the car approaching him in the short distance and took a deep breath.

The white Cadillac STS came to a stop in front of the Durango, and Guy Tony stepped out from the driver's side carrying a small bag, which J-Dogg assumed was the money and items he needed to leave town.

J-Dogg was upset that Supreme sent one of his henchmen instead of coming himself. "Yo, where the fuck is Supreme?" he shouted.

"He got caught up in somethin' and sent me," Guy Tony said.

"Nah, fuck that! He told me he would be here." J-Dogg had the gun near his side with the safety off. If Guy Tony was to flinch wrong, he was ready to put a few hot bullets in him. "But that's my money?"

Guy Tony kept his cool and acted casual while taking a few careful steps closer to J-Dogg. "I'm just the messenger," he exclaimed calmly.

His trigger finger itching, J-Dogg quickly looked around and stepped out of his car. He was hungry to snatch the bag from Guy Tony's hand and drive off, but hesitated to take any steps closer.

"Why the fuck he send you, Guy? Huh? Somethin's up?" J-Dogg continued to look around the area nervously.

"I told you before, he got caught up wit' somethin'. Now, I ain't got all day, J-Dogg. You want the bag or what?" Guy Tony shouted.

"Yeah. Just toss me my shit."

Guy Tony tossed the small brown duffel bag over to J-Dogg, and it landed at his feet. He then took a few steps back and said, "Open it and see if we good."

Uneasily, J-Dogg crouched down near the bag, slowly unzipped it, and saw thirty thousand dollars in small bills stuffed inside, along with what appeared to be his fake driver's license and a few other items. He nodded.

Before J-Dogg could look back up at Guy Tony, a shadowy figure crept up behind him with the swift motion of a cheetah. J-Dogg didn't get to turn and see what was happening. He just felt the cold steel of a Desert Eagle pressed to the back of his head, and it fired without any delay.

Boom! Boom! Boom!

J-Dogg's brain matter was scattered across the shaded street, and his body laid sprawled out face down on the concrete, three huge holes in his head.

Guy Tony ran up to the body and quickly snatched up the bag of cash and everything else, while the mystery killer disappeared into the shadows from where he came.

A few minutes later, Supreme's truck slowly rolled by the deadly scene with Apple seated in the passenger's side. He pointed out J-Dogg's body and said, "See, love? There's your justice. I promised you that."

Apple looked down at the body with an expressionless gaze. She took the entire scene in slowly and knew that Nichols' killer would rot in hell.

Feeling like her king and hero, Supreme smiled. He had orchestrated everything perfectly. He placed his hand on Apple's uncovered thigh, with her skirt riding up her legs, and massaged her lightly, eager to move it farther up her legs.

"You ain't gotta worry about the bullshit anymore. I'ma take care of you, Apple. I told you I would make it right, and as you see, I made the shit right."

Apple looked at Supreme with a slight smile and rested back in her seat, remaining quiet. Supreme drove off the block, heading toward I-95/New Jersey Turnpike with plans on taking her on a trip out of town. Maybe wine and dine her, take her shopping, and introduce her to the finer things in life. He was rooted in her head and planned on staying there for a long while.

Chapter 17

Nichols' funeral was a simple one, with a few friends, family, and residents from the community coming together and collecting donations to assist with the burial. After a short ceremony, she was about to be buried in a Bronx cemetery. It was a cloudy day with graying skies, and a gentle breeze pushed through the small crowd gathered around the casket.

Kola stood next to her teary-eyed mother, who was dressed in a black V-neck dress with black shoes and constantly wiping the tears from her eyes with a handkerchief. Kola wore a short black dress, revealing her substantial cleavage and long legs, while sporting a pair of six-inch Christian Louboutin stilettos. Feeling no desire to comfort her crying mother, she stood near her sister's casket, wearing a pair of dark Gucci shades to hide her crying eyes. She stood still, taking no one's hand, as the preacher led the group into a prayer.

Remaining aloof, Kola's eyes focused on the dark brown casket that she'd paid $1,500 for. The funeral was a little costly, but Kola wanted her little sister to go out in style. She clenched her fists, her eyes fixed on the three dozen white roses that decorated Nichols' casket.

The preacher and others in attendance recited the Lord's Prayer, but Kola played no part in it, refusing to say any verses. She was furious, not seeing Apple at the wake or the burial. In fact, it had been almost a week since she had seen her sister, and she almost went berserk thinking about how disrespectful Apple was. *How fuckin' dare she!* Kola thought.

People were asking her continuously, "How is Apple holding up? I haven't seen her around. Where is she?"

Kola tried to ignore the questions concerning her sister. She didn't want to hear about that bitch at all. Her beef with Apple was far from over. She felt Apple left her stranded with their mother, who was in shambles. Kola felt Apple should be bearing the burden that she'd caused their already dysfunctional family. But she was MIA.

After the burial, Kola didn't stick around to speak to anyone, not even her mother, who called out for her. She trotted off the grass-covered cemetery and headed straight to Danny, who was waiting for her in the truck parked some distance from the internment. Once inside the truck, Kola sat back in her seat and instructed Danny to drive off. Danny nodded and turned the Tahoe off the green meadow and exited the cemetery into the busy Bronx street.

Kola sighed. "Wait till I see this fuckin' bitch! It's fuckin' on! She don't fuckin' come to our sister's funeral?

She's a dumb fuckin' bitch! I swear, I'ma hurt that bitch when I see her. I'ma fuckin' hurt her, Danny. She's so fuckin' disrespectful."

Danny allowed Kola to rant as he steered the truck back to Harlem. Feeling the same way, he nodded in agreement with everything Kola said about her sister.

Within twenty minutes, they were back in Harlem. Danny parked in front of Lincoln Projects and waited for Kola to go inside to get a few things.

Kola had decided to leave her mother's apartment and shack up with Danny at his place in Washington Heights. The day before the funeral, she'd cleared everything out of her bedroom with Danny's help, tossed her things into a large trash bag, and threw it in the back of the Tahoe. Now, she was returning to pick up the few things she'd left behind. She only took clothes, money, shoes, and other accessories she needed, telling herself everything else could easily be replaced.

On her way to Danny's apartment, Kola told him to pull over for a moment, and he did without question. She stepped out of the truck and peered out at her Harlem hood from an uphill block that had a phenomenal view of her urban world. Kola looked down at the city and smiled, thinking about the illicit business she was putting together with her young stable of hoes. With Mike-Mike locked up, she was still going to continue on with it. It was her dream to get paid and one day run the city, and Nichols' murder gave her that extra push.

She then got back into the truck with a mission to

accomplish. She closed her eyes and was ready to go to her new home, which was a decent distance from where tragedy had struck her family.

That same night in Danny's studio apartment, he ate her out like it was his obligated duty. Now that Mike-Mike was locked up, Danny wanted to take his place. He wanted to be the one Kola relied on, for everything.

Kola wanted to get her mind off the past and her heartache, and sex was the only way she knew how. The duo was butt naked and all over each other, stirring up the white sheets with sex and sweat.

Kola tasted the tip of Danny's thick dick, licking all around it like it was a lollipop. She then ran her tongue up and down the base, causing him to squirm with delight from the sensation. She sucked him so good, Danny nearly busted a nut in her mouth, but he held back and allowed her to straddle him so she could feel him deep inside of her.

Kola dug her nails into Danny's chest as he plunged into her aggressively. Then he flipped her over and continued. He held Kola tightly, panting and twisting between her thighs. Soon, he came inside her, shuddering between her legs. Kola panted too with a spent look, while lying underneath Danny's sweaty body.

Kola needed that release, but it didn't fully cure her anger and bitterness over the loss she'd suffered. Still, she knew that in due time, she was going to be OK. She refused to let her world fall apart, and getting money was on her mind. Getting money would be her remedy.

When Apple opened her eyes in the late evening, Supreme was navigating his truck down the busy DC streets, with its hectic rush-hour traffic and network of grid-like streets named after the different states. She had slept for a long time but wasn't expecting to be in a different city when she woke up. The four-hour drive was her first real trip out of town, not including the short venture into New Jersey for Summer Jam.

She looked out the window in awe at the city's magnificent structures, from the soaring Treasury Building to the United States Capitol. She yearned to get a glimpse of the White House, thinking about the country finally having a black president in the Oval Office.

As the evening continued on, DC became illuminated in a mixture of colors that extended for miles. Like lights on a Christmas tree, it captivated Apple's eyes.

"You like?" Supreme asked.

"I never really been out of New York before," she informed him.

"It's fun. You'll like it here."

"We're staying here?"

"Nah, just taking some time away from New York to get us situated. I know you don't wanna be around that bullshit back home."

Apple didn't answer him. She just continued to look out the window, taking in the city's scenery one block at a time, her mind far removed from home and her family. With the smile she had on her face, it felt like Nichols' murder didn't even happen. She was too caught up in Supreme and his promises.

Supreme drove Apple sightseeing around the lively city, taking her from Foggy Bottom to the National Mall, where millions of men and women had stood in the subzero cold to witness President Obama's inauguration. Apple was wide-eyed when she saw the White House from a distance. She wondered if the president was actually home.

"Oh my God! I can't believe I'm actually this close to seeing the White House," she exclaimed with joy.

"Yeah, there it is. Shit, we can be the first couple and shit," Supreme joked.

Apple didn't know Supreme had a humorous side. He wasn't the monster loan-sharking pervert from her Harlem neighborhood; he was actually kind to her, smiling and treating her like she was his woman. Apple became more relaxed around him and didn't know how she'd ended up in a different state with him. Miles away from home now, it didn't strike her that she had missed her little sister's funeral. In her mind, Supreme had helped her escape the poverty and harshness of her old life, which she wanted to leave behind.

As Supreme merged onto the 395 expressway, Apple asked, "Where we goin'?"

"It's a surprise," he stated with a pleasant smile. He inserted a Jay-Z CD into his truck's system.

Apple was relaxed. The night was covering the city, and the traffic on 395 was slowly breaking away from the earlier traffic jam, making the lanes easier to drive through.

Forty minutes later, Apple found herself at the Gaylord National Resort and Convention Center located at National Harbor, a few miles south of DC. It was a phenomenal-looking place, where they were met by a suited valet at the front entrance of the largest non-gaming hotel and convention center on the East Coast.

Apple stepped out of the truck and looked around in astonishment. She had never been anywhere so classy in her life. She followed behind Supreme and entered the atrium, which offered a panoramic vista of the Potomac River, two-story replicas of a colonial-era mercantile shop, and the thousands of plants and trees that provided a magnificent atmosphere. Apple had her eyes fixed on the indoor water fountain with its synchronized lights, special effects, and patriotic musical score.

"Oh my God!"

"Wait till you see the rooms," Supreme told her.

He walked up to the lavishly designed front desk made of rich oak and marble, where there was a string of hotel clerks ready to check in the guests. Supreme addressed a young, smiling girl in a burgundy blazer and tie, with her name tag reading, *Michelle*. She began the process of reserving one of the suites for the night. She smiled, wished him a good evening, and began processing his information into the computer.

Apple just marveled at the resort as she stood behind Supreme. The place was the size of a football field, maybe larger, and the height extended far beyond anyplace she'd ever been. It was a sure thing that she wasn't in Harlem anymore.

The two soon made their way through the atrium, with Supreme holding the room keys, and they walked toward the elevators. Apple strutted through the reception area in her short denim skirt, heels, and tight top. She had no change of clothes, but since Supreme had promised to take her shopping the minute they were settled in, she was ready for a new look.

Their room was located in a maze of a hallway, with its miles of dazzling red carpeting spread throughout the corridor like the yellow brick road. Supreme got one of the best suites possible, to impress Apple. He knew she had never been anywhere and wanted her to feel like he was the best thing to happen to her. He wanted to have his enemy close. It was fun for him. In fact, he marveled at how easily he had Apple wrapped around his finger.

Soon, they found their room, which was located many doors from the elevator. Supreme walked in first, turned on the lights, and then Apple followed inside, looked around the room with a thrilled smile. "Wow!" she uttered.

She wanted to run around the two-bedroom suite like a three-year-old, but she kept her composure while admiring the room, with its king-sized bed and mini-bar stocked with snacks, wet bar, and plasma TV in the living room. She enjoyed the city's canvas and the spectacular view of the flourishing mid-Atlantic panorama from a distance through the large bay windows.

When Apple walked into the bathroom, her mouth dropped open at the marble bath with its relaxing oasis, featuring a deep soaker tub, brass accents, and a separate glass shower. Immediately she ran a bath, adding the complimentary shower gel for bubbles. Overnight, she went from the shitty, roach-infested project apartment to something royal. She couldn't wait to sink herself in the tub and unwind for the night.

Supreme walked up closely behind her in an intimate manner as she stood gazing at the bathroom. He wrapped his arms around her waist and then moved his hand up her shirt. Squeezing her juicy breasts, he kissed her gently on the neck and slowly began undressing his young prize.

Apple went along with the program, his touch traveling along her curves, moving down her waist with much impatience.

Supreme slowly unzipped her skirt and allowed the material to drop around her ankles like a puddle. Then he started stimulating her clit with his two fingers, causing Apple to gasp.

Supreme moved her closer to the sunken tub and removed her panties then her top. Apple stood naked in front of her adult lover and was ready to spread her legs for him. Supreme smiled, marveling at her naked curves and long, defined legs. He eyed her with a lustful appetite, ready to take pleasure in every inch of her young body and bury himself within the depths of her youthful loving.

With the water teeming with bubbles, the two slowly slipped into the soothing warm tub, and Apple, little by little, straddled Supreme's mega inches, feeling her walls opening up with his firm thrusts. With his back pressed against the granite tub, he explored Apple's insides. She clutched Supreme's strapping frame snugly—her arms wrapped around him for support—panting and cringing from the crazy fucking they were doing, her face warped somewhat from the thick, long dick tunneling deep into her.

Their episode went from the bathroom to the bedroom. Apple was now on her back, her legs spread like wings against the silk sheets, while Supreme pressed on top of her, sucking on her luscious light-brown nipples as he gripped her thighs.

Apple dug her nails into his back and felt herself ready to burst, her legs quivering next to Supreme's sides, feeling every bit of him close to her. She cried out, "Oh shit! Ugh! Shit!" Apple came so hard, it felt like her heart had stopped from overindulgence.

Supreme then flipped her over onto her stomach and fucked her hard from the back until he got his nut. Spent, Apple lay pressed on her tits. Her face was in the pillow, and her pussy felt like it needed fixing from the pounding.

Supreme got up and walked into the bathroom. Apple heard the water running but couldn't move from where she lay, her breath taken and her body numb. She closed her eyes and soon was fast asleep, naked in the bed, looking forward to a new day.

❧◦❧

The next morning was bright. Through the bay windows, the dazzling sun slowly stimulated Apple and Supreme from their slumber. They were meshed with each other, clothes scattered across the floor, their naked bodies still tingling from the previous night.

Apple was the first to rise up. She stretched, got out of bed, and walked toward the window, where the sun beamed on her through the glass. She felt the warmth of it on her naked breasts and peered out at the scenery. She looked down at a distant DC from high up and couldn't wait to explore the city. She stood looking out the window for a long moment, until Supreme called out to her.

"Nice morning, right?" he said amiably. He jumped out of bed with all his glory hanging between his legs, his chiseled structure looking like a plate of armor on him.

Apple turned to greet him with a grin that the eyes couldn't hide; she'd had the time of her life last night.

Supreme approached her, pulling her into his arms and loving the way her soft, smooth skin rubbed against him. She was only seventeen, yet her pussy was sweeter than anything he'd ever had. It was like candy. He moved his hands down her curvy backside and rested it on her round, succulent ass cheeks, which felt like a cushion in his hold.

He looked Apple in her eyes and saw how childlike she was despite her womanly exterior. Even though she was from the projects, rough in a way, and had been with men before him, Supreme knew she hadn't experienced anything outside of Harlem. She was grown in her own way, but fresh to the world outside of her own. Supreme preyed on that, knowing that when you show a young girl like Apple something new and make her believe in you, she'll be eternally indebted.

"You hungry?"

Apple nodded.

"A'ight, we'll get something to eat first, and then I'll take you shopping. We gotta have you looking fresh in DC."

Apple smiled. She couldn't wait to try on some new threads. The last few pieces of clothing she had purchased were from the local booster, Jay-Ray. Now Supreme was promising her a whole new wardrobe.

First, the two had morning sex. This time was different. Supreme pushed her against the bed and slowly inserted his morning hard-on into her. He proceeded gently, as if he knew her vagina was still sore from the previous evening. Apple just laid on her back, and Supreme did all the work, from eating her out until she came multiple times, to him actually making love to her—soft and tenderly.

After they made love, Supreme left Apple to rest it off for a moment. "I'll be in the shower," he said, staring down at her with contentment.

Apple nodded as she curled into the fetal position. The morning sun still twinkled down on her with its warmth, and the only sound in the suite was the shower running in the bathroom. Hypnotized by the immense silence, she turned onto her back and sprawled out. She didn't want to go back to Harlem anytime soon. She tried to block out her past, turn away from the trouble she'd endured. She wanted to have a new identity, become someone else entirely. She was tired of poverty. Tired of the negative abuse coming from her mother. Yes, she had love for Denise, but she was more like a peer than a real mother.

Apple lay there until Supreme came out the bathroom wrapped in a towel, his well-built body glistening with droplets of water. She looked up at him and couldn't help but admire his physique. She no longer saw Supreme, the malicious loan shark that tormented her with the debt she owed, but the man that took her away from her problems and placed her into better circumstances.

"Hurry up and get ready," Supreme commanded lightly.

Apple jumped up and went into the bathroom, while Supreme began getting dressed.

An hour later, they both walked out the atrium to the shiny black Escalade that the valet had pulled up front. Supreme tipped the slim, pale young boy twenty dollars, causing him to smile, saying, "Thank you, sir. Thank you so much."

Supreme nodded. "You ready?" He looked over at Apple and marveled at the sudden transformation he made happen. He remembered a week ago she hated his guts and was repulsed by just the sight of him. Now the gleam in her eyes was a clear indication that she wanted to be close to him. It was brainwashing at its finest.

Supreme drove off the resort and headed toward 295 N, which would take them into the DC area. Forty minutes later, he parked his truck on the streets of Georgetown and took Apple into every store she could imagine. Apple was wide-eyed while strutting through the dozens of exquisite boutiques and stores in the colorful, diverse Georgetown shopping district, a truly unique experience for her.

She was ready to expand her wardrobe with the chic, trendy offerings of Tory Burch, Fendi, Diane Von Furstenberg, Gucci, Prada, and Donna Karan. Apple and Supreme walked down M Street and Wisconsin Avenue, enjoying what the shops had to offer. They also indulged in the variety of foods from the eateries in the area. They went into Burberry, Juicy Couture, Diesel, Lacoste, Chanel, and many other stores that Apple had only heard of through commercials, word of mouth, and print ads, if she had heard of them at all.

When they went into the jewelry store, she picked out a *doppio cuore* pendant in 18-karat white gold with full diamonds and a pair of 5-karat diamond studs. She began wondering just how much money Supreme had, as he pulled out wads of cash to pay for the high-priced clothing and other items she'd picked out. The tremendous spending didn't seem to faze him one bit.

By early evening, Apple had about a half-dozen bags in her hands and was ready to shop some more, so she dumped them into the trunk of the truck and continued shopping. Supreme had bought Apple Chanel sandals, Christian Louboutin stilettos, Gucci bags, Diesel jeans,

Diane Von Furstenberg dresses, and items as simple as a Prada wallet to hold all the cash he was going to throw her way.

In Supreme's eyes, Apple was becoming his young protégé. He didn't mind spending money on her. It was an investment to him, with a greater interest later on. Supreme was always about money, and he liked Apple's style.

After shopping, they had drinks and dinner at Sea Catch Restaurant, right off M Street. Apple was taken aback by its stone walls and narrow archways. The raw bar afforded a serene view of the canal and its towpath. In the dining room, oil-burning candles were situated on the sphere-shaped tables, and there was a 40-foot oak backed by a rough stone wall.

Supreme and Apple dined on the deck overlooking the canal. She had one of the live Maine lobsters that were in the tank by the door, and he ate the filet mignon and walnut-crusted chicken breast.

After dinner, they retreated to their suite at the Gaylord Resort, where Apple tried on her items of clothing and jewelry. She stared at herself in the mirror, finally thinking she was on the come-up. She had clothing and jewelry that would easily outdo anything Kola owned. Apple wished Kola was around so she could boast about her new clothes.

Supreme rested on the bed, watching Apple with a smile. "Try on some of the lingerie I bought you," he suggested.

Ready to please him with a show, she willingly went into the bathroom to become eye-candy for him for the evening. She stripped from her stylish outfit and slipped into a black stretch lace micro-chemise with the off-the-shoulder scalloped neckline and body-conscious shape. She stepped out of the bathroom with a pair of clear stilettos to top off the outfit and slowly modeled for Supreme where he sat.

"Nice." He nodded in approval and watched how her curves complemented the lingerie she wore. "Nice."

"So I take it you like the way it looks on me."

"I'm ready to take it off you."

Apple smiled and then went back into the bathroom to try on another scanty outfit for Supreme. She wiggled out of the first and easily slipped into a red flyaway baby doll in a mix of sheer silk chiffon and lush velvet, with the velvet burnout bikini beneath. She put on some fiery red pumps to match. She walked out of the bathroom feeling like a queen bee.

Supreme loved this outfit even more. "Yeah, I like that one, baby. It looks so good on you."

Apple smiled. She loved it too. She loved it so much that when she went back into the bathroom, she stared at herself for a long moment and thought about her future. Apple was sure of one thing. She didn't want to go back to her old way of living—broke, unemployed, and scared. Even though she and Supreme had their bitter differences, he made her feel special, like his queen, and opened her up to a whole new world. It seemed like, overnight, she had gone from an unspeakable nightmare to a living Cinderella. She looked at her image strongly and vowed to never go back to her old way of living; it was too painful. She wasn't going to ever be that poor nigger girl coming up in the ghetto. She had gotten a taste of the good life, with the shopping spree, touring DC, and dining at classy restaurants, and yearned for more.

Chapter 18

ONE MONTH LATER ...

Harlem was in a full-blown heat wave. The streets felt like they were melting, and the sun felt like it was personally giving Harlem a bear hug. Fire hydrants were on full blast on almost every block, with children and some adults trying to keep cool. Other residents downed ice-cold bottles of water, some in little to no clothing, putting themselves at risk of getting arrested for indecency, the men walking around shirtless, the women in short shorts and skirts, revealing tops, and flip-flops.

The streets had been calm, violence somewhat on the low, but the tension between the two rival crews was still felt in the air. It could've been the calm before the storm. At any rate, police were on constant patrol, trying to keep the streets safe.

After having been gone for a month, Apple returned to Harlem a transformed woman. She enjoyed living it up in DC with Supreme and took advantage of the best her new life had to offer. She had forgotten about her family for a moment, but when she went to visit her mother, she was quickly reminded of the harsh reality she'd left behind.

Supreme accompanied Apple into her old apartment. When she entered the place, it still looked the same. Nothing had changed—the dirt, the clutter, the roaches.

Denise was in the kitchen smoking a Newport, when she noticed her daughter walk into the room. She eyed Apple from head to toe, noticing the sudden change, and for a quick moment thought Apple was Kola. But a mother could always tell her twins apart. Apple was profiling in a short, stylish skirt, a tight Fendi top, thousand-dollar shoes, and her jewelry gleamed like the sun itself.

Denise screwed up her face, and with a growl in her voice, she said to Apple, "So the fuckin' chicken comes back home to roost." She took a long pull from her cigarette and kept her eyes steady on Apple. Then she sharply turned them on Supreme, who stood in the center of the kitchen doorway looking nonchalant.

"Whateva!" Apple snarled back. "I just came to see how you were doing."

"What did you fuckin' do, huh? You leave here, don't go to your fuckin' sister's funeral, and then you bring this nigga into my home. How dare you, bitch!" Denise screamed.

"Ma, you need to chill right now. I came up," Apple replied.

"I need you to get this muthafucka out of my house. How dare you disrespect me like that? You done lost ya fuckin' mind, Apple! But I see you good now. You got this nigga taking care of you now, huh, Apple? After what you said he did to us, you betray your family and run into his fuckin' arms! Your sister needs to be here to kick your fuckin' ass!" Denise's screams echoed throughout the rooms. Then she added, "The police came talking to me and shit, and where were you?"

"They came to you about what?" Apple asked.

"This nigga here." Denise pointed at Supreme. Then she screamed at him, "You took her from me!" Enraged, Denise charged at him.

But Apple grabbed her mother by the arms and held her back a few feet, stopping the assault on her newfound man. She tussled with her mother then pushed her into the sink and shouted, "Ma, relax ya fuckin' self!"

Supreme decided to intervene, stepping between mother and daughter with a strong presence. He then looked down at Apple's mother, his eyes set in a caring manner, and said to her, "Look, I'm sorry about what happened to your daughter, and I know there are some things being said about me. Shit ain't true, but I'm here to make things right wit' you."

Supreme reached into his pocket and pulled out a wad of bills. Then he counted out five hundred dollars and pushed it into Denise's hands as a peace offering.

A surprised Denise looked over at Apple and asked with her eyes, *Is he for real?*

Apple smiled. A good sum of money could easily shut her mother up and change her mood.

"And there's more where that came from," Supreme said, "if you just chill wit' things. I'm not here to cause any trouble for you. I just wanna make it right."

Denise took a seat at the weathered kitchen table and counted her money. She then took another pull from the cigarette, looked up at Apple and Supreme with a shift in her attitude, and asked, "So where you been at, Apple?"

"DC."

"I would like to go next time. I never been anywhere."

Supreme smiled. "Then I won't forget you when we leave again."

Denise smiled warily. The two women quickly reconciled with each other and decided to put their past behind them.

⌘

It wasn't long until Apple started to learn the loan-sharking and bookkeeping business with Supreme, who picked up on her skills and wanted to bank on it. Apple was fresh, but had ideas herself, and she saw how Supreme made the bulk of his money—using intimidation to get debtors to pay him back at a high interest.

Within weeks, Apple came to realize just how successful and devious Supreme was with the illicit business he ran. She began doing bookkeeping for him, managing his organization, and maintaining some of his debt collection records. She also managed a few of his real estate holdings. She saw the money he was bringing in and was turned on by it.

One of Supreme's major loan-sharking schemes was through the restaurant businesses that occupied Harlem's busy streets. He had implemented the scheme about a year earlier. He would take patrons' credit card information when the failing restaurants couldn't make their loan repayments. Sometimes, if the owners couldn't pay him back, he demanded the credit card information of their customers by brute force and threats of death. Supreme would walk into several of the struggling businesses and lend the proprietors the money they needed to keep their businesses afloat, charging them exorbitant interest rates. Some he hit with the "juice" system—If a business received a loan of $10,000, then Supreme required them to pay an extra four points, which was $4000 or more a week.

The owners, scared to get any help from law enforcement, did what they needed to do to survive. Supreme would walk into the establishments under his domain, and he and his goons would eat for free, creating bills in the hundreds, sometimes thousands.

Supreme also had scouts going out into the streets of Harlem, and occasionally downtown Brooklyn, to look for potential victims he could invest in. His young scouts, young boys and girls ranging from ages fifteen to nineteen, would walk into different stores looking for the unfortunate ones who couldn't afford the items and mostly window-shopped. His scouts would strike up a conversation with the customers, and with influence and game, before day's end, get them to borrow the cash under the "juice" system, depending on the size of the loan. The customers had a certain amount of time to pay back the money borrowed, with the points added.

Supreme profited well from both schemes. If they couldn't pay in time, then intimidation and violence followed. Sometimes he would threaten to kidnap family members and loved ones, guaranteeing to the debtors that every week they were late with payment, they would receive a piece of their loved ones in the mail. The women, they had two choices—Pay back in cash or work it off sexually. Supreme's goons would rape them or occasionally force them to work as prostitutes or hostesses in sleazy nude underground spots throughout the city to pay off their debt.

Supreme even brought misery to hard-up families by offering loans to tide them over. One terrified client of his was so scared, he hung himself after his $500 loan spiraled to $3,000. Sometimes the borrowers were paying more than $500 a week in interest. Supreme wanted his money and he wanted it fast.

Apple and Supreme soon became an item, the hood speculating and gossiping about her involvement in his operation, from corner to corner. She became the most talked-about girl, and when they didn't see her at Nichols' funeral several weeks earlier, they began to have their doubts about her.

Before long, Apple started doing some of the debt-collecting herself. Supreme taught her how to be hardhearted and not to let anyone slide out of debt, explaining, if you let one individual pass on a debt, then the others would be looking for a pass too, or a fucking handout. He let it be known that he wasn't running a charity case and had convinced Apple that anyone late with payment or refusing to pay was taking money out her pockets as well, which meant no new Gucci or Prada for her to style in, or no riding around in the drop-top Benz.

As August began, Apple became known as Supreme's main chick around the way, confronting those that didn't pay, like a pit bull in a skirt, carrying around a nickel-plated .22 and a small razor for any problems that sprung up in her line of work. She'd easily cut and pistol-whipped a few bitches that tried her, spreading her reputation on the streets of Harlem. Too bad, they chose to learn the hard way that she meant business.

With the women, Apple made it clearly known that there wouldn't be any more sleeping off their debts with Supreme or any of his goons. Having to duck and hide from Supreme herself not too long ago, she'd quickly learned the tricks of the trade. They either had to pay up or sell their ass on the corners to pay back what they owed. No exceptions.

It was a new day, and Apple was at the top of the food chain for once.

When her cell phone rang, she hesitated before she answered it.

"Whaddup?"

"What's up, this Cartier."

Apple's mood soured. "Where you been? I called you ages ago about Nichols."

"I was shot, bitch. Me and my daughter, so I couldn't get right back."

Apple didn't like the tone in Cartier's voice, but knew better than to react. She'd already heard about Cartier's run-in and how Bam had gotten murdered; the streets don't keep no secrets.

"Oh, my bad. But you OK, now right? You and baby-girl?"

"Yeah, we good but I heard from Kola and you wildin'."

"Fuck that bitch! She just jealous, that's all."

"Nah, I don't get that from her. Kola said she was tossin' up Harlem for Nichols while you went MIA. She said you let dick come between fam. The streets are talkin' 'bout you and 'Preme, and so is Kola."

"How you gonna take her side over mines?" Apple was spent. She thought she was closer to Cartier than her sister. "I can't really talk over the phone, but the Nichols situation got handled. That was all me!"

"Look, we peoples, but fam is fam. You don't go against the grain for no fuckin' body. Kola wanted me to come through to help her tie up a few loose ends, but I'm heading OT for a while, but wanted to touch base to make sure you and Kola would squash your beef."

"Oh, no doubt. It's ain't that serious," Apple lied.

"You sure?"

"One hundred."

Apple couldn't wait to hang up with Cartier and get right back to her empire. But she did make a mental note to readdress her feelings toward her mentor at a later date. She respected Cartier and all, but gone were the days that she'd let anyone—including Cartier—speak to her like she was less than a boss.

Chapter 19

It was the middle of August, and Apple hated that she had to collect a certain debt from someone, but business was still business, no matter who fell prey to their system. She waited patiently behind the steering wheel of her powder blue Benz with the top down and kept an eye out. It was late evening, and the block was quiet.

She sat back in her seat and took a few pulls from the blunt she was smoking. She exhaled, enjoying the way the kush worked itself into her system. The chick she was after had been ducking her and Supreme for weeks. Tired of the nonsense, she took it upon herself to handle the matter personally. She wanted her money, and she wasn't trying to hear any excuses. With interest and the four points, the $900 loan had easily grown to $1,620, and Apple planned on getting back that money one way or another.

She toyed with the radio, flipping back and forth from Hot 97 to Power 105.1. She stopped at Hot 97 upon hearing her boo, Drake, singing "Find Your Love."

Apple nodded, thinking about the time she saw him perform at Summer Jam with her friends, Ayesha and Mesha. But those were old times. Times had changed for her now.

She looked at herself in the rearview mirror and saw such a difference in herself. She felt she had matured more, and the diamond earrings in her ear made her feel like she was royalty.

A half-hour later, Apple shut her car off, locked her doors, and went into the building, where she took the elevator to the fifth floor. She thought maybe Mesha went into the building through the back, giving her the slip. She banged on Mesha's door.

Ms. Thomas, Mesha's elderly grandmother, answered. She was wearing a housecoat and clutching a wooden cane for support. "Hey, Apple. How are you?" she asked in her caring, gentle tone, her eyes lighting up on seeing Apple.

"I'm good, Ms. Thomas. Is Mesha around?"

"Oh dear, she didn't get home from work yet. You wanna come in?"

"Nah, Ms. Thomas, that's OK. How you been, though?" Apple asked with concern.

Before Ms. Thomas could answer, she let out a terrible cough. She leaned beside the doorway and clutched her cane tighter as the heavy coughing continued. For a moment, she looked out of breath, like she was ready to collapse at Apple's feet, but she got herself together and continued on with her talk.

"I'm so sorry about that, Apple. This poor ol' body

is trying to wear out on me," she said, a little winded, attempting to smile.

"You OK?" Apple asked.

"I've been better."

<hr>

Ms. Thomas was a frail-looking woman. Despite her high spirits, her health was declining fast. She'd been diagnosed with cancer a few months earlier, and it was spreading fast throughout her body. Uninsured, and with little income coming in, her hospital bills were piling up every month.

Mesha was stressed over her grandmother's health, and the sales job she had at the mall barely covered the bills. She was soon forced into a corner when they received an eviction notice on their door. On top of that, her grandmother's long hospital stay in the late spring put them in so much debt, she felt she needed to look to other resources. The first thing she did was go to her boyfriend, but he didn't have any savings. He had worked as a paralegal for the City of New York, but right before he completed his probationary period he was let go. Not enough money in the budget for all the new hires. With the horrible economy, he'd been out of work for months.

She soon turned to Supreme for the money to stop the eviction from happening, since being homeless with a sick grandmother wasn't an option for her. Supreme lent her the money, and then shortly after, her debt, like everyone else's, began spiraling out of control.

Mesha was ready to fuck Supreme to cancel her

debt when she couldn't afford to pay it back, but Apple quickly put a stop to that, and the threats followed right after. Mesha was shocked that her once best friend could turn on her like they were strangers, and they got into a small confrontation a week back.

❧

Apple had said to her, "Yo, it's just business, Mesha. It ain't personal."

"Business? You gonna do me like that, Apple? I thought we were friends."

"We good, but we'll be even better if you pay me my money that you owe."

"After all these years, the shit we did together, and you know my grandmother is sick? Apple, where the fuck I'm gonna get almost two thousand dollars from? Shit, I only borrowed nine hundred."

"Look, Mesha, like I said, it ain't personal, it's just business—"

Mesha shouted, "It *is* fuckin' personal! How can you just do me like this after all the shit I fuckin' done for you? Are you fuckin serious?" She wiped the tears that streamed down her face. "You used to stay at my house when your fucked-up moms used to run you out."

"Look, Mesha, I don't wanna have to fuck you up. I know we go way back. That's why I gave you some time, but you got a week."

"A week?"

"Yeah."

"And then what?" Mesha asked with attitude.

"Then it becomes personal wit' you and me." Apple turned to walk away.

Mesha stood there fuming. Then she shouted, "Fuck you, bitch! Get the fuck away from my crib! How dare you! What? You Supreme's ho now? Huh, bitch? You his dumb fuckin' bitch?"

Apple ignored the insults and kept it moving. She could still hear Mesha cursing her out when she trotted down the pissy stairway.

～⌒～

A week later, now Apple was back at Mesha's door, talking to her sickly grandmother like things between her and Mesha were good. Apple remembered the many days she'd spent at Mesha's crib when staying at her own place became too hectic to deal with. But she quickly blocked out that memory and focused on getting her money.

"Ms. Thomas, you take care of yourself. I'll catch Mesha some other time," Apple said with a smile.

"You too, Apple. Take care, and please come by more often. I haven't seen you around," Ms. Thomas said, unaware of the beef between her granddaughter and Apple.

"I'll try." Apple smiled.

When Ms. Thomas closed her door, Apple didn't leave right away. Instead, she lingered near the stairway, being shadowed in the corner. Looking at the time on her watch, she knew Mesha would be on her way home from work soon. Determined to confront her about her debt once more, she waited for a moment.

When Apple heard the sound of the elevator reaching the floor, she figured it was Mesha and was ready to face her like a raging bull. She stayed poised near the elevator. The second Mesha stepped out of it, she would be on her like stink on shit.

The solid doors slowly slid behind the walls, giving access to the iron lift. The minute Apple saw Mesha step out, holding onto her purse, fumbling with her house keys, looking exhausted after a long day at work, she jumped on her, pushing her back into the elevator with force.

"Where the fuck is my money?"

Caught off guard, a look of shock registered across Mesha's pretty light-skin face. Apple moved in on her with the speed of lightning. Before Mesha could defend herself, the nickel-plated .22 in Apple's hand came across her face with a vicious blow, dropping her back and stunning her. The contents of her purse spilled out onto the floor when Apple knocked her to the ground with the second strike.

"I told you, bitch—Stop fuckin' wit' me!"

Mesha cried out and pleaded for her to stop, but Apple wasn't budging. She stood over Mesha with the .22 in hand and kicked her in the ribs. Mesha wailed, and with her body balled up, she fell over onto her side.

Apple kicked her again. "Bitch, where's my fuckin' money?" She picked up Mesha's purse and dumped the remaining contents out, looking for anything valuable. She saw the money from Mesha's cashed paycheck. She counted it, and it only totaled $350. Upset, Apple waved the money in her hand and shouted, "Bitch, this is it? Are you serious?" Apple gave her one swift kick again to her side.

Mesha cried out, "Oowwww!" Still curled up in the fetal position, her side felt like it was on fire. She began crying and begging Apple to stop the abuse, but Apple just looked down at her ex-best friend with cold, callous eyes and pointed the gun at her head.

"Mesha, you better do somethin', 'cause I ain't toleratin' this shit. You come up wit' our money. I don't care if you gotta sell your pussy on the streets—You come up wit' my twenty-five hundred that you now owe, or your grandmother gonna be the one burying you. Then who's gonna take care of the sick bitch when you're rottin' in the fuckin' ground?"

Mesha cried out, begging Apple for more time, but Apple wasn't changing her mind about anything. She robbed Mesha of her paycheck, iPhone, iPod, and earrings, and then left her and her things on the floor of the elevator. Apple hurriedly took the stairs, adding up the stuff she snatched from Mesha. With everything she had taken, she figured it totaled $500, and with the paycheck, her take was $850.

The next night, right after working long hours in the mall, Mesha came home and quickly changed into a snug skirt and tight top. After slipping on her high heels, she rushed back out the door.

An hour later, she stood on the grungy street corners

in the shadows of the block, trying to sell her body to the passing cars. Afraid for her life, she was willing to do whatever to get Apple off her back. She shivered as she dried her tears. Mesha was a fresh young girl, and the horny men easily took the bait, snatching her up. With her light skin, hazel eyes, and long legs, it didn't take long for a trick to stop his car and for her to jump in.

Mesha was such eye-candy, she didn't get much of a break between her tricks, reluctantly giving head and spreading her legs in the backseat of over a half dozen cars that night.

Within five days of shamefully selling her ass on street corners, she had Apple's money in full. It was the worst five days of her life. She got no rest and had no peace. Every night when she came home, she would linger in the shower for an hour or more, trying to wash away the filth and shame. Her tears would mix with the shower water, and sometimes Mesha would drop to her knees, trembling. She could still feel the painful penetration from the tricks that violated her.

After a visit to her local physician a week later, Mesha found out she had herpes. Her world came crashing down on her, and she didn't know what to tell her boyfriend. She cried for days, hating Apple with a passion.

Denise sauntered around Harlem in her new clothing and jewelry, compliments of her daughter, boasting about Apple's success to everyone, leaving a bitter taste in everyone's mouth. She felt like she and her daughter had finally come up. But everyone looked at the mother and daughter with disdain. The residents once felt sorry for Denise and Apple for their tragic loss, but when the mother and daughter started to act as if Nichols' death never happened, their feelings changed toward them. In fact, there were rumors of foul play within the family.

When Kola found out that Apple was now Supreme's wifey, she was livid. What upset her even more was that her mother was riding with Supreme and Apple because of the money and gifts they flaunted. It seemed like Apple was buying her mother's love, or maybe silence.

Kola finally confronted her mother late one evening at their old apartment, where she was running a card game out the place, though her new home was with Apple in a magnificent brownstone on the West Side. Denise, grateful for her daughter's generosity, stayed in the basement. She didn't know why Apple put her up in a home and bought her the finer things in life with the ill-gotten wealth. She had put her daughters through hell, and wasn't about to complain or bring up the past now that she was finally living the life she had always dreamed of, and had muthafuckas kissing her ass.

Hearing the blaring music from inside, Kola banged on the apartment door of her former home. She stood back, waiting impatiently, ready to kick it down. *The bitch changed the fuckin' locks*, she thought. She banged on the door again.

A moment later, the apartment door opened up, and

Denise stood in front of her daughter, holding a glass of wine in her hand. She was dressed in a pair of tight leather pants that accentuated her curves and a mohair-blend camisole sweater that had delicate pointelle stitching with a bit of sparkle. With her new weave reaching down to her back, she looked like newfound money.

Kola's mouth dropped open.

"Kola, why you here?" Denise asked, surprised to see her.

Kola glared at her mother, wanting to ram her fist down her throat, but she kept her cool. "So this is you now, huh, Ma?"

"What?"

"Ma, how the fuck you let that shit ride like that? What is wrong wit' you?"

Denise stepped farther into the hallway, closing the door lightly behind her, so her company wouldn't hear the dispute. Resenting Kola's words, she got up in her face. "Kola, Nichols is dead, OK? I'm trying to move on with my life, and this is me moving on."

"You movin' on how, Ma? By letting your fuckin' daughter fuck that nigga? You pimpin' her now, Ma!"

"My business is my fuckin' business, and you need to stay the fuck out my business! Look at us, Kola. Look how I'm living now. Fuck it! We came up."

"Came up? Look at you! You're a fuckin' joke! You and Apple, ya'll some dumb bitches!" Kola screamed out.

"You watch your fuckin' mouth, Kola. You always been the stupidest one out of all my kids!" Denise shouted.

BAD APPLE THE BADDEST CHICK

"Whateva, Ma. Nichols ain't been dead two months yet, and you're actin' like she never existed, but I swear on Nichols' grave, I'ma see you and Apple."

"Bitch, how dare you threaten me! I'm the queen bitch, Kola! I gave birth to your fuckin' ass! You hear me, bitch? I gave birth to Nichols, and I'm allowed to mourn her in my own fuckin' way. I wish you were the one rottin' in the fuckin' ground!" Denise shouted as she followed Kola toward the elevator.

Though hurt by her mother's words somewhat, Kola kept it moving. She dried the few tears that fell from her eyes and exited her old building, a vengeful spirit dwelling inside of her.

Denise cursed the ground Kola walked on and went back into the apartment to continue her wild card game; smoking, drinking, and partying like it was New Year's Eve. She decided not to give Kola and her foolishness a second thought. She loved her new life. The clothes and jewelry were the best. *Fuck that bitch*, she thought to herself.

⚬⚬⚬

Kola got into her black BMW 5-Series and started the ignition, her heart ice-cold toward her family. She thought about Nichols every day and was ashamed to see her family acting like fools, disregarding what had happened to her little sister.

It'd been two months, and still Nichols' murder was unsolved. Kola had heard about J-Dogg being gunned down in the Bronx, but it was bittersweet news. She knew he might have been the triggerman, but he wasn't the only one behind the murder. She felt in her heart that the real culprit was tearing her family apart, and even though her family was dysfunctional before the tragedy, she felt like they were even more fucked up now.

Apple was the talk of the town, but Kola was the gangsta in the family. People knew not to fuck with her. Still, Apple had a growing reputation, and Kola was reminded of it daily. She'd heard about her sister pistol-whipping bitches or cutting up their face if they were late with payment. Kola was somewhat stunned at her sister's sudden change of character.

Who knew the bitch had it in her? Kola said to herself.

In her eyes, Apple still couldn't fuck with her. Though Apple was getting money, she was making her ends too. Yet, it pained Kola's heart to see her twin sister sleeping with the enemy. She knew Supreme was no good. He was a creep who'd manipulated her sister with money to cover up Nichols' murder.

Kola couldn't worry about her sister and mother at the moment. She was having a party that night. Her sex-selling business was taking off. For the past month and a half, things had been booming for her. She had the finest girls in the city under her influence and the best locations anyone could think of—rooftops, penthouse suits, and lavish clubs. In fact, she was becoming well known for her business and profiting greatly from selling sex throughout Harlem and the rest of New York. Once you went to one of Kola's party—a sex 'n' play gathering, she called it—you didn't want to fuck with anything else.

Kola had a close-knit team of women that helped her organize things, and she ran her business like a corporation. She had her ladies on salary, with tips, had them all tested for any STDs, and the only way into her parties was through membership fees, which was paid in advance by either cash or credit card via her business account that she had set up. Once membership was paid up, the members would receive the time and location of her next hardcore event via e-mail or text. She made sure never to stay at one location too long, knowing if she kept changing venues, it would be harder for law enforcement to raid her business. She always kept her parties on the low and made up to five to ten thousand each event from selling sex, liquor, and ecstasy.

Kola pushed her 5-Series toward her home in Washington Heights. It was getting late, and she had to be ready in time for her party at a downtown Manhattan loft in SoHo. The venue was big enough to hold up to one hundred and fifty people, which was perfect. She needed the space, since her parties were growing because of increasing membership. She had fifteen girls arriving, and they were all ready to get things popping. None of her girls were ugly, because she'd handpicked them herself. Ranging from ages eighteen to twenty-two years old, they were all cute, thick, and curvy in the right places, and were the best at what they did—making men buy into a sexual fantasy that they'd never forget.

It was almost nine in the evening when Kola arrived at her cozy one-bedroom apartment off Broadway. She double-parked her car outside the building and rushed inside. Her place was quiet, with an unflustered and comfortable silence that took time for her to get used to. She'd decorated the place with lovely accent furnishing, including a large overstuffed Candice Olson designed couch, a Horchow modern glass dining table, a vintage canopy bed, and off white-colored walls that enriched her living room. The large plasma screen was mounted on her wall like a painting, and the unique Bistro Loft aerial rug, though it had cost her a small fortune, made her place a little more welcoming. In fact, the design on the rug was stunning enough to have been a piece of artwork on her walls.

Kola kicked off her shoes and went straight into her bathroom. She needed to wash up before attending her event. She turned on the water to her marble sunken tub and began stripping out of her clothes.

She made a few phone calls from her cell phone to make sure all the preparations for her party had been taken care of. Mostly, she talked to Gina, her trusted assistant, and Gina let her know that everyone was ready and everything was in place.

Kola's parties started late—midnight or after. She liked it that way because it gave her more time to arrange everything. Besides, she knew the freaks mostly came out at night.

She smiled as she slowly submerged herself in the steaming, relaxing water. Then she turned on the small sound system embedded in her bathroom walls to listen to some R&B. Soaking in the tub, she tried not to think about her problems with her family, as she focused on her business and the streets.

Meanwhile, Mike-Mike was locked up in Rikers Island, and Danny was on the run. He had caught a murder charge a month earlier and decided to flee the city, but Kola didn't stress it. She was only seventeen and living better than most adults.

Chapter 20

The porn-style party, taking place in SoHo, Manhattan, got into full swing after one in the morning. The cast iron building, tucked away on a quiet cobblestone city street, with sparse traffic outside, was the perfect location for a sex 'n' play gathering. Inside the large room with the high ceiling and large-covered windows, with the brick, ductwork, and beams exposed, and a soaring view of the city, young scantily clad women in stilettos, some nude, moved around the loft, looking to please the many men available.

The men were just as loosely dressed as the ladies, some shirtless or in their underwear, and drooling at the slim, curvy, long-legged beauties. The loft came to life with sex. It was a free-for-all to do what you please with any of the ladies. There were two makeshift back rooms for privacy, or if a couple was bold enough, they could create their own show for everyone to see. Couples paired off in some corner or against the brick walls, in full view of one another.

The 15-inch club-size speakers situated throughout the loft played the smash hit by Ludacris and Trey Songz, "Sex Room." All the grinding and touching going on got the ladies wet, and it didn't take long for the downtown loft to literally become a sex room.

A handsome, young executive got his chance to be sexually entertained by Bunny Rabbit, one of Kola's favorite girls. She was raw at the party, walking around butt naked in some six-inch heels and feeling up on all the fellows daringly with a teasing smile. Her long black hair danced around her shoulders, and her voluptuous curves got many stares from the men and women. She gave an enthusiastic member a blowjob right on the floor, sucking his thick, long, pink penis so good that after he came, he took a seat on the floor to catch his breath.

"You OK, honey?" Bunny Rabbit asked with a smile.

The man nodded. "Shit! That was fuckin' awesome, man!"

"That's what I'm here for," Bunny Rabbit told him.

Kola knew who to pick for memberships. She went after the men with big bucks and lustful appetites. Her networking skills were that of a champion. She would hit up Wall Street, corporate events, and industry parties, and then start to talk. She disguised her age, carried herself with true professionalism—classy, but with a little aggression to push her business—and had the men believing she was a young madam. She would take their business cards or give out hers, promising them the time of their lives. A few days later, they'd discuss membership fees, and then two days before the party they would get a text or e-mail containing the details.

Kola's first event went off very well. She had a great crowd come through, and all her ladies did their thing. The men couldn't get enough of her girls. Kola had hosted the event at a vacant Brooklyn warehouse, where everyone was treated to champagne, wine, even liquor, and there was so much sexing going on that, at the end of the night, used condoms were found all over the place.

Within weeks, Kola's party spread by word of mouth, and everyone wanted in. But Kola was very careful in screening her clients. She was shrewd and meticulous, and had a good eye to spot bullshit. She did background checks and watched everything carefully, knowing that one slip-up could cost her plenty, especially if the police were watching her.

❦

Bunny Rabbit happily guided the tall, dark, handsome, suit-and-tie-wearing man by the hand, leading him to some place more discreet in the congested loft. She knew he was kind of shy and new to Kola's parties.

Since the two rooms were occupied, they had to fuck out in the open. Bunny Rabbit liked his swag. He was dark-skinned and well-built with short hair and a thin mustache. He didn't talk much, but she knew he wasn't interested in having a conversation with her. She noticed he'd been ogling her since he arrived, so she took the initiative to start something with him.

She went up to the tall stranger and whispered in his ear, "Follow me," and took his hand, guiding him through the crowd. The man didn't protest. He willingly followed Bunny Rabbit to wherever she was taking him.

They soon were hugged up on each other in a dim corner of the loft, near one of the large, covered windows. Little by little, Bunny Rabbit began grinding her thick backside into him, feeling his dick growing in his slacks. She smiled, reaching around behind her, and let her hand travel south, grabbing his package. The man moaned and wanted her to continue.

"You like that?" Bunny Rabbit asked, turning to face him.

"Yes."

With her naked body pressed against him and her large tit cupped in his hand, Bunny Rabbit began unzipping his pants. She reached inside for his hard-on and pulled it out so she could please it better.

The man moaned with gratification, feeling Bunny Rabbit's soft, manicured hand gripping the tip of his erection. With his dick still in her hold, she stroked him lightly and pressed against him more with her naked breasts touching his suited chest.

She leaned into his ear and seductively asked, "You want me to fuck you, suck you, or both?"

The man's breath was sparse with excitement, and Bunny felt his dick throbbing in her hand. She wanted to enjoy it either way—in her pussy or in her mouth. She continued to stroke and toy with his dick. Her nipples were hard as rocks, and her lips were soft like cotton.

"You choose," he said.

Liking his response, she smiled before dropping to her knees and taking his hard, pulsating, penis into her mouth. As she rocked her head back and forth into him, the stranger gasped, reclining and rolling his eyes into the back of his head. He ran his hand through Bunny Rabbit's thick, black hair and felt his knees about to buckle as she sucked his dick like the professional she was. It felt like his dick was in a vacuum tube.

Soon after, she gave him a condom, curved herself over to grip the brick wall, and waited for the penetration. He thrust himself into her, but it was a quick fuck. Bunny Rabbit had gotten him so excited, he came shortly after entry. He pulled out, somewhat embarrassed.

Bunny Rabbit smiled genially and said, "Don't worry, honey. My pussy has that effect. You ain't the only one." As he pulled up his pants and smiled back, Bunny Rabbit noticed her boss Kola arriving.

Kola arrived at her party an hour after it started. She walked through her event with a proud smile. She was well liked and respected. She was greeting her girls, admiring the turnout, and looking stunning in a sheer black dress, embellished with sequins and cut to hug the body, underneath a sheer robe with long sleeves and shimmering sequin trim.

She also wore a thong panty, and her long legs strutted around in a pair of six-inch stilettos. Kola moved through the loft with authority, making sure everything was in order, from the music, money, and liquor, to making sure her regulars were satisfied with the girls.

She stood around talking to Gina and marveled at the orgy she put together. Screaming orgasms roared throughout the loft, and the different positions that a few men and women were entwined in looked like something out of *Kama Sutra*.

Two hours later and the party gave no indication of dying out anytime soon. It was even more vibrant.

Kola noticed Cross in attendance. She was surprised to see him at her event, especially since he wasn't a member. She watched him for a moment as he mingled with one of her girls. He looked finer than ever in his True Religion jeans, and old school red and white Adidas jacket and white T-shirt underneath. His long Cuban link chain with the diamond-encrusted pendant gleamed around his neck, and his long stylish braids portrayed him as the thug he really was. She hadn't seen Cross since Mike-Mike's arrest.

She downed the shot of vodka in her glass and walked over to him to say hello. She tapped him on his shoulder, and when he turned around, she asked, "What brings you to my party?"

"I see you doin' ya thang, Kola. I like this," he replied.

"How did you find out about it, Cross? I keep my shit on the down low."

"I got my ways, baby. You know me, Kola. If I want in, I want it. I keep my ear to the streets," he said arrogantly.

"I see." Kola smiled.

The two locked eyes for a moment, and Kola couldn't help but to become that little girl around him. It was her party, and she was that chick handling her business, but like her sister Apple, Cross had a way of making them feel like putty when he was around.

Cross looked at Kola with a hint in his eyes that he was pleased with what she had on. "You lookin' really nice, Kola. Damn! Really fuckin' nice."

Kola blushed, which she rarely did, and responded, "Yeah, stop playing wit' me, Cross."

"Nah. Look at you. You runnin' ya own thang. Shit, girl, you a natural born hustler. I like that. You came up."

"I learned from the best," she replied with a smile.

"You did, huh?"

She nodded.

"When was the last time you visited Mike-Mike?"

"Two weeks ago. He doin' a'ight," she answered.

"Yeah, I would go see my nigga, but wit' the heat on us and shit wit' these murders, I gotta fall back and chill."

"I know. You ain't gotta explain it to me, Cross. You know I'm always on the block."

"But, look, I know things been rough wit' you, wit' your sister's murder and everything, but if you need anything, you know to come holla at me, right?"

"I know. But I'm good for now, Cross. Thanks."

"Yeah, I see you holdin' your own. I see what Mike-Mike always saw in you. He always had good taste in women." Cross stared at Kola with an urge to snatch her into his arms.

"You think so, huh?"

"Yeah, I know so."

Kola felt her panties getting wet, and her legs quivered lightly with the bass in his voice and his towering presence. Her heart started to beat faster.

"You came for anything else, Cross? What you lookin' for?" she asked, flirting.

Cross smiled. "Yo, is there some place where we can talk in private?"

"Yeah, follow me."

Cross followed closely behind Kola, moving through the place and walking up a spiral stairway. They entered a small room decorated with burning candles, a small bed, and incense.

Kola pivoted on her stilettos to stare at Cross closely. "So, what do you want to talk to me about?"

Cross shut the door to the room and walked up to Kola. The look in his eyes made it clearly known. He didn't want to talk. He noticed something different about Kola. She was advanced in her own way; mature.

Kola placed her hand against Cross' chest, admiring his muscular physique, and felt her heart beating like African drums. She looked up at him, her eyes simply giving her away, telling him that she was his to play with for the night, so Cross pulled her into his arms and instantly began caressing her.

Kola unbuckled his jeans, slid out his dick, and went to work on it. She pushed him down onto the bed, taking control, laying him flat on his back, and began sucking his dick with such expertise, she had Cross squirming under her spell, speechless.

When she was done, they quickly stripped off everything, and she mounted his ample erection with a thirsty obsession to fuck the man her sister had loved for the longest. When Kola felt the fast thrust into her, she gasped and clawed Cross' thick chest, grinding into him and feeling every inch of him digging deep inside of her.

When they were done, the two quickly got dressed. Kola went back to hosting her party, and with his mind continually replaying their brief encounter, Cross left.

Chapter 21

I t was the beginning of September, and Apple's vicious reputation was growing daily. She tormented and severely abused her once close friends. Everyone felt that she was out of control, and her mother wasn't any better, supporting her daughter's reckless ways because it kept her fresh in clothes, money, and jewelry. Apple had growing confrontations in Harlem, from her sister to the males and females that hated her. She was always too stubborn to back down from a fight and threatened anyone that crossed her. She looked at herself as improved from how she used to be—naïve and broke—and vowed never to struggle for a dime ever again. She was heartless with her .22 and small razor, leaving her trademark across half a dozen ladies that dared her.

She drove around Harlem in her pricey powder blue Benz and boasted about her wealth, sporting the nicest clothes and jewelry that money could buy. Money had changed her for the worse. It had gotten so bad for her that one night she exited a local diner from taking her mother out to eat and found her car keyed up, both front tires slashed, and her windshield shattered. Apple was highly upset, but she knew it was only part of the program. *Collateral damage,* she said to herself. Apple was somewhat glad she had haters. It meant she was relevant.

Apple woke up suddenly around three in the morning in a cold sweat, screaming out from a nightmare she'd been having continuously. She lifted herself out of bed, and welcomed the dim light coming from the television. She felt like she couldn't breathe, and the room was spinning, the walls closing in on her.

Apple found herself alone once more in the luxurious brownstone that she and Supreme shared. Her mother was out gambling till the early morning hours again, and Supreme was never home, which was starting to trouble her. She'd heard rumors about him fucking other girls, and even though she put the word out that there was no more sleeping off a debt, it had gotten back to her that Supreme had fucked Ayesha a few times when she couldn't pay back the five hundred dollars she borrowed.

Apple fumed at Ayesha getting with her man and made a mental note to check her when she saw her in the streets. Apple wasn't having it; she wasn't going to be played like some fool. She felt she had worked too hard to get the finer things, and Ayesha wasn't going to take the easy way out. She planned to confront her at her home and tell her that she still owed the money, even though she'd fucked Supreme to clear herself from the debt.

And she was ready to cut Supreme. They hadn't fucked in two weeks because Apple felt he was too busy occupying himself with the whores on the streets. She was afraid that maybe he was getting tired of her. She was doing all of his dirty work, while he was basking in the glory.

❧❧❧

Right now though, Apple had bigger problems to deal with—her nightmares and her guilt. She was having the same recurring dreams about Nichols. In her dreams, Apple was alone, frightened, and being dragged into a dark, terrifying pit—maybe hell—where she'd hear blood-curling screams from Nichols as she cried out to her in anguish, "Why? Why? Why you let him do this to me?"

It pained her to hear Nichols' gut-wrenching voice. She felt this paralyzing chill overcome her that she couldn't escape. Some demonic force would depart from the depths of hell to seize her sadistically and pull her into a long suffering. She would try to scream, shake, bite, and fight her way out of the dark entity's control over her, but the more she fought, the weaker she became, until finally she'd give in. That's when she would feel herself sinking down into hell and hear Nichols' chilling voice fading in the distance. She would stir wildly from her sleep and have to catch her breath. Her nightmare seemed too real, and she would be paranoid for the first ten minutes after waking up.

It was the sixth nightmare she'd had within two weeks, and it started to bother her. She thought about seeing a doctor, but then she didn't want to be looked at as crazy.

With no one around to talk to or comfort her, Apple got out of bed and went into the bathroom. She turned on the faucet and splashed cold water on her face to calm her nerves. She lingered on her reflection in the bathroom mirror for a moment and noticed the change in her eyes, which were now cold and daring.

Next, she walked into the kitchen to fix herself a late-night snack. She figured having something in her stomach would ease her nerves a little more. She made herself a turkey and cheese sandwich, poured a large cup of iced tea, and returned to her bedroom to try and relax. She rested against the headboard, stuffed her face with food, and turned the volume up to see what was good to watch on cable at three in the morning. It was mostly paid programs and movies she'd already seen.

Nothing of interest caught her eye, until she turned to The History Channel and caught the beginning of an hour-long documentary on Stockholm syndrome, which she wanted to know more about. She didn't know why the show had caught her eye, but she focused on the program.

At first, the host talked about the syndrome—"the psychological occurrence where hostages show admiration, worship and praise and have unreasonable positive feelings toward their captors, given the endangerment and risk."

The program stated that the FBI's Hostage Database System showed that almost 30% of victims show signs of Stockholm syndrome, an extraordinary phenomenon in which a hostage begins to identify with and grow sympathetic to his captor.

Apple's young eyes stayed glued to the program. The program then went on to talk about Patty Hearst, the heir to a publishing fortune who in 1974 was kidnapped by the Symbionese Liberation Army. Unbelievably, Hearst aggressively participated in a robbery just two months after she was captured. Patty was convicted and sent to prison, but in 1979 her sentence was commuted by President Jimmy Carter, and in 2001 she received a pardon from President Bill Clinton.

After the program ended, Apple started wondering if she was suffering from the same condition. Was it Stockholm syndrome? She was in awe, still staring at the TV in a trance-like state.

The tears started to flow from Apple's eyes like a waterfall. It was like she was meant to watch that documentary. She had become a willing participant in covering up her sister's murder by cohabiting with her murderer. Supreme had used her, taken advantage of her when she was vulnerable, and left her blinded from the reality that he was still a murderer. After killing her sister, now he was using her for his own purposes. And he would probably discard her when he had no more use for her.

Apple knew she was fucked in her own way, though, without any real proof linking Supreme to her sister's murder. Besides that, she figured the police weren't likely to help because now she was known to be an accomplice in Supreme's criminal enterprise.

That same night, Apple logged on to the Internet and continued to read more about Stockholm syndrome. She stayed up till morning reading about it and learned that hostages who develop Stockholm syndrome usually see the culprit as the giver of life simply because they spared it. The captor automatically becomes in control of the captive's need for survival and the victim's overall life.

Apple thought about Supreme taking her to DC, buying her things to make her happy, and not killing her when he had the chance. He'd provided her with material things and made her look to him for her survival.

She continued to read on. "The perpetrator threatens to murder the victim and paints the picture of having the capability to do so. The hostage figures it safer to align with the captor, bear the adversity of captivity, than to resist and face murder."

Apple ended her research by reading some more. "When realization from the hostage seeps in that their life was spared, the hostage sees the perpetrator as showing some degree of kindness. Kindness is the basis of the Stockholm syndrome; the condition will not develop unless the captor exhibits it in some form toward the hostage. However, the hostages often misinterpret a lack of abuse as kindness and may develop feelings of gratitude for this supposed compassion."

Apple thought about how Supreme had once threatened her and her family, and then sucked her into being in a relationship with him with his gifts, sex, and charm. She felt Supreme had manipulated her over the summer. Suddenly feeling disgusted and used, she ran into the bathroom, fell to her knees, positioned her face over the toilet, and began vomiting.

"Fuck me!" she uttered.

She stayed in the bathroom staring into space for about an hour. Then she got up, washed her face, collected herself, and devised a plan to get back at Supreme. He'd brought hell and shame upon her family, and for that he needed to pay with his life.

The following day, Apple got into her Benz and drove to Lincoln projects. Even though she had a sudden disgust in her heart and despised Supreme, she loved her newfound life and wasn't about to give it up. She still had business to take care of.

The first thing on her agenda for the day was confronting Ayesha. Apple had got word that not only did she fuck Supreme to cancel her debt, she was also talking shit about her.

Ayesha let it be known in public that she wasn't scared of Apple, shouting out, "I remember when she used to be a dumb, broke bitch! That bitch ain't shit to me!"

Apple didn't take too lightly to the insult and wanted to teach Ayesha a lesson. She parked her Benz and strutted into the building in her tight Seven jeans and stylish top, her .22 and small blade concealed. When the locals saw Apple around the way, they knew to expect trouble. She only came through to either collect money or whip a bitch's ass.

Apple walked up to two passing young ladies and

asked, "Any of y'all seen Ayesha around?"

"No," they replied.

Apple kept it moving and continued to ask around for her, but no one knew where she was at. She was beginning to think they were covering for her, knowing she was there to hurt Ayesha for the gossip she was spreading.

An hour later, Apple still didn't have any luck finding Ayesha, so she decided to call it quits and come back the next day to continue her search. She stood beside her Benz, the sun slowly dropping below the horizon. The streets were teeming with people, from the young to the old, and with the first day of school right around the corner, the young ones were trying to have fun for the last few days of summer vacation.

Apple lit up a cigarette, leaned against her Benz, and looked around at her old hood. She didn't live too far from it and didn't miss it at all. She hated the sight of her old building—too many memories for her. She wanted out of Harlem, period, but the only place she'd been to was DC.

She exhaled the smoke, took a few more pulls, and was ready to extinguish her cigarette and get into her car. Just then, she noticed Cross' gleaming black Range Rover coming to a stop across the street from her. Her heart fluttered, and she couldn't keep her eyes off his truck. The windows were tinted, and his chrome wheels shined like a brand new dime. Apple knew it was Cross' truck because she knew that man's ride from blocks away. She missed staring at her eye-candy. Apple so badly wanted to jump his bones, and in a heartbeat, she was ready to become his woman. The way he made her feel, it should be considered a crime. She would have done anything for him.

Apple watched from the short distance of three lanes of traffic, as Cross stepped out of his truck clad in a bright red velour sweat suit, matching Jordan's, and his long chain gleaming with diamonds. She smiled, feeling like she had the courage to finally holla at him the way she wanted to, but her smile was short-lived when she saw Kola step out from the passenger's side of the Range Rover. Apple looked on with bewilderment, which soon turned to bitterness and hate when she witnessed Cross pull Kola into his arms like she was his woman, hugging and kissing on her in public.

"Oh no, this bitch didn't," she whispered under her breath in total disbelief.

Apple was fuming and couldn't keep her eyes off Kola hugged up on Cross. It was apparent that they had become a couple. She wanted to know how the fuck it happened. She just stood there watching the two enter the Chinese takeout spot. For a moment, Apple was lost. It seemed like her nightmare was never-ending. She couldn't believe how Kola betrayed her. Kola knew of her feelings for Cross.

She tossed her cigarette and hurriedly moved across the street, not caring about traffic, and stormed into the Chinese establishment.

"Bitch, how fuckin' dare you cross me like that!" she shouted, attracting the attention of other customers.

Kola was hugged up on Cross as they waited for their

food. When she saw Apple barging into the place, she smirked. Then she suddenly slid from her man's arm and rushed toward Apple with that same fury. The twin sisters were up in each other's faces, while the customers stood around watching the two identical twins size each other up.

Kola shouted, "I just stepped up on somethin' that you were too scared to push up on!"

"Nah, fuck that! You knew how I felt about him! How you do me like that, Kola? You a foul bitch!"

"Bitch, fuck you! Don't come up in my face talkin' about betrayal, after what happened to Nichols! You ain't got no fuckin' right!"

"Why you gotta keep throwing that in my face?"

"'Cause you and Mommy are some dumb bitches. But it's all good, 'cause you gonna get yours, bitch!"

"Kola, don't fuck wit' me!" Apple was so close up on her sister, she could see the pores of her skin.

Cross got between the two. "Y'all need to chill." He grabbed his woman away from Apple, who was crushed when she saw how Cross took hold of Kola in that caring manner.

"Yeah, I got him, bitch. He's wit' me. You hear me, tramp? I got him. So go and continue fuckin' wit' that rapist killer, 'cause I'm doin' better!"

Apple exited the food spot with tears in her eyes and rushed across the street to her ride. She hastily got in behind the steering wheel, started up the car, and peeled off without caring about oncoming traffic, causing an approaching car to slam on its brakes to prevent crashing into her Benz.

Apple raced back home and hurried through her front door. She cried out for Denise, but she wasn't home. She peeled off her clothing, leaving a small trail from the living room to the bathroom. She suddenly needed to cleanse herself in the steaming hot water. She got into the shower and let the hot water cascade off her rich light-brown skin, wishing she could just wash the pain and heartbreak away. She was fucked up. Just thinking about Kola fucking Cross made her want to go insane. It wasn't supposed to happen like that. Cross was supposed to be her man. She was the one he was supposed to wife up.

Apple remained in the shower for a long time, wanting to make the pain go away, scrubbing herself and letting the water soothe her. So much had happened in the past three months. In fact her life had gone a quick 180 degrees in such a short time.

After spending an hour in the shower, she stepped out the bathroom, wrapped in a towel, to find that Supreme and Guy Tony had arrived and were lingering downstairs.

Supreme looked at her and asked, "Where you been at?"

"Out."

"What you got for me then?"

"What?" Apple responded, confused.

"I heard you was out today trying to collect. So where it at?"

"I didn't collect shit today, Supreme, and right now,

I'm not in the mood for your shit."

Supreme glanced at Guy Tony and then glared back at Apple with a look that let her know he didn't like her response. His hulking figure moved closer to her. "Bitch, who the fuck you talking to like that?"

"Supreme, just step the fuck off! Fo' real!"

Apple wasn't in the mood for his nonsense and had enough to deal with. She spun on her heels with an attitude and was about to go back into the bedroom, but Supreme grabbed her from behind with brute force and tossed her into the couch like he was a tornado.

"You dumb bitch, watch your fuckin' mouth wit' me!" he yelled. "Remember who the fuck you talking to! You work for me! I fuckin' made you! You fuckin' understand me? Everything you got is 'cause of me."

Apple lifted herself off the couch, but Supreme knocked her back down with a quick backhand slap. Then he snatched the towel from around her, leaving her stark naked in front of company.

Guy Tony didn't turn his head. Instead, he stared at Apple's lovely figure.

Apple clutched the side of her face and wiped the little blood from her mouth. She flaunted a defiant stare and mockingly replied, "Yeah, that's the fuckin' Supreme I know. I guess the honeymoon is over now. Huh, baby?"

"Apple, don't fuckin' test me. I'll fuck ya whole world up!"

Apple didn't know where his sudden rage came from, but she knew for sure that Supreme had to die, either by her hands or someone else's. He had gotten away with too much, and he needed to expire promptly.

Supreme stood over Apple with the towel gripped tightly in his hand. His eyes were cold and his demeanor so chilling toward her, one more wrong word and she wouldn't leave the house alive. "Get dressed," he told her. "We goin' out."

Apple didn't say another word. She slowly picked herself up off the couch, with every inch of her petite, curvy body exposed to Guy Tony, and slowly made her way into the bedroom, knowing Guy Tony's eyes were glued to her backside.

～～～

That same evening, the trio walked into a chic soul food eatery on the West Side of town. Supreme had gotten word through the streets that the business was failing, and the owner, Bobby, was reluctantly ready to take a buyout from a few willing investors. Supreme knew that Bobby had put his heart and soul into the business for eight years, but he was hit hard during the recession, and business was never the same. The neighborhood's soul food restaurants had long been losing business as a result of changing tastes, intensifying health concerns, and rising costs, and with the current economic downturn, many Harlem businesses were declaring bankruptcy.

It was the opportunity Supreme had been waiting for. He wanted to offer the owner his proposal when the business was at its worst, make Bobby believe that a loan from him could boost things up to where they used to be.

Then when he was locked in, he would go in for the "juice" system, and Bobby wouldn't see it coming.

Apple sat down with Supreme and Guy Tony at the eatery, where everything from Southern-style biscuits and smoked pork chops to homegrown collard greens were served the way mama made it. Supreme admired the place with its Southern feel and the black baby grand piano situated in the back for the nights when the band entertained the customers with jazz and blues. Supreme wanted in.

The trio ordered their meals, and when they were halfway through eating, Supreme asked the waitress for Bobby by name. She nodded and walked off.

Apple remained quiet and barely touched her catfish and beans.

A moment later, Bobby came walking out of the kitchen following behind the waitress. The two men instantly recognized each other, and Supreme stood to greet the owner.

"Supreme, it's been a long time," Bobby said with a halfhearted smile.

"I know. Too long, my friend."

"And what brings you to my place?"

"How's business?"

Bobby looked at Supreme with cautious eyes. "It can always be better."

"I know. But is there someplace private where we can talk?"

"In my office."

"Then you lead the way." Supreme gestured with his hand.

Bobby looked reluctant at first, but he knew Supreme didn't take no for an answer. The two men disappeared into a back room, leaving Apple seated with Guy Tony.

When Supreme was gone, Apple looked at Guy Tony and asked, "So did you enjoy the show earlier?"

"What you mean?"

"You like what you saw?" Apple asked, referring to when Supreme stripped her of the towel and left her naked.

Guy Tony just smiled bashfully and took a sip of his drink.

"I know you did. You can never keep your eyes off me. Why's that, Guy? Huh? You wanna fuck me?"

"You're Supreme's lady, and he's like a father to me."

"And? He don't own me."

"I see different."

"You do, huh? And what you see different?" Apple asked with a smile.

"I see you a fuckin' tease," he spat. "So just let it be."

"A tease, huh? Well, wit' you, I don't have to be."

"What you gettin' at, Apple? Huh? You tryin' to have me killed? You know how Supreme feels about you. Why you doin' this?" he demanded with a serious tone.

"'Cause I'm tired of him and his shit. And I know you are too."

"What?"

"I see how he treats you, looks at you. You been under

his wing for how long, and he still got you pushing him around like you in *Driving Miss Daisy*. And what you got to show for yourself? Nothing much. Don't you want more outta life, Guy? I mean, I been wit' him for nearly three months, and he done showed me more love than his right-hand man. I know you see it, Guy. Don't try to ignore it."

Guy Tony didn't respond, but Apple knew she had him thinking about her words. She leaned back in her chair, crossed her legs underneath the table, and looked at him with such an intense seductive stare, he had to turn his head in order to control his hormones.

"Stop playin' wit' me, Apple. I'm not that nigga to fuck wit'," he warned lightly.

Apple chuckled. "I never said you were." The two locked eyes across the table, and Apple made it clear by her look that she was available to him whenever he wanted it.

Guy Tony felt uncomfortable. He squirmed in his chair, finding it nearly impossible to fight the urges he'd felt for Apple ever since they'd first met.

Apple continued teasing. "It's your move, Guy. How do you want it?"

"You're playin' a dangerous game, Apple."

"If you think so."

The conversation quickly ended when Supreme returned to the table gloating.

"Shit is good," he uttered to Guy. "It's fuckin' good."

"Everything good, boss?"

"Yeah, it is. I can see us running this place in three

months or so. That burnt-out Bobby ain't gonna be able to keep up wit' this shit. But I'll let him believe so. It's all good, my nigga."

Apple kept quiet and took a few sips from her drink.

Supreme looked down at her. "You finish eating?"

"I've *been* done," Apple returned in a sneering, but subtle tone that Supreme didn't catch.

She pushed herself away from the table and walked ahead of Supreme and Guy Tony to smoke a cigarette. While standing outside the restaurant, she thought about her future. She wanted out of the relationship, but not out of the lifestyle. She had grown addicted to it.

When Supreme and Guy Tony exited the eatery, Apple was ready to go home. As she and Supreme waited for Guy Tony to pull the car around, she kept her mouth shut. She'd had enough of Supreme and didn't feel like arguing with him.

During the ride home, Apple sat in the backseat, while Supreme rode shotgun. She noticed Guy Tony glancing back at her every so often. She smiled at herself and knew it was only a matter of time before things went her way.

Chapter 22

Apple's seduction finally paid off. Guy Tony was now grinding between her soft, thick thighs in the bedroom of her brownstone home in the early afternoon. Supreme was out of town on business, leaving Guy Tony alone with Apple to keep watch over, but the two fucked passionately during his absence.

Guy heatedly panted while rocking on top of her, pressed against her snugly and thrusting in and out of her love hole. He gripped the sheets like a man being electrocuted, crying out from the feeling of her good pussy when she ran her nails down his back, pressed her thighs into his sides, and whispered in his ear.

Apple had continually teased Guy whenever he was around the house, walking around in tight booty shorts, showering with the door ajar and even drying off with the door open, leaving the door open while naked in the bedroom, allowing him to catch a peek of her. Whenever she got the chance, she would rub up against him and stare at him with a look that said, *Fuck me!*

Guy Tony couldn't resist his urges any longer, and while Supreme was away on business in DC, that's when he started to play. The first night they fucked, Guy Tony was quick—in and out of Apple like a minute-man. Their second encounter, Apple sucked his dick so good, his legs felt like jelly afterwards. Her pussy was the best.

But Apple couldn't say the same for the dick. He wasn't big like Supreme, but less than average, and his strokes didn't hit the bar. He was pretty much whack in the bedroom. But Apple tolerated him, and each passionate night together, Guy was falling more in love with her. She was constantly in his ear, trying to persuade him to do the unthinkable—murder Supreme so they could take over the loan-sharking and bookkeeping business. But Guy Tony was against it, reminding Apple that Supreme was like a father to him.

The more they fucked, the more Apple manipulated Guy Tony to believe the illicit business would be better off run by the two of them, proclaiming that Supreme was getting sloppy and old. She promised him that they could become the next Bonnie and Clyde, lovers and partners in crime.

The pussy had Guy Tony possessed. The way Apple fucked, he just couldn't get enough of it.

"You're asking the impossible, Apple. Supreme taught me this business. He always looked out for me."

"And now it's time for you to implement it and get from under his wing," she replied.

"Easier said than done."

Guy Tony had been in business with Supreme since he was fifteen. He remembered the day when he had no one, and was homeless and starving on the cold city streets. He was willing to steal just for a meal and slept in the parks during the coldest days, trying to keep himself warm by bundling up in layers of clothing. Guy's parents were both killed on the streets when he was eight, and there was no other family to take him in. He was put into foster care, but ran away when he was thirteen, and had been surviving on the streets ever since then.

Supreme pulled him off the streets, put clothes on his back, and fed him. He put money in Guy Tony's pocket and treated him like a human being, while everyone else just ignored him and looked down at him like he was shit they were trying to scrape off from the bottom of their shoes. Guy began to resent society and thought about suicide most days, but it was Supreme who brought him back to life.

Supreme's generosity came with a cost, though. Guy Tony began doing Supreme's dirty work, beating up men and sometimes women who failed to pay on time, even setting up and shooting people who crossed his boss. Supreme had Guy Tony in the trenches, hustling and working in the same streets he had rescued him from.

Guy Tony was once a humble and shy young man, but his years of working for Supreme had changed him into something that most days he wasn't proud of. He had witnessed things in the past four years that kept him up at night. One such thing was Nichols' murder. He hated having witnessed what Supreme's goons did to that young girl. He wished he hadn't been there. Yet, being the loyal disciple he was, he kept his mouth shut, not wanting to be a snitch.

∽∾∾

As Guy Tony lay between Apple's legs after climaxing, she gently stroked his ego and low haircut, asking, "You love me?"

He looked up at her and sincerely replied, "Apple, you know that I've loved you since grade school, but shit changed. I ain't that young boy anymore. I've seen and done things that I'm not proud of, but to go against the man that brought me life and hope . . . yo, you asking too much."

"Am I, Anthony?" Apple said, calling him by the name she once knew him by when they were kids.

He laughed. "Nobody's called me that since I was ten."

"You remember when we would play together and how close we used to be? We were young, but you promised to look after me, like in the fairytales we used to read. You were my prince. How did things go so wrong between us?" Apple was kicking game.

"I don't know."

The two had grown up together, but felt like strangers because it'd been so long since they'd shared words together. While they talked, Apple kept stroking him like he was a soft puppy in her arms. Convincing him to go along with her plan was harder than she'd expected. Supreme had seriously brainwashed Guy Tony. Still, she was determined to get through to him.

Two weeks after their affair started, Apple continued trying to win over Guy Tony to go along with her agenda. They continued to fuck, but with Supreme back home, they had to be more discreet.

Supreme started to become more abusive toward Apple, and when her mother would try to stop him, he would threaten to take away everything she had and beat her too, forcing Denise to look on helplessly while her daughter suffered. But Denise cared more about the good life than saving her daughter from the hands of a monster.

Guy Tony hated that Supreme suddenly started to beat on Apple for every little thing she did wrong. Apple would try to fight back, but Supreme always overpowered her. Guy Tony would stand there watching the abuse, which reminded him of the way he stood there watching her little sister suffer the same way. Guy Tony kept his composure, but his eyes became more menacing.

One night, Supreme attacked Apple so bad that he'd left her unable to move in the living room. He stormed out of the apartment, leaving Guy Tony to watch over the badly beaten Apple.

Guy Tony picked her up and took her into the bedroom to lay her across the bed. He then tended to her wounds.

When Apple looked up at him with her black-and-blue eye, and bruised cheek, he said, "I'll do it."

Apple smiled, weakly.

She now had Guy Tony where she wanted him—doing the dirty work. She knew she couldn't pull the hit off by herself. With Supreme out the way, a new day would dawn. Apple felt she was skilled and vicious enough to fill his shoes in the illicit business he had built.

Smiling, she rose up to passionately kiss Guy Tony like he would be the only man she would love from now on.

Guy held Apple in his arms affectionately, not wanting to let her go. He was ready to do the unimaginable for her—murder Supreme, the man who he had looked up to like a father since he was fifteen. The wheels started to turn, and Apple was ready to solidify her destiny in the underworld.

Several days later, Apple was so horny and intoxicated with sexual pleasure that her voracious lovemaking pushed her physical boundaries that night—from biting, pinching, and slapping to autoerotic asphyxiation and creative breaches of body cavities. She became a beast. It turned her on knowing that Supreme would soon meet his demise at the hands of the man he once trusted and even called his own son.

So she fucked Supreme like never before, riding him with the bed shaking wildly and feeling his thick erection rooted in her, filling her up. It was the point of no return for her.

Apple's legs quivered uncontrollably against his sides.

She curved frontward, locking eyes with her lover, and dug her nails into his chest. Then she attacked his neck with bites, feeling the dick plunging in and out of her.

Supreme loved every minute of it and wondered what caused such animalistic behavior in his girl. He rested on his back, gripping Apple's sweaty thighs, and felt himself about to explode. "Ugh! Ugh! Ugh shit! Ugh! Ah! Ugh shit! Damnit!" he grunted with ferociousness, feeling Apple's sugary walls shrink around his length.

"You like it, huh? You like how this pussy feels?" Apple asked, working her hips into him.

He crushed her sides with his massive grip, and his facial expression turned ugly like death because the pussy was too good to him.

"Fuck me!" Apple cried out. "Fuck me!"

And Supreme did just that. He pushed Apple off him and speedily repositioned her on her stomach. Then with the technique of a snake, he slid his concrete dick back into her froggy-style.

Apple pushed her face into the pillow and groaned from the harsh entry, her legs spread open like the letter V, and his dick plunging inside of her like a piece of machinery.

Supreme fucked her in that position until she purred and squirmed underneath his solid physique, feeling sandwiched between a piece of good dick and the mattress. Soon after her nut, she felt Supreme's dick throbbing intensely inside of her, knowing he was about to come. He moved against her like an android, focused on his nut and nothing else.

"Ugh . . . yes. Ugh . . . yes. Damnit! I'm fuckin' comin'!" he screamed out, one hand tangled in her hair and the other pushing against her side as he swayed on top of her, brewing his nut.

"Aaahhhh shit! Oh shit! Come for me, baby! Come for me," Apple exclaimed through closed eyes and gritted teeth. She felt the final thrusts into her, and then came the explosion.

Supreme shook wildly on top of her and then, sweaty and exhausted, fell on his back next to Apple. "Shit, baby. You need to start fuckin' me like that more often," he said, breathing hard.

"I assume you enjoyed it," she replied with a light smile.

"Fuck, yeah!"

Hiding her contempt, Apple looked at him, massaging his chest with care, nestled against him like he was a soft, giant teddy bear. She threw her naked leg on top of him and began kissing her man with a counterfeit love.

Supreme was none the wiser to her plot to kill him. He thought everything was all good. He slowly closed his eyes and felt relaxed enough to fall fast asleep with Apple beside him.

Once his eyes closed, however, Apple's pleased gaze instantly changed to a scowl, and she removed herself from his reach and quickly donned her robe. She looked down at him sleeping soundly and felt the need to just spit on him. She walked out the bedroom and decided to wait for the opportunity to come knocking.

A half-hour later, Guy Tony came walking through the front door of the brownstone dressed in all-black. He had a nervous look about him, but Apple's sweet touch and smile made him want to carry out the hit.

"He's upstairs sleeping," she informed him.

Guy Tony nodded. He gripped a .45 with the latex gloves and proceeded up the stairs. When he got to the bedroom, which was silent and dark, he saw Supreme sleeping under the white sheets, out cold.

Apple moved behind Guy Tony, gently wrapping her arms around him, to assure him, and said, "Baby, just do it. Now is our chance."

Guy Tony glanced back at her with a deadpan expression. Then he sighed quietly and advanced into the room. He stood over Supreme's sprawled figure and pointed the gun at his head, but he couldn't look at his boss straight on, knowing he was about to snatch his life away. He gently placed the white sheet over Supreme's face, to avoid freezing up on the job, and then he fired at point-blank range into his face.

Bam! Bam! Bam!

Everything felt still.

Apple walked into the bedroom and stared down at the white sheets stained with crimson blood. She observed the blood dripping from Supreme's skull onto the floor, leaving a small puddle on the carpet. She smiled. "We need to get rid of the body," she said.

Guy Tony nodded, and the two then went into action,

securely wrapping Supreme's body in the sheets, putting duct tape around his legs, face, and wrists. The mattress was soaked with blood, and the carpet was ruined, so Apple and Guy Tony began to do a massive cleanup. After moving the body into the corner, they removed the bloody sheets and bed, and then tore up the carpet. It took them until morning to clean everything up, and they would have to dispose of the body the following night, since they couldn't do it during the day.

That same morning, Guy Tony and Apple had breakfast at a local diner and tried not to mention Supreme's murder at all. Apple dined on her meal like she was one of the regulars enjoying the day, while talking to Guy Tony in their corner booth tucked away in the back of the diner.

Apple noticed Guy Tony to be somewhat distant from her. She knew he was thinking about the killing. She took a swig of orange juice, her eyes fixed on him. "Look, don't worry about it. We gonna be a'ight. You hear me?"

"Yeah, I hear you."

"It needed to be done."

Guy Tony just looked at her, and it was then that he realized how cold and calculating Apple could be. She didn't flinch about the murder at all. She didn't care. It was obvious she didn't have any remorse for taking a life.

After breakfast, Apple went shopping on 59th Street, spending a small fortune on clothing and jewelry in Bloomingdales and a few boutiques in midtown Manhattan. She strutted around in her high heels and stylish outfit, carrying a few shopping bags, and like Scarface, she felt the world was hers.

The following night, she and Guy Tony continued on with their mission in covering up Supreme's murder. After the midnight hour, they carried the body out the door and stuffed him into the back of the Escalade. Guy knew of some men that would help dispose of the body for a sizable fee, no questions asked. They linked up with them in New Jersey, made the exchange, and before dawn were driving across the George Washington Bridge back into New York.

The past two days had been exhausting for Apple, but the deed was finally done. Now she was on her way up. Throughout that week, after Supreme's murder, she put the hit out on anyone who she felt might become a threat or a problem for her. She needed Guy Tony to have her back because he was well-liked and respected. Apple knew once he confirmed that she was "official business," the others would soon follow in line.

With Supreme MIA, people became suspicious and came to their own conclusions about his unexpected disappearance. There were arguments and speculations about Apple's quick rise to power, but Guy Tony quickly put the doubters in check—even if it meant putting the murder game down.

The one thing Apple's mother always taught her so well was, if you fuck a nigga the right way, he'll give you the world. Pussy made things happen. Apple couldn't be more proud of herself, because her sweet pussy had acquired her power and wealth.

Apple had one last thing to accomplish. Something personal. She wanted to send out a strong message.

It was a late Sunday night, when she rode shotgun in the Escalade, Guy Tony driving and another one of his goons seated in the backseat. The truck stopped in front of St. Nicholas projects on Eighth Avenue. Apple took a few pulls from the cigarette and watched the area as the goon in the backseat got out and tucked a .380 down his pants. He then disappeared into the projects, while she and Guy Tony waited patiently in the Escalade.

A short moment later, Ayesha emerged from her building and began walking toward Eighth Avenue in her tight jeans and trendy tight top that accentuated her ample breasts. Clutching her Gucci handbag, she was ready to catch a cab to meet her date, who was waiting for her in Times Square. She planned on having dinner at Planet Hollywood and then catching a comedy show with someone she really liked.

As Ayesha neared Eighth Avenue, Apple's hired goon quickly crept up behind her, raised the .380 to the back of her head, and fired twice into her skull, sending her smashing into the ground face first. The loud shot echoed throughout the projects, rousing residents and startling those close by. The goon ran off and jumped in the truck, leaving Ayesha's body spread out on the hard concrete, a pool of blood forming around her torn skull.

"Dumb bitch!" Apple stared at the body of her once close friend. "Talk that shit now."

Guy busted a U-turn on Eighth Avenue and sped up the block.

Apple wanted to send out a strong message to the community that doubted her power and wanted to talk shit about her. *Don't fuck with me!*

After Ayesha's murder, everyone soon got the message. They soon realized there was a new sheriff in town. Some thought she was even more vicious than Supreme.

Chapter 23

It was the heart of October, and Apple wasn't the only sister to step her game up. Kola felt she needed to outdo her sister.

Kola and Cross were an item in the hood. It was like the ultimate merger when they'd linked up. Kola was the envy of every chick throughout Harlem, with her being the first woman that Cross wifed up, and she made it known every day that Cross was her boo by styling in his Range Rover and being in his arms constantly. When they'd started doing business together, Cross realized she was smart and fierce, like a female version of him.

Kola and Cross obtained a contemporary three-bedroom single-family home in Yonkers, not too far from Yonkers Raceway. Their place was far enough from Harlem's active streets, but was a short enough drive to allow them to continue taking care of business.

Kola was happy. They were making money in every direction. Becoming a high-priced madam, her sex parties were continuing to blow up, and Cross had gotten a new drug connect, still having the hood on lockdown with product and muscle. Still, he had rivals who wanted to see his downfall, and he never knew when and how the feds were watching him.

Cross couldn't afford to have any slip-ups, so the couple kept everything discreet. No direct phone calls, no meetings with anyone that they didn't know personally, and no unnecessary violence, to avoid unwanted attention.

While Kola and Cross tried to keep a low profile, Apple was a different story. She was becoming the Tony Montana of Harlem, making enemies in every which way.

The sisters had their 18th birthday approaching soon, and Kola wanted to celebrate her birthday big, popping bottles and looking good, the way music moguls did. She wanted the biggest club, the jamming crowd, and the best DJ their money could get them, wanting to bring in her 18th birthday like a superstar.

She and Cross began putting everything in motion. It would be the party of the year. Kola's birthday bash was going to be held at, Cipriani's, a posh location in the city. She didn't want to spare any expenses and was ready to throw the wildest party, like she was P. Diddy himself. She felt she deserved it. The year had been good to her, despite the tragic loss of her sister. She still couldn't forgive Apple for it, and in her mind, both her sisters and mother died that day. She didn't want any dealings with them. And, though some time had passed, the pain was still fresh in her heart.

Apple had changed so much that the hood was saying

they could no longer tell the difference between the two sisters, both of them now in the same in style of dress and with fierce attitudes. Apple used to be the nonchalant, quiet one that the neighbors liked better. Now the only way the community could tell them apart was by the cars they drove—Apple in her powder blue Benz or Kola in her BMW 5-Series. The other distinction was by their boyfriends, Kola being with Cross, and Apple with Guy Tony.

It had been over a month since Supreme's death, and Apple was growing tired of Guy Tony's complaints. She thought he was bugging out, losing his mind. Every day it was the same thing with him. His conscience was eating him up inside, and he reminded Apple constantly.

"Shit is fucked up, Apple," he would say. "He's haunting me, yo. He is. I can feel him coming after me."

At first, Apple thought the feeling would pass, but with it being October, Guy's paranoia was becoming a problem for her. She knew he had killed before and wondered why he was suddenly bugging out over one murder.

"Guy, he's dead! He ain't comin' back! He's fuckin' dead!"

"Nah, you ain't the one that bodied him. I was. He's pissed at me, Apple. What we did was fucked up. You knew he was like a father to me. He helped me out, and I turned my back on him. Now his spirit is after me."

Apple knew the only way to shut Guy Tony up was

through sex. She would fuck him so good, his paranoia seemed to fade for days at a time, and he would be back to his normal self. Then the two would continue to get money through their loan-sharking and bookkeeping in Harlem and elsewhere, with Guy Tony being on point when he wasn't going loco.

But then a week or two later, it would be the same with him. Apple was growing tired of hearing his grievance about death, his guilt, and ghost stories. She once had the same horrid nightmares about Nichols, but with time, she had gotten better; money and power helping to relinquish the anguish.

Now she had a business to run, and Guy Tony wasn't making it any better with his antics. She needed him, though, because he was still her backbone, her muscle in the streets. She fed off of his reputation, while building hers.

Apple was enjoying the fruits of her hard labor, frequenting the top clubs in the city from downtown to uptown, sitting in VIP, popping bottles, dancing with the cuties, and flaunting her wealth. With tons of cash to spend, she had the world at her feet and felt unstoppable.

From Club Velour in midtown to the Versace Palace in downtown, Apple was the baddest chick making a name for herself. She didn't wait on any long lines or have to deal with the security. She and her crew would just roll up to the front entrance of the clubs in their motorcade of high-end cars, sometimes with more than a dozen people, and bypass the wait to get inside the happening party that night. Apple loved the nightlife like she loved sex. She worked hard during the day, and partied even harder when the lights went out.

She sat in the VIP section surrounded by her crew in Club Velour on Sixth Avenue, a sexy two-floored lounge housed in a candle-lit space with chocolate-brown walls and a Spanish-inspired décor, and a bar on each floor. The upstairs DJ had set the mood with '80s- and '90s-style hip-hop and rock. Apple had bottle service the entire night and admired the state-of-the-art technology with twenty large flat-screen TV's.

Apple, her long, black hair dancing around her shoulders, was dressed in a very tight Dolce & Gabbana dress that accentuated all her curves, and sported a pair of Versace shoes that seemed to give her long, defined legs six more inches.

She sat next to Guy Tony, who seemed removed from everything going on around him. He sat back in the VIP area and took a few sips of Moët.

"Guy, you a'ight?" she asked.

He nodded. "I'm good," he replied flatly.

Worried, Apple looked at him. He hadn't been himself lately. She was hoping he didn't bring up Supreme's death tonight. She just wanted to have a good time and enjoy the club scene. She downed Moët and Cristal, eyeing a few cuties that passed her way.

The manager didn't care or ask about her age. Apple knew that money talked and bullshit walked, and with the small fortune she was spending in Velour, the staff,

NISA SANTIAGO

security and management just looked the other way.

The DJ played Drake's "Find Your Love," and Apple jumped from her seat, swaying her hips to the beat and singing along to one of her favorite tracks. With the half-empty bottle of Moët clutched in her hand, the seventeen-year-old showed the boys her rhythm on the dance floor as she moved to the beat, keeping up with the other girls.

The men stood back and watched the show she put on, craving to push up on her smoothness, place their hands upon her soft thighs, and grind against her for some pleasure. But her reputation had preceded her, and she intimidated a lot of the men standing around.

One individual quickly caught Apple's eye in the crowded spot. She noticed him by the bar standing next to a few goons, sipping on drinks and displaying that hardened thug image. Apple hooked her eyes on his smooth, dark skin and long braids that fell behind his head like tightropes. He was tall, well-dressed in a crisp white jacket and jeans, and sporting a pair of fresh white "Ups." From afar, the man had Apple's undivided attention without having to say one word to her. His demeanor kind of reminded her of Cross'—unconcerned about anything or anyone because their presence was authority enough to shut things down.

The two locked eyes, and it didn't take long for her handsome stranger to leave his goon's side and push his way through the crowd to approach her. Apple waited patiently for his arrival. She continued to dance, taking sips from the Moët. When he got near, she looked at him, but didn't say a word.

He leaned in close to her ear and asked, "What's your name?"

"Why?"

"I don't need a why," he boldly spat back. "Just my question answered."

Apple smiled, admiring his approach. It was stern, and to the point. She knew he was hood by his conduct. He towered over her, styling with his 18-karat Rolex watch, long, sparkling diamond chain, and diamond-encrusted earrings in both ears.

"Apple," she said. "And yours?"

"Chico."

Chico took Apple by her wrist and began dancing against her without her permission. He removed the Moët bottle from her hand and put it into the hands of a stranger next to them that dared not ask why. He moved against Apple with the same rhythm, keeping up with her flow. Apple worked her ass and hips against him, loving that he was on beat, unlike most niggas in the lounge.

They danced tightly together for a few songs and then moved to the bar, where Chico offered to buy her anything. When he invited her to his VIP section of the club, Apple didn't hesitate to join him, forgetting about her own section. The two hit it off right away and conversed about everything.

Chico was from Washington Heights and was the man in the area. He was a four-key-a-week nigga with a vile crew underneath him, and he was articulate and smart.

"So you're into loan-sharking and bookkeeping, huh?" Chico laughed.

"What's so funny?" Apple asked.

"I just can't see a beautiful woman like you shaking niggas down, especially in that dress."

"What they say, never judge a book by its cover?"

"Yeah, but I'm ready to turn your pages." Chico smiled.

"I'm not some weak bitch, Chico. I worked my way up and got mines just like the rest of you niggas out here."

"And I'm not mad at you, Apple. I respect that. Shit, I don't respect a lazy broad with her hand always out for something. You understand?" he replied, seriously.

Apple nodded.

"So, no boyfriend?"

"No. And yourself?"

"Nah. Can't find a woman able to keep up with me."

"And what is it that you're looking for?"

"The female version of me," Chico joked.

"You might've just found her," Apple said, staring at him with meaning to her words.

Chico chuckled. He sat back in his seat, took a swig of Cristal, and looked at Apple with eyes that showed the thug in him. And Apple matched his with her own.

"I like you, Apple. You're my kind of girl."

"I try to be."

Chico poured her another glass of the flowing champagne, and the two continued their talk. Apple was nestled next to him, feeling that tingling sensation between her legs as Chico spoke the sweetest things into her ear that she needed to hear. He made her pussy jump. Chico was too sexy and exciting. He had all the qualities that she desired in a man—strong, fine, confident, and powerful. She wanted to fuck him.

Chico made Apple forget about Cross and Kola. In her eyes, Chico was better than Cross, or so she tried to convince herself. But the two men had the same qualities, and with Chico running Washington Heights with his drug crew, Apple saw the perfect business opportunity for herself. If they were to link up and become a couple, she would definitely be the queen bee in the city. Chico would become her country with an army.

Chico admired everything about Apple and didn't care for her age, though Apple did inform him that she had an eighteenth birthday coming up. He was young himself, twenty-three, and a woman like Apple on his arm would be the ideal match for him.

As the night continued on, she laughed and drank with him, music blaring in their ears. Everything was all good, except for the jealous eyes that peered over at Chico as he mingled closely with Apple.

The scowl on Guy Tony's face was evident. He disapproved of Apple flirting with Chico and wanted to intervene, but he downed his brew and blended in with the crowd of revelers.

With dawn looming and the lounge's crowd slowly dwindling, Apple decided she wanted to spend the rest of the night with Chico. They were going to stop and eat at a diner. Then she would see his place in Washington Heights.

Apple followed Chico to his cocaine-white 745 BMW sitting on polished chrome rims. Their short walk to his car was interrupted when Guy Tony called out to Apple from the exiting crowd of Velour.

"Yo, Apple! Where you goin'?" he shouted in a not-so-friendly demeanor.

Apple spun around on her heels and shouted back, "I'll be back, Guy! Just chill out!"

Chico looked at Guy Tony and figured the man would a problem later on. He'd noticed the way Guy Tony stared at him throughout the night, his eyes showing a trace of hate. Chico smirked at him and continued to guide Apple toward his car.

"Apple, I need to holla at you!" Guy Tony called out again.

Apple, frustrated with his nagging, spun around on her heels and shouted, "What the fuck you want, Guy? I need to talk about business!"

Guy Tony walked up to the two, ignoring Chico and focusing his look on Apple, and said, "I need a word wit' you."

Apple sighed. She then turned to Chico. "Give me a minute, a'ight?"

Chico nodded.

Guy Tony directed Apple away from Chico, and they walked to the corner.

She glared at him. "What the fuck is wrong wit' you?"

"What the fuck is wrong wit' *you*?" he barked through clenched teeth. "You goin' to fuck that nigga?"

"No, I'm goin' to talk business with him."

"I don't believe you."

"Look, Guy, I'm a grown fuckin' woman. I don't need you babysitting me. I can handle my own, you fuckin' understand me? Now let me handle my shit, and I'll talk to you when I get back." Apple strutted off, leaving him standing there.

Guy Tony wanted to believe that she was actually going to talk business with Chico, but that feeling in the pit of his stomach told him otherwise. He watched her climb into Chico's BMW, and it sped off.

∽∞∽

Apple found comfort in Chico's exclusive two-bedroom apartment in Washington Heights, New York. Chico's spot was tricked out with 46-inch flat-screens, high-end stereo system, a fine leather furniture set, granite bathroom with a sunken tub, and a king-size bed in the sizeable bedroom.

Apple wore one of Chico's throwback Giants jerseys, being naked underneath, and lay in his bed smoking a cigarette and staring at music videos on the LCD after the intense fuck she had with him. The dick in her couldn't have been any better. She felt fortunate that he was packing—eight inches and better—and that he knew how to work it.

Chico stepped out of the bathroom shirtless, parading a few tattoos on his chest and arms. His lean physique wasn't as muscular as Cross' or Supreme's, but he was still able to hold his own. He removed a Newport from the dwindling pack and lit one up. He then exhaled and took a seat on the bed next to Apple.

"Damn, I like your style." He smiled at her. "You know how to fuck, fo' real."

"I'm here to please. So what now?"

"What you mean?"

"I mean, am I just a fuck and a throwaway? Or you wanna make it happen?"

Chico looked at her. "Damn! You're blunt with it, I see."

"I mean, I'm not tryin' to waste your time, and I know you ain't tryin' to waste mine. I'm about my business. Hopefully, you are too."

"So what you wanna make happen?"

Apple snuggled close to Chico and kissed him on his back. "I want you and me to happen. I like your style too. I know we'll go good together."

Chico took another drag and thought about her proposal. "I don't even know you."

"You knew me well enough to bring me to your crib and fuck me."

He chuckled. "And if you know me, I don't bring broads back to my crib . . . especially ones that I meet from the club."

"Well, I'm special like that."

"I guess you are."

Apple held him in her arms and felt the warmth of

his body against hers. She ran her hands across his chest, touching him with sensitivity. *He is the one*, she thought. Chico was the one she needed to complete her. Kola had her Cross, the nigga that she'd loved since forever, so now she wanted and needed Chico.

Chico continued to smoke, thinking about it. He then turned to face Apple, kindly moving himself from her sensuous touch, and looked at her carefully. "Seventeen, huh?"

"Do I fuck like one?" she grilled back with attitude.

Chico chuckled. "I see you're a wild one."

"Then let me show you how wild I can really get," Apple replied with a teasing smile. Dropping to her knees, she situated herself between Chico's legs. She took a hold of his thick penis and slowly began stroking him with her firm grip. Then, without hesitation, she took his dick into her mouth.

Chico groaned from the feel of her lips that were soft as cotton. She went down on his throbbing dick to the base, raised herself up, and toyed with the mushroom tip with her tongue.

"Oh shit! Oh shit! That feels good," he moaned.

Apple continued to mouth-fuck him, massaging his nuts while doing so and going into overdrive on his dick.

Chico clutched his bed sheets tightly with the feeling that, if he let go, he would fall from the bed. It didn't take long for him to explode, some of his semen landing on the side of Apple's face.

"Damn! You suck some good dick!"

She laughed as she wiped her face clean. "Is that wild enough for you?"

Chico knew Apple was the one that was up to his speed. From the time he'd met her in the club, he knew there was something special about her. She carried herself differently from other girls he'd met. She didn't fear him, and she wasn't scared to be herself. He liked that she was real and on the come-up. Chico was a rich nigga, and he needed a superstar by his side. Apple quickly proved herself to be the one.

He lifted her off her knees and tossed her on the bed, where she bounced and giggled. "Your turn," he stated.

Apple smiled, spread her legs for him, and gasped as he ate her pussy.

❦

The next morning, Apple was fully dressed and willing to take a cab home, but Chico volunteered to drive her. She climbed into his Beamer, and they drove into the West Side of Harlem. She got out with a smile. Her business with Chico was official, and with his backing, she knew she would definitely become the queen of New York.

It seemed like she and Kola were going neck and neck in a win-all race for Harlem, both sisters feeling like they needed to be better than the other. Kola already felt she had a big enough head start, but Apple was gaining fast.

Apple walked through her front door early that morning, and her mother was coming home right behind her. Denise got out of a green Durango and staggered up the steps behind her daughter. She was dressed like she had come from the strip club—short mini-skirt, tight crochet halter top, shoes in her hand, and her hair in disarray, like she had just fucked the nigga in the backseat of the truck.

She looked at Apple and asked, "Who dat in the Beamer?"

"None of your business."

"Well, damn, Apple!"

"Ma, I'm tired. Not now wit' your shit."

"I was just asking."

Apple shouted. "Ma, just leave it alone! Damn! You don't know how to fuckin' close your mouth sometimes! Stay the fuck out my business!"

Denise twisted her face at her daughter. "Oh, so you think 'cause we ain't in the projects anymore that you can disrespect me like that?"

Apple stared at her mother and harshly replied, "Yeah." She then walked into her bedroom, leaving her mother dumbfounded in the living room. Chico was on her mind that morning, and she didn't want to think about anything else.

Apple kicked off her shoes, and after checking a few things in the bedroom, she just wanted to lie down for a while, but her cell phone ringing prevented that. She looked at the caller ID and saw that it was Guy Tony calling. She sighed, wanting to ignore his call. However, she knew it would only piss him off even more. So, reluctantly, she answered.

"What, Guy?" she spoke halfheartedly.

NISA SANTIAGO

"You just now getting home?" he asked.

"Why you care?"

"You fucked him, right?"

"Guy, you need to really chill."

"Don't fuckin' tell me to chill, Apple!" he screamed. "I did a lot for you, you fuckin' hear me?"

Apple became a little worried.

Guy Tony continued, "I'm telling you, Apple, don't fuckin' play me. I did Supreme for you 'cause we supposed to be together."

"Guy, is you crazy? I'm hanging up now. You wildin', nigga . . . over the phone. Is you fuckin' sick? Good night." Apple hung up and tossed her phone aside.

It rang again, but she refused to pick it up. She knew it was Guy Tony calling back. She was really growing tired of his antics. She sat at the foot of her bed in her quiet room, deep in thought about the situation with him. He had gotten her this far, but she worried about him. It was getting to the point where she thought, if push came to shove—with his jealously and hallucinations about his guilt and ghosts—she would have to do the inevitable and have him killed also. She had come too far to be pulled back down.

Chapter 24

Apple was on cloud nine, with her eighteenth birthday approaching soon, and her newfound relationship with Chico. Word had gotten out quickly about the couple, the new Bonnie and Clyde of the hood, the two of them almost inseparable. Business was good, and her love life was even better. Still, the tension between her and Kola was increasing on the streets. There was conflict wherever she turned, bloodshed right around the corner.

When news of Apple's relationship with Chico, a well-known rising kingpin, reached Kola and Cross, Cross was furious. Chico was the man responsible for trying to move in on his turf. They were at war for Harlem—with dead bodies on both sides. Cross felt that Apple was disrespecting him by sleeping with the enemy.

Apple's response back to Kola and her man was, "Fuck you!"

❧

Cross wasn't the only one unhappy about Apple's new relationship with Chico. Guy Tony sat in his car with a loaded pistol in the seat next to him. He downed a bottle of Mad Dog 20/20 and mumbled to himself. Slumped in his seat, he gazed at the heavy rain cascading off his windshield. He reflected on his past. His life had never been easy. Still, he felt the ultimate betrayal. His mentor was dead, and the burden he carried made him feel like he was sinking into the concrete.

Guy Tony finished the bottle and tossed it to the floor. He picked up his pistol, looked at it like he was examining it for inspection, and cocked it back. "That fuckin' bitch!"

The heavy rainfall engulfed his car and fogged up his window. He couldn't think rationally and felt the walls closing in around him. Placing the gun back on the seat, he took out his cell phone and quickly called Apple, who answered after the second ring.

"What, Guy?"

"You fuckin' owe me, Apple."

"What's wrong wit' you? What are you talking about?"

"*You* is what's wrong wit' me. You're a connivin' bitch. You think I wouldn't find out the truth about that nigga?"

Apple sighed heavily. "It is what it is, Guy. There's nothing else I can tell you."

"You used me, bitch. You fuckin' used me and hurt me. You got what you wanted, huh? That nigga got your back now, so there ain't no need for me anymore."

"You sound drunk, Guy. You need to get the fuck off the phone and get yourself together."

"What I need is you. You know I fuckin' love you."

"Nigga, move the fuck on. I don't love you. Can't you

see that, muthafucka? We about business, not love."

"So it's like that? You fuckin' used me to get what you want, and now ain't no love for me anymore? You fuckin' that nigga, huh? You think he's gonna have your back, Apple, when shit hits the fan?"

"Guy, get yourself right. You're a fuck-up right now, always have been. You let Supreme use you, and I just came along and did the same. Face it, nigga—You're a follower, not a leader."

"Fuck you, Apple!"

"But look at the bright side, Guy. You got to fuck me, right? I mean, I'm the best you ever gonna have . . . and you're almost better than most. It was good while it lasted, but you need to move on. There ain't gonna never be an *us*."

"So you're feelin' untouchable now, huh, bitch, since you spreadin' your legs for that cornball nigga? You feelin' that you can't get touched, bitch?" he shouted. "Well, let's see how untouchable you are when I go to the cops and start runnin' my mouth. I ain't scared of jail, bitch. I'll turn myself in and give you up at the same time. Tell the police everything. Shit, maybe I'll even tell the feds about it all . . . you and me."

"Guy, shut your fuckin' mouth."

"Yeah, I'll tell the feds how we killed Supreme while he slept. I go down, you go down."

Apple barked, "You blackmailin' me, muthafucka?"

"I want you back, Apple. I want us to be like it was."

"There was never any *us*! Get that through your thick fuckin' skull!"

"Well, if there can't be an us, then I'll do it. I'll march down to the nearest precinct and tell 'em everything. Supreme was like a father to me, and you convinced me to kill him. But I'll get over this guilt and change my mind if you give me another chance, Apple. I want us to be together, but if we can't, then I'll give myself up and you. I'll do the time. I don't give a fuck!"

Apple felt trapped. She couldn't allow Guy Tony to bring her down because of his jealousy. Her tone suddenly changed with the fear of him really being that stupid and turning himself in. Her mind spinning, she tried to reason with him.

"Guy, look, shit just been a little fucked up these past few weeks. Let's say we get together and talk about this in person, just you and me."

"I don't wanna talk. I want you. I want us to be together, and unless your answer is yes, then there ain't no fuckin' talkin'."

"I need time to think, Guy."

"Bitch, what your answer? I ain't fuckin' playin' games wit' you!"

Feeling trapped, Apple answered, "Yes, OK. I'm sorry, baby. I'm sorry that I hurt you. I don't know what I was fuckin' thinking."

Guy Tony laughed. "That's my girl."

"I need to see you."

"I wanna see you too, baby. We need to make up for lost time," he said joyfully.

"Yes, we do."

Guy Tony laughed again, a clear indication to Apple that he was drunk and irrational. Apple felt that Guy Tony was definitely a threat to her freedom and livelihood, and without giving it a second thought, she began plotting his murder. He needed to go, like Supreme. It didn't matter to her that they'd been friends since grade school. The only thing important to her was survival, so that meant her enemies had to fall.

"Guy, where are you now?"

"In my car, thinking about you. We can make it work, baby. I know we can."

"I know we can, and believe me, I'm gonna make things right between us very soon."

After Apple got off the phone with Guy Tony, Chico walked into the bedroom. She stood by the window and gazed outside at the heavy rainfall. Guy Tony had her worried, and it was a situation she needed to deal with immediately.

"Who were you on the phone with, baby?" Chico asked.

"Nobody special, just something I need to get rid of," Apple said with a genuine smile.

Chico smiled at his woman and went closer to her while she stood by the window seemingly fascinated by the downpour. Apple, wearing a silk chemise that shaped her body very nicely, turned to him, and Chico smoothly pulled her into his arms and embraced her warm, soft body.

"You got a problem, baby?"

"Nothing I can't handle on my own, Chico. I got this."

He nodded. "That's my baby. You know how to hold your own. But if it's something serious, then let me know. No secrets, right?"

"Of course."

Chico kissed his woman passionately and then carried her to the bed, positioned her on her backside, and began undressing. While she watched her man undress, Apple thought about how Guy Tony didn't even come close to her boo. In just a few minutes, she had devised a scheme to have him killed and was ready to implement it.

Several days later, Guy Tony was sitting in his truck by Morningside Park near 123rd Street waiting patiently to see Apple, who soon pulled up in her Benz, parked, and quickly jumped in the truck with him, her .22 and a small blade concealed, just in case he became violent.

Apple put on her perfect smile and charm, hugging Guy Tony when she greeted him. "Baby, you OK? I've been worried about you."

"I'm good. I was fucked up the other night, but I'm good."

"That's good to hear."

Guy Tony looked at her, his eyes staying on her long legs a little too long, with Apple's skirt riding up her thigh. He licked his lips. "I missed you," he said. He leaned in close to her, placing his hand on her thigh.

"I know you did. I missed you too."

Apple didn't flinch upon feeling his touch, but kept

her composure. She knew she needed to play his game and convince him that everything was OK, until the deed was done. So she continued with her fake smiles and positive attitude toward him, becoming that Academy Award-winning actress for the day. Inside, she felt disgusted by him and figured once the threat was gone, she could breathe easily.

As they talked, Guy Tony began to relax, feeling like his old self once more. Still, Apple could no longer trust him. She continued on with her role, and to seal his trust, she took his hand and placed it farther up her skirt.

She didn't resist the sexual gesture, feeling the warmth between her thighs, and as his reach advanced, he realized she wasn't wearing any panties, which aroused him. Guy Tony's eyes danced with excitement.

Apple let his fingers explore for a short moment, but was unmoved by his finger pushing inside of her. She pulled his lips close and locked onto him with a strong kiss. She could feel his heart racing. The taste of his breath made her want to puke, but she went along with the program, maintaining her calm, trying to avoid cutting open his throat. She couldn't afford to get her hands dirty.

She suddenly pulled away from him, leaving him yearning for her to continue. With the foreplay out the way, she wanted to get back to business. "I got some business for you," she said. "I need you to do a pickup for me."

"Where?"

"Tomorrow. That spot over on a Hundred and Forty-Fifth Street. Munchies owe me a payment, five stacks. I trust you with it."

"A'ight, I'm on it."

Apple smiled. "It's good to have you back, Guy."

"Like old times, right?"

"Of course." To seal the deal, Apple kissed him once more. She felt his lips lock onto hers so tight that she thought he would pull her tongue from her mouth. She pulled away, smiled at him, and exited his truck.

While walking back to her Benz, she felt the urge to wash her mouth out with soap. Guy Tony had never been a good kisser. He was sloppy, too wet, and it always felt like he was trying to swallow her whole.

Looking in her rearview mirror, she watched him pull off and hoped by tomorrow night, he wouldn't be a problem for her anymore. He was just too stupid to realize he was walking into a trap.

Apple continued to look into her rearview mirror while touching up her lipstick that Guy Tony had smeared. She then stared at her eyes. They had changed into something so cold and calculating. She had transformed into a completely different woman after her little sister's murder. A year ago, she wouldn't even have thought to have someone murdered, but now it came easy to her, like child's play.

∽∾∽

Guy Tony stopped in front of Munchies' spot just as the night was about to cover the city. The streets were still busy with people and traffic, the fall gradually changing the color of the leaves on the trees. He got out his truck, a 9mm hidden underneath his Völkl jacket, and looked around. The block was slowly losing the day's traffic of shoppers and residents, who moved up and down the block like they were programmed.

With a determined mindset to get the job done and satisfy Apple, Guy Tony stared at Munchies' worn-out spot, with its fading green awning and dilapidated front entrance that was slanted on the hill. He yearned to have Apple in his arms again.

After collecting from Munchies, his next big move would be to take out Chico. It was a risk he was willing to take, especially for love.

Guy Tony moved to the front entrance in a confident stride; he was well known in the area. When people saw his face, they didn't know what to expect from him. Sometimes he was an understanding and reasonable man, other times he was violent and cold. It was his unpredictability that made him feared. He could be lenient, but then again heartless.

After walking into the soul food spot that ran numbers and gambling in a secret back room, he looked around for the owner. The restaurant wasn't busy, but Guy Tony knew where they got their true money. He could hear dishes and pots moving around in the kitchen. The tables were old, the lighting dimmed, and the flooring tattered. The place was in need of a serious renovation. Despite its raggedy appearance, the food was excellent. Munchies had been around for years, and was famous for its peach and sweet potato pies, fish sandwiches, and crab cakes.

Munchies had hired a nice little staff and management, and soon got rich off his cooking, but greed overcame him. Wanting more, he ran numbers in the back of his place and had late-night gambling downstairs in the stonewall basement. He had his own Atlantic City casino going on, being under the radar of law enforcement for years. Supreme had muscled in on the business two years back, when Munchies was overwhelmed with gambling debts himself and had the IRS investigating him. However, with the help of Supreme, he was able to pull himself out of a slump and get back in business.

Munchies thought, with Supreme gone, he would be able to profit fully from everything, especially with a young girl trying to take over the business. He shunned Apple and taunted her, exclaiming, "I don't deal wit' little fuckin' girls!"

Days later, Apple stepped into Munchies' spot flanked by three hard-hitting, baseball bat-swinging thugs, and accosted Munchies in front of his patrons. They held the overweight Barry White lookalike to the floor and went to work on him with the bats, hitting him everywhere, except the face.

Munchies wailed out from the pain, hugging the floor. After the beating, Apple placed her heel on his bruised chest, glared down at him with a hardened stare and said to him, "I'm the new bitch in town. Young or old, I'm that bitch that will fuckin' kill you. Don't ever doubt me again, you fat fuck!"

Munchies grasped that she meant business, and Apple never had a problem with him again. He soon became her little bitch, doing anything she told him to do.

～～～

Guy Tony asked the young waiter for Munchies, and she quickly went into a back room. A short moment later, Munchies emerged and greeted Guy Tony with a smile.

"Guy, yeah, she said that you were coming. You hungry? Thirsty?" Munchies asked in good spirits.

"Fuck the hospitality! You know what I'm here for, Munchies."

Munchies nodded. "I got that for you in the back. Follow me."

Guy Tony walked behind him, and the two moved down a short, narrow hallway and entered one of Munchies' back rooms. Munchies, clad in a white-and-red Sean John warm-up suit, with diamonds dripping off his wrists, neck, and ears, placed himself behind his desk. He liked to be flashy and loved money more than anything else. He reached into his desk drawer and tossed Guy Tony a small brown lumpy envelope stuffed with cash.

"That should cover me, right?" Munchies asked.

Guy Tony took the package in his hand and opened it to inspect the contents. It was filled with twenties, fifties, and hundreds.

Munchies began smoking a cigar and pouring himself a drink.

Guy Tony looked at him suspiciously. He was soon overcome with a nervous feeling. For as long as he knew

Munchies, he never gave up a large sum of money without bitching first, always exclaiming, "Y'all fuckin' breakin' my pockets, man. Highway robbery, that's what it is. Robbery." But Munchies still paid what was owed.

Guy noticed he seemed a little too cool handing over five thousand dollars without a mumbling complaint. "You OK, Munchies?" he asked.

"I'm good." Munchies smiled and downed his drink. "Never been better."

Guy Tony looked around, quickly studying every detail of the cluttered room. He noticed the closet door behind him was ajar, and that suddenly became his point of interest. He had a feeling someone was hiding in the dark, waiting for him to let his guard down.

"Guy, have a seat. Drink?" Munchies offered.

It was another giveaway that something was wrong. Munchies never wanted him to stay longer than he had to.

"Nah, I'm good. I'ma take off." Guy Tony watched Munchies' eyes and noticed them focusing on something behind him, looking toward the closet door, possibly signifying they weren't alone in the room. He placed his hand near his weapon, ready to strike.

"You sure, Guy? I mean, you ain't gotta rush off too soon," Munchies said loudly.

Guy Tony's survival impulse kicked in, and in one rapid motion, he pulled his weapon from his waistband and rushed to the closet and saw a figure trying to emerge from it. He slammed the door shut on the stranger's arm, which had a .357 attached to it. There was a loud scream.

The man was trapped inside the closet with his right arm crushed in the door, as the gun fired wildly in his hand. Guy Tony put more pressure on the door and heard the stranger's arm snap like a twig, and then another loud scream.

Guy Tony became aware of Munchies reaching into his desk for a weapon, but before Munchies got the draw on him, he fired, striking him in the abdomen and causing him to double over from the sudden shot.

"Ah shit! Fuck!" he cried out, falling back into his chair, holding his wound.

With Munchies out of commission for a moment, Guy Tony focused his attention back to the gunman trapped in the closet. Swiftly, he swung open the closet door, aimed, fired, and the man dropped dead at his feet, a gunshot wound to his head.

"Muthafucka!" Guy Tony looked down at the man sprawled out lifeless at his feet and fired another shot into his head. Breathing hard, he turned his attention back to Munchies with a bitter stare, the smoking gun at his side.

Munchies sat slumped in his chair, looking somewhat disoriented. He looked up at Guy Tony standing over him with the gun trained at his head. He pressed his hand against his bloody wound and coughed, a look of defeat on his chunky face.

"Don't kill me, man," he pleaded. "It wasn't me."

"Who told you to set me up?" Guy Tony shouted.

"I was just doing what I was told."

"Who, muthafucka?" Guy screamed, stepping closer, the gun aimed at Munchies' head.

"It was Apple, man. She's the one that put the hit out on you. I swear, man. I didn't wanna do it, but she promised me that if I took you out, my debt with her would be wiped clean."

Guy Tony couldn't believe it. For a split moment, he felt like his world didn't matter anymore. He regretted taking out Supreme to help Apple rise, when Supreme was actually the lesser evil. He felt he had been played one time too many, so now it was war. He vowed to destroy Apple by any means necessary.

"Yo, Guy, please, man, I'm sorry. It wasn't personal with you. Just business, man. I'm just trying to survive," Munchies said.

Guy glared at him, the 9mm still trained at his head. His eyes showed no remorse for the victim. He mockingly replied, "You was tryin' to survive." He fired point-blank into Munchies' forehead, killing him instantly.

Munchies' blood splattered everywhere, even on Guy Tony, who calmly exited the room, leaving Munchies slumped in his chair and his friend lying face down on the ground, a thick pool of blood forming underneath him. Guy Tony needed to leave right away. Since the shots were loud, he knew someone had probably called the police. He swiftly moved past curious employees, some of whom noticed the blood on him and panicked.

"Oh my God!" a man shouted. "Somebody, call nine-one-one!"

Guy Tony pushed past the nosy men and women and rushed outside to his truck. After tucking the gun safely into his waistband, he climbed into his SUV and sped off. Guy Tony was so furious, he almost hit a parked car. He sped toward the Westside Highway and hit the clear stretch of highway going south.

"I swear, I'ma kill that fuckin' bitch!" he cried out to himself. "Oooh, I'ma fuck her up!"

Chapter 25

"How did he fuck it up?" Apple screamed out. "It was so fuckin' simple! Kill him and we would be good!"

"Well, Munchies and his boy are dead now. Guy fucked them up real good. He gave Munchies somethin' for his fat ass to chew on," the caller said.

"You find this fuckin' funny?" Apple spat.

"Nah, I'm just sayin'—"

"Just shut the fuck up!"

Apple paced back and forth in her living room, the cell phone glued to her ear. She knew it would only be a matter of time before Guy Tony came looking for her, that there was no fixing the situation with him this time.

"I'll call you back."

She hung up her phone and then smashed it into the wall. She stormed through her living room and knocked over a lamp, causing it to smash against the parquet floors. "I don't believe this shit!" she screamed out.

Apple went outside into her backyard and lit up a

cigarette. She took a few quick pulls and was upset that she got the news about the failed hit on her eighteenth birthday. She exhaled, leaned back against the patio door, and figured she had to step up her security team. Guy Tony knew too much about her—her home, her business, and her personal life. He pretty much helped her put everything together, so Apple felt she needed to change up her habits. She was too vulnerable for attack.

Her first priority was moving from where she was living. She planned on selling the house and relocating somewhere out of Harlem, maybe Queens or Brooklyn. Second, she needed a bigger gun, so she took Chico's Glock 17 from out the closet and kept it close to her. Third, she had to make herself ghost for a while and lay low. There was no telling where Guy Tony might come after her. Apple knew he would be lurking and plotting. She was going to put the word out to her people and Chico's crew—$25,000 on Guy Tony's head.

Despite the bad news and drama, she was going to have a good time that night. She planned on crashing Kola's big birthday bash at the upscale Cipriani's. She had been hearing about Kola's party through the grapevine for weeks and heard she went all out for the celebration and wasn't sparing any expenses.

Apple felt she had the right to be at the party too. After all, it was her birthday also, and she figured that for one night, she would let bygones be bygones with her sister because she wanted in on the party—the VIP, the champagne, and the limelight. It was a night she didn't want to forget.

In an attempt to calm her nerves, Apple went back into her home and ran some bathwater. She submerged herself into the sunken tub, unwinding in the warm, soothing water, with the warmth of the sun shining through from the skylight above. She took a deep breath, closed her eyes, and began pleasing herself with the plastic dildo while Chico was out of town meeting his connect. Afterwards, she planned on getting ready to attend Kola's party in style.

The line and crowd outside of Cipriani's was remarkable. Hundreds of people were waiting to get into Kola's birthday bash on the breezy October night. High-end cars lined the city street from corner to corner, while security tried to maintain crowd control by the front entrance. The ladies were adorned in the most eye-catching, scantiest clothing, the shortest skirts, mini-dresses, and plunging tops showing ample cleavage, while the men were decked in urban wear and bling, some flaunting their wealth like it was going out of style.

Kola's bash would soon become the most talked-about event. The venue was able to hold up to 2,500 people. Inside the 40,000-square-foot landmark, with the hottest New York DJ spinning his mixes above the massive crowd, were half-naked models walking around the crowd with painted-on bikini tops, serving drinks and dazzling the revelers. There was a seven-foot-tall champagne fountain of flowing Cristal centered on the stage, flanked by two exquisite, colossal ice sculptures, one engraved with *Happy*

Birthday, Kola and the second, *Queen Bee.*

The loud music was streaming and had everyone dancing, while suspended above the revelers' heads were several giant LCD monitors that displayed different images of the birthday girl.

Kola had reserved a VIP area, one of six separate lounges, for her more important guests. She sported a beautiful ruby charmeuse slip dress with rhinestone studs and a pair of matching stilettos. And she styled her hair into a well-designed French bun with a few strands falling over her eye, giving her a sophisticated appearance and making her look twice her age.

She sipped on Cristal and mostly kept company with Cross, who paid for the entire event, taking balling to a whole new level. She loved him so much that when she looked into his eyes, it was hard to turn away without a smile. He was her joy, her kingpin that had promised to give her the world, and he was making good on his promise. He presented Kola with a few lavish gifts for her birthday—one being a pair of bezel hoop earrings with diamond drop briolettes that cost him ten stacks. His other gift to her was the black, drop-top BMW 650. Kola loved it all and was having her best birthday ever.

Cross wanted to make his boo happy and get her mind off whatever had been troubling her over the past few months, one being the problem with her sister and mother. He wanted his girl to feel like the queen she was to him. He showered her with gifts and power. Their names rang out simultaneously through the streets of

Harlem. They'd bonded and fell in love so fast, Cross even thought about proposing to his young love.

Dressed in a pair of black slacks and a white button-down with a pair of dark wingtip shoes, his bling gleaming and his braids long and fresh, Cross had the eyes of plenty ladies in the crowd, but he only had eyes for one. He moved through VIP with authority, his crew of thugs not too far from him. The couple popped numerous bottles of champagne, danced like they were on *Soul Train*, and did it up like it was the end of 1999.

"Happy birthday, baby," he said to Kola then kissed her deeply.

"Them my niggas right there!" one of Cross' soldiers shouted out. "Y'all muthafuckin' clap for them. That's fuckin' love right there!"

Among applause, the two kissed passionately for the crowd to see. VIP was the banging spot in the club. It was decorated with a dozen "Happy Birthday" balloons, a string of colorful ribbons, and there was a continuous flow of food and liquor. Scantily clad women swarmed to Cross' clique and danced provocatively against the men, hiking up their short skirts and grinding on them.

The DJ unexpectedly started to play 50 Cent's "In Da Club," and the crowd went berserk. Those seated quickly stood up to join the others on the dance floor. Kola and Cross began to dance together closely, while the crowd started singing along with 50's raunchy verse.

Champagne was being poured, and it seemed like the music had gotten louder. Not a soul was sitting or hugging the walls. Every foot moved, and every arm swung around with joy. Kola was in the mix of the party, having the time of her life. She was eighteen, but looked like she was in her mid-twenties. She was young in age, but more mature in the mind than anyone could imagine. It was her night, and she was going to celebrate until she couldn't party anymore.

〰️

The dark green Lincoln Navigator with tinted windows slowly moved its way down Third Avenue and then turned on Eleventh Street with a slow crawl before coming to a stop near the club, where so many people were gathered outside. The four doors opened up like it was orchestrated, and Apple and her goons climbed out of the truck, making their way to Cipriani's.

They pushed through the thick crowd, by-passing the long line, and approached the team of security. Apple went up to the doors, and the main bouncer shook his head in disbelief, thinking he was seeing double. He looked at the twin in awe. They were too identical, from their beauty to their thick curves.

"This my sister Kola's shit, right?" she asked the bouncer.

"Twins, huh?" the beefy bouncer responded.

"I'm in there," Apple said.

"She got you on the list?"

Apple gave him a hard look. "What the fuck you think? I'm her twin sister, right?"

The other bouncers looked dumbfounded, but to

assure they would grant her entry, Apple handed the man a large stack, leaving him wide-eyed. "That's all for y'all. Don't spend it all in one place," she said with a teasing smile.

The bouncers looked confused, but were easily bribed with a thousand dollars. They unhooked the velvet rope and allowed Apple and her small entourage of scowling goons into the mix of things.

Apple walked through the grand foyer and was greeted with a multiple of doors leading into a clubgoer's paradise. The lighting, thick crowd, earsplitting music, and décor were fit for the birthday queen. Suddenly, Apple was overcome with jealousy. Her sister outdid herself, she had to admit. Seeing Kola's name everywhere, in lights, on blocks of ice, and on the LCDs above, made Apple hate on her sister.

"Bitch thinks she's P. Diddy now," Apple joked lightly.

Her and her people moved through the jumping crowd, pushing their way toward the bar and catching wrongful looks from a few partygoers they nudged the wrong way. Apple managed to get herself a small VIP section, since she was ready to pay for bottle service.

"Fuck it!" she said to herself. "It's my fuckin' birthday too!"

When some of the attendees saw her, they thought she was Kola. They rushed up to her eagerly, shouting out, "Happy birthday, Kola!"

Apple sharply replied, "It's Apple's birthday!"

She made it clearly known that she was in the house,

with her crew of thugs circled around her, shouting out, "It's ya birthday! Go, Apple! It's ya birthday! Fuck that bitch 'cause it's ya birthday!"

Apple mingled among everyone, wearing a short leather mini-skirt that flaunted her thighs and legs, a tight, tiny, plunging-neckline metallic halter top with a unique o-ring, and a pair of six-inch stilettos. She moved to the music like she was a video vixen. And she and her boys were popping bottles, bumping into people, and causing a small scene with their vulgar antics. Apple's presence with her goons was an obvious "Fuck you, bitch!" to Kola.

❧

Kola was seated in a lounge chair, feeling the best she had ever felt while talking to one of her friends, when Bunny Rabbit approached her with a sense of urgency. Kola looked up at Bunny Rabbit coming toward her and knew by the look on her face that there was something important she needed to tell her.

Bunny Rabbit leaned over and said into Kola's ear, "Your sister is here."

"What?"

"She's down at the party. Got her own VIP section, and her and her goons are showing out right now, Kola. It looks like it's about to get ugly."

Kola was furious. She ultimately felt disrespected that Apple had the audacity to crash her party and show out. She sprung from her seat and looked around for Cross, but she didn't see him. So she decided to confront her sister and kick the bitch out.

With a small following behind her, Kola stormed out of the room and rushed into the grand ballroom, her people parting the large crowd so she could pass through with ease. She spotted Apple in one of the cushioned sections of the club, where she stood among her goons and a few bitches, with bottles all around. She glared at Apple and was ready to pull out every root from her head. The sisters were soon eye to eye.

"Bitch, what the fuck you doin' here?" Kola shouted.

Apple smirked. "Enjoying my birthday, that's what."

It was clear Apple was a little tipsy and was going to be a problem. She continued dancing on one of the ladies next to her, clutching a bottle of Moët and staring at Kola with a daring look.

"Apple, get the fuck outta my party! I don't want you here!"

"Bitch, it's *our* fuckin' birthday. I see you doin' it all big and shit. Fuck it! It's my birthday too!"

It didn't take long for Cross to hear the news, and he joined Kola, with his crew having his back. The tension between the two sisters and their followers became so thick, security came rushing over. Both sides looked fiercely at each other.

Apple slapped her sister, and Kola responded with a right hook to Apple's face. And, just as quickly, a melee between both sides erupted. Bottles were smashed against skulls, with swinging fists and kicks flying everywhere. Soon, everyone was forced outside into the streets.

Kola was fuming that Apple had ruined her party. It

was supposed to be her night, and she was being dragged outside kicking and screaming by bouncers.

The fight continued outside, with more people getting into the mix. It was starting to become too big for the bouncers to handle themselves.

Apple was holding her own, knocking out a few bitches that were for Kola. She even kicked off her stilettos and fought in the streets barefoot.

Onlookers were shocked at the sudden rumble. Bouncers were soon fighting instead of trying to break things up.

Kola tried to look around for her sister, but she felt herself being pulled away from the chaos. She spun around angrily to see that it was Cross.

"C'mon!" he told her.

That's when Kola heard the dreadful sound of gunfire. *Boom! Boom! Boom! Boom!*

The crowd began to disperse like roaches after the lights were turned on. Cross pushed his woman down to the ground and covered her from any harm. He looked around to see who was shooting, but the crowd was still too thick to tell. It was pure panic, the pushing and shoving causing a few people to get trampled.

Kola was a little bruised herself. She was in tears, seeing that Apple had ruined her party. When the smoke cleared, Kola was even more shocked to see two of her friends sprawled out dead on the concrete from gunshot wounds, Bunny Rabbit and one of Cross' soldiers.

Chapter 26

News of the shooting at the club had spread in Harlem quickly and was talked about for days, creating high tension between both cliques. When Chico returned from out of town and heard of the incident, he wanted to gun everyone down. Apple was ready for war, and everyone was on high alert. Within months, Apple had created so many enemies in her life, she was on everybody's official shit list.

Apple sat in the cut, her guns close and loaded for action. Her mother was nagging her about her beef with Kola. They had been arguing all day, and Apple was ready to slap the shit out of her. Apple let it be clearly known that she was in control of everything. She stared at her hip, thirty-seven-year-old, ghetto-fabulous mother bitterly and wondered why she put up with her.

She heard the doorbell and cautiously went to see who it was. She was surprised to see Kola standing outside her door, and a few thugs lingering by her car. She wondered how Kola knew her address.

Apple cocked back the Glock 17 and shouted out, "Bitch, get the fuck away from my door!"

"I wanna talk to you," Kola exclaimed.

"There ain't nothin' to talk about," Apple shouted. "I'll see you on the streets, Kola."

"Bitch, open the fuckin' door so we can talk," Kola shouted back.

Denise heard her daughter outside and rushed to the door, telling Apple, "Just open it."

"Ma, step the fuck back!"

"No. I wanna see her."

"Ma, get the fuck away from the door," Apple warned again.

But Denise was too stubborn to listen to anything her daughter had to say. She swiftly pushed Apple aside and unlocked the front door.

Kola burst into the home and marched up to Apple. Before she could throw the first swing, Apple smashed the gun over her head, and Kola stumbled back a little dazed.

"Apple, is you fuckin' crazy?" Denise shouted.

While Apple was distracted, Kola charged and knocked the gun out of her hand. She pushed Apple into a wall, and followed that up with a series of blows to her face and midsection.

Apple and Kola tore into each other like two ferocious lions, knocking over furniture and breaking precious items in the home.

Apple soon got the upper hand, grabbing Kola by her long hair and knocking the wind out of her with a hard right uppercut. Kola, her mouth full of blood, lost her footing and fell over a chair. She hit the ground like she had received a blow from Mike Tyson.

Apple pounced on her like she was a stranger in her home. "I told you, bitch, don't fuck wit' me! Look at you! I'm that fuckin' bitch now!" she screamed out, landing a series of vicious blows on Kola.

Denise ran to aid Kola. She grabbed Apple from behind and flung her across the room, screaming out, "Apple, stop it! Stop it!"

Apple fell over the couch, surprised by her mother's strength. But she was more hurt to see Denise helping Kola off the floor. Apple's eyes stretched with shock. She couldn't believe how, out of the blue, her mother actually became a mother to Kola, asking if she was OK.

Kola pushed away from her mother, shouting, "Get off me!" She wiped the blood from her mouth and looked at Apple with so much contempt, if looks could kill, Apple would have been torn apart. The sisters' intense gaze at one another was deadly. But Kola dared not continue the fight because Apple had the Glock 17 gripped in her hand and looked wild.

"You gonna get yours, bitch. I ain't playin' games anymore," Kola warned. "The only sister I ever loved is six feet fuckin' deep."

Kola's crew of thugs was at the front door, making sure she had a protected exit. She exchanged hard looks with her sister and mother once more then left the house.

Apple's living room was in disorder, but she didn't

breathe lightly after Kola left. She focused her hard stare at her mother. "Get the fuck out my house!"

Denise was shocked. "What?"

"Bitch, you ain't deaf! Get your shit—Nah, fuck that! Just get the fuck out!"

"Apple, you ain't serious."

"I am. After all the fuckin' love I showed you, Ma, you take her side and diss me. I fuckin' hate you. I thought I had your loyalty, but I guess I was wrong," Apple said with tear-filled eyes. "I put you up and gave you nice things, and this is how you repay me?"

Denise looked at her sternly. "I'm not going anywhere."

"What? Bitch, you think I'm playin' wit' you!" Apple shouted. She raised the gun and fired suddenly, and the bullet whizzed by her mother's ear, startling her.

"Apple, are you fuckin' crazy?!"

"Yeah, I am."

Denise saw the seriousness in her daughter's eyes. She knew there was no changing Apple's mind.

"Don't take shit wit' you, bitch, 'cause I bought all that. Just leave my crib wit' the fuckin' clothes on your back and take your ghetto-fabulous ass back to the hood and stay the fuck out of my life!"

"You're gonna regret this, Apple."

"I don't think so. My only regret was taking you in, but now I'm done wit' you."

Denise slowly backed her way toward the door and walked out the brownstone with a heartrending look. She had nothing to go back to; she quickly went from something to nothing.

With her mother gone from her home, Apple slammed the door and gazed at herself in the mirror that hung by the doorway. She looked a mess. Her hair was a mess, her face was bruised, and her outfit torn and ruined. Still holding onto the gun, she felt she didn't need anyone. She was on top of everybody, and nobody could tell her a damn thing. It felt so good to finally whup Kola's ass. She was definitely the baddest chick, and Kola had better recognize.

Epilogue

With Thanksgiving right around the corner and so much money still in her grasp with business being good, Apple decided to treat herself. So, with the help of Chico and his business manager, she went to an upscale Mercedes dealership in Long Island, and Chico purchased her the sleek, pricey, silver McLaren. A one-of-a-kind. When Apple got behind the wheel of the stylish car, with its lustrous aero design and 5.5L V8 engine, she knew she would be the most envied person in the city.

As Apple drove the car off the lot that afternoon, she couldn't wait to flaunt her new ride in Harlem and elsewhere. She wanted to turn heads, show the whole hood how much she came up. She went from having a bus pass to driving one of the best-looking cars that Mercedes ever made.

It had been weeks since her fight with Kola, and she had been laying low for a while. Chico had moved them out of the city, about an hour and a half away from Harlem, and into an upstate four-bedroom mini-mansion with a sprawling green lawn, a hilltop driveway leading to a three-car garage, and a picturesque view of the river. Apple loved every inch of her new home.

For a while, her life seemed easygoing and separated from the war going on in Harlem, where she still ran her loan-sharking and bookkeeping business. Guy Tony had disappeared for a moment, and she hadn't seen or heard from Kola or her mother in weeks. It seemed that her beef had died down a little.

Wanting to show off her car, she decided to take the long drive back into the city and cruise around Harlem on this sunny fall day. She looked good, styling in the gleaming McLaren and smiling at all the heads that turned to get a peek at her new ride.

Apple didn't give a second thought to all the drama she had stirred up and the lives she'd turned upside down. The only thing she cared about was how fly she looked driving the expensive car that only celebrities and athletes could afford. She wanted all eyes on her. She loved the hate thrown at her, because it was proof that she was doing her thang and doing it right. Like Dave Chappelle, she wanted to shout out, "I'm rich, bitch!"

For an hour, Apple drove around Harlem, block to block, showing off her new car. She parked in front of her old building, stepped out in her designer jacket and heels, and profiled in front of her McLaren like she was in a video shoot. She lingered in her old hood for a moment, enjoying being seen, mostly gawked at by bitches that wanted to be her, and niggas that wanted to fuck her. A few residents stopped to chat with her, admiring her car, but she warned them to only look, not touch.

Apple soon got tired and decided to leave. She had made her statement loud and clear. For her, it felt so good to show off. She was about to get back into her ride, feeling invincible and accomplished, ready to make the two-hour drive back upstate, but the sudden calling of her name made her turn to see who was asking for her.

As she turned, a crackhead, who had been paid to do the deed, threw a cup full of acid in her face before running away.

"Aaaaaahhhh!" she screamed, clutching her burning face in agony and falling to her knees, the acid eating away at her beautiful face.

A small crowd gathered around her as she squirmed around on the concrete in pain, her cries echoing throughout the streets. Some were happy about the incident, watching her suffer with a pleased smile, thinking that the bitch got what she deserved, others felt sorry for her and tried to help.

As her face burned, Apple vowed to get revenge on whoever disfigured her beautiful face. She knew it could have been anyone, from her sister to Guy-Tony. Or it could've been just a random act of jealousy.

Apple was quickly rushed to intensive care, where she soon found out that her face would be disfigured for life.

To be continued . . .

An Excerpt from
Coca Kola: The Baddest Chick (Part 2)

Prologue

The midnight staff at Harlem Hospital was busy with an influx of incoming patients. The trauma unit was understaffed, and the hallway was lined with the sick and injured that needed to be treated. The echoes of the men and women in agony seemed never ending to the doctors and nurses that were bustling back and forth from one patient to the next. The EMS was daunted with nine-one-one calls. It seemed like everybody had either fallen ill, gotten shot or stabbed, or were complaining about some unknown sickness, and had come to Harlem Hospital for treatment.

The third shift working the trauma center was exhausted, hungry, and swamped from wall-to-wall with the ill, some who needed to be restrained and some fighting to be kept alive from their injuries. But, the following patient that the Ambulance brought in screamed the loudest and was definitely out of control. She was barely strapped down to the gurney and had suffered serious burns to most of her face.

As the staff hurried her into the center, she constantly screamed out, "I'ma kill that bitch! I'ma kill that fuckin' bitch! Aaaah, shit, it hurts! It hurts! It fuckin' hurts!"

Apple was in sheer pain. The medical team wanted to treat her as quickly as possible, but Apple wasn't allowing them to do their jobs sufficiently as she kicked, screamed, and squirmed on the rushing gurney.

"Get the fuck off me! Get off me!" Apple yelled, sounding crazy.

"Ma'am, just calm down. We're trying to help you. Just stay calm," the night RN said, while trying to hold Apple down on the gurney with the help of the others.

"What happened to you?" another nurse asked.

Apple refused to be cooperative, though. She continued kicking and screaming, feeling her face melting away painfully like the wicked witch from *The Wizard of Oz*.

She screamed out, "My fuckin' face! My fuckin' face! I'ma kill that bitch! Aaaah!"

"She needs to be sedated," the doctor said.

After wheeling Apple into a private room they started prepping her for an emergency surgery. The sedative was being prepared, and the doctors wanted to tend to the burns right away. By the looks of her injuries, they were confident that Apple would need some severe skin grafting.

The screaming continued, echoing through the trauma center. It took security and four staff members to hold Apple down while the RN tried to stick the syringe filled with a sedative into her arm. But, Apple put up a tough fight; she kicked one of the nurses into a shelf filled with medical supplies that spilled over.

"Hold her down!" the doctor screamed out.

"Get off meeee!" she yelled.

She tried to bite the second nurse, but her arms were forced to her side with physical force by security. The RN quickly thrust the syringe into Apple's right arm, hoping it worked promptly.

Apple's chest heaved and dropped like a winded athlete, with her facial expression looking more soothing and the wildness in her slowly fading. There was finally some calm in the room.

"Shit!" the RN exclaimed, shocked that the teenage girl was so strong.

Immediately, they began working on her burns. The doctor tried to operate the best he could on her face, but the acid had done severe damage. It would take a miracle for Apple to look the way she used to.

Hours later, Apple lay in the room and slowly opened her eyes to find her face heavily bandaged. She touched the dressing slowly and gently. She was still loopy from the sedative, but realizing how ugly she must be, she started to cry. It had to be a nightmare for her.

When she closed her eyes to try and stop the crying, she heard a nurse say, "You need to rest."

Turning to look at the short, round nurse clad in blue and white scrubs, Apple yelled, "I want a plastic surgeon." When the nurse hesitated, Apple screamed, "Now, bitch!"

"Ma'am, you need to rest."

"Fuck that! Look at me!" she cried out.

The shaded, but saddened look on the nurse's face said she felt sympathy for the young girl. She wanted to console the eighteen-year-old, but thought against it. Instead, she checked Apple's IV flow, jotted something down on a clipboard, and walked out the room, leaving Apple feeling alone and disgusted.

She fell asleep again and woke up hours later in the burn unit. She was alone in the room, and the only thing on her mind was revenge. Every time she touched the bandages that covered most of her burned face, she fumed with rage and then began to cry with the realization that she was no longer beautiful.

Chico rushed into the hospital searching for his woman. He argued with security and then a few staff members, shouting, "Where's my fuckin' girl?"

One of Apple's doctors escorted Chico toward the burn unit where she was recuperating and heavily sedated. He stopped at the doorway with a look of shock registering on his face. He couldn't believe it. She looked like a mummy as she lay in bed.

"What the fuck," he uttered.

Apple slowly turned to see her love, Chico, standing in the doorway, but she didn't say a word to him. The medication in her system was making her drowsy and delirious. Her burns were itching and painful, but she couldn't scratch.

Chico rushed into the room, took Apple's hand into his, looked at her with that firm love in his eyes, and demanded to know, "Baby, who the fuck did this shit to you? Just give me a fuckin' name, and they dead. I promise you that."

Apple locked eyes with her boyfriend and constantly repeated, "Kola . . . Kola . . . Kola."